Robert, the son of a Royal Navy Officer, was born in the West Riding of Yorkshire. Retired and having sold his own successful business, he took up writing in 2017. He is now living in rural Leicestershire, England.

Yang Qun

my spirit . my love . my life .

Robert Pierré Donarté

jACK©
BOOK 1
jASPER

AUSTIN MACAULEY PUBLISHERS™
LONDON • CAMBRIDGE • NEW YORK • SHARJAH

Copyright © Robert Pierré Donarté **YQ** 2019

The right of Robert Pierré Donarté **YQ** to be identified as author of this work has been asserted by him in accordance with section 77 and 78 of the Copyright, Designs and Patents Act 1988.

All rights reserved. No part of this publication may be reproduced, stored in a retrieval system, or transmitted in any form or by any means, electronic, mechanical, photocopying, recording, or otherwise, without the prior permission of the publishers.

Any person who commits any unauthorised act in relation to this publication may be liable to criminal prosecution and civil claims for damages.

A CIP catalogue record for this title is available from the British Library.

ISBN 9781528922173 (Paperback)
ISBN 9781528963695 (ePub e-book)

www.austinmacauley.com

First Published (2019)
Austin Macauley Publishers Ltd
25 Canada Square
Canary Wharf
London
E14 5LQ

I would like to thank my two younger brothers, John and Paul, for all their support during the writing of this book.

Table of Contents

Chapter 1 .... **13**
   Suburbia..

Chapter 2 .... **17**
   The Kettle..

Chapter 3 .... **19**
   Doctor Doogood ....

Chapter 4 .... **22**
   69, Ponsbury Close ....

Chapter 5 .... **25**
   Where to Next?..

Chapter 6 .... **29**
   Welcome Home ....

Chapter 7 .... **33**
   Indications..

Chapter 8 .... **39**
   Time for Change ....

Chapter 9 43
Daisie ....

Chapter 10 47
Skepton General Hospital ....

Chapter 11 53
The Plan ....

Chapter 12 60
Dinner for Two ....

Chapter 13 65
Notice ....

Chapter 14 73
Room 166 ....

Chapter 15 77
Fate Takes a Hand ....

Chapter 16 83
A Breath of Fresh Air ....

Chapter 17 89
Beryl Heatherley ....

Chapter 18 94
How Far Should I Go? ....

Chapter 19 99

The Journey Home ....

Chapter 20 104

The George & Dragon ....

Chapter 21 119

Mother ....

Chapter 22 127

Decadence? ....

Chapter 23 131

Temptation ....

Chapter 24 142

Fences and Forecasts ....

Chapter 25 157

A Lesson Learnt ....

Chapter 26 164

That's Ludicrous ....

Chapter 27 188

Grace Nightingale ....

Chapter 28 191

The Contract ....

Chapter 29 206
  Reunion ....

Chapter 30 216
  The Ridings ....

Chapter 31 226
  Digital Decadence ....

Chapter 32 235
  Life Begins Again ....

Chapter 33 241
  Yang Li ....

Chapter 34 244
  Landlord ....

Chapter 35 253
  Level 17 ....

Chapter 36 256
  Revelations ....

Chapter 37 260
  Las Vegas ....

The End 270

Chapter 1
Suburbia

Suburbia starts at one end of the road spreading itself wherever the house-builder takes you, a cul-de-sac, an avenue, even estates sometimes. That is where Belinda and Neville live, 69, Ponsbury Close, on the outskirts of Skepton in the West Ridings of Yorkshire.

A cosy four-bedroom detached house with en-suite bathroom and a conservatory overlooking the open countryside of the ridings, with only the car on the drive, the curtains and the patterned block paving made it stand out against their neighbours, the Redgrave's at number 67 and the Marshes' at number 71.

It was spring time, April 2018.

Idyllic, no suburbia, clicky suburbia. Belinda was a snob.

She sat at her dressing table, pulling her face from one side to the other, parting her frown, her forefinger on her dimple, her cheeks smothered in dollops of mid-life elixir, for middle age. Well, that is what the label on the jar was telling her. She rubbed harder where the wrinkles were more pronounced, although it did not get rid of the red spot near her left ear. She rolled her forefinger over it, wishing it wasn't there. She would deal with that later from another jar, another cream. She was late getting ready for work. *Sod it, look at the time,* she said to herself, glancing at her *Gucci* watch and her Pandora bracelet, a love heart. Neville bought it for her 30-something birthday last year. She lied even to herself. She was forty-four, but still in good shape for her years, tall, bright blue eyes and long blonde hair, attractive, with a hint of elegance. Although most people would think she had that authoritative business woman appearance, some people would find daunting. She liked to dress with a measure of risk – short skirts, plunging necklines. Her demeanour deterred all but the fearless. She had that ability to put fear into people's hearts with her strong personality, although she had an equal amount of charm when it was needed.

She made one last stretch and took one last look at her make-up before she stood up, allowing her dressing gown to slip from her shoulders and fall to the floor, naked.

She arched her back in an attempt to stiffen her breasts. That sagging feeling had already started in her mind, edging menopause. She pushed her face nearer to the dressing table mirror, making one last swirl with her fingers perfecting the face cream, a spread of bright red lipstick and she was ready for her underwear, a matching thong and bra, over the top for the office, be prepared, the boy Scout instinct, ever the opportunist, but that was her, the real her, the praise-seeker,

Oh my god! Look at the time. Where are my shoes? She dashed from the bedroom, searching the landing, *Not there.* She raced to the bottom of the stairs, heading straight for the lounge door, remembering where she had taken them off last night. No, it wasn't her. It was Neville sucking her toes. He was the last one to see them. *Dirty sod!* He loved playing that game. *Me lying on my back, my legs reaching upwards, him spreading them apart, opening them wide, ogling my bush and my swollen lips nestled inside, hiding until he had spread me wide enough to reveal my excitement, my lust.*

"No time for lust and dirty thoughts, where the fuck are they?" she shouted to the room. It was then that she saw it rising from behind the arm of the sofa. She stopped dead in her tracks, unable to speak as she stared at the vapours rising upwards. It reminded her of the morning cup of coffee, steaming hot.

Her instinct told her something was wrong. A chill ran down her back. Fear gripped her throat as she forced herself to look down behind the arm of the sofa. She gulped, almost vomiting with fear and disgust, putting her hand to her mouth.

Fucking hell, she shouted. No reply. The pile of dog shit said nothing, and I mean a fucking pile, Great-Dane sized.

She ran to the kitchen hitting her side on the door frame, ignoring the pain. *Jasper, Jasper! Where are you?* she screamed. Seeing no sign of him in the kitchen, she pulled the blind back, searching the lawns as she peered outside. Nothing. Neville must have taken him for his early morning walk down by the canal. She wondered why she hadn't heard him messing about over coffee in the kitchen. They both liked it there by the canal, a little bit of peace and quiet and fresh morning air.

Jasper, a two-year-old lively and boisterous Dalmatian full of playful life, was Neville's friend. *I'll give them what for when they get back here,* she told herself, to make sure she opened the front door. She sighed. The car was not there. *Fuck it,* she slammed the door shut.

She raced back up the stairs to her dressing table, grabbing her phone. *Neville, you need to come home. Now.* No reply. She rang for the third time before throwing her phone onto the bed, screaming, *AHHHHHHG! Where the fuck are you when I need you most?* The tears began. She felt dirty, pulling her thong down and unclipping her bra, letting them fall to the floor and then kicking them away in disgust. It was the embarrassment of it rather than the event that controlled her thinking now as she raced for the bathroom, turning on the taps. She needed to cleanse herself. She wanted to be sick, holding her face in her hands her, mind wondering how the fuck could it have happened. *God only knows.* She asked herself, searching her mind. Jasper never goes into the lounge, out of bounds. Everything was too expensive, not the place for dog hairs, Neville's dog hairs. *He will have to go,* Jasper that is spite now taking over her thoughts. *Five minutes, a pile of shit and the dog is up for sale. What a start to the morning and I am fucking late for work.* She glanced at the clock on her bedside table, almost 9 am. The tears were flowing now. She screamed again. *You've no fucking right doing this to me. This is my house, you bastard! My fucking house,* she was openly sobbing.

She returned to the bathroom, closing the taps, feeling the water with her hand as she poured a generous amount of *Revelations* bath gel before paddling the water with her free hand, creating an ever-increasing mountain of soap suds. She stepped into the bath, lowering herself into the hot water, bubbles popping as she laid full length, wanting to clean every little bit of her body. She sat up creating a waterfall as the water washed down between her breasts, wondering if she would ever be totally clean again.

She opened her legs, her hand searching for the soap when she touched it. The water immediately coloured as she disturbed whatever it was. Small crusts of it rose to the surface. She screamed and screamed, pulling herself out of the water, traces of shit just below her knee and on her fingers. *Oh my God! What's happening?* She was sobbing, uncontrollably shaking with fear now as she stood at the side of the bath, watching as a muddy cloud began to consume the surface of the water, spoiling her view. In desperation, she pulled the bath plug, watching as the water raced away down the plughole, leaving just the frothy bubbles only to reveal a pile of crap in between where her legs had been. The bubbles clung to the irregular shape of the turd like frogspawn, bubbling as the water rushed away. She reached for a towel, wiping the shit from her hand and leg. The pile of crap making its statement, disturbed but still there, unmoved.

Her mind was out of control now. She fell to the floor, drawing her knees up against her breasts, her head hiding in her cleavage, wanting Neville, sobbing and afraid. *Help me,* she cried. *Help me.*

*****

Chapter 2
The Kettle

Jack liked cooking. He first cooked through necessity in his university years, with independence and all that jazz, sometimes wishing he was still living with his parents. You know that world where everything is free and on schedule, breakfast at eight, dinner at six, a kiss from his mother and a sandwich box as he went out of the door to university. Now he enjoys it. In today's menu, the ingredients all laid out on the island work surface, washed and prepared, ready for cooking.

Menu: asparagus with chicken breast fillets,
Ingredients:
Free range chicken breast
English asparagus (Worcester) cooked in butter
Italian vine tomatoes
Portobello mushrooms
Lemon and rhubarb Jus
A bottle of Chablis in the fridge

He glanced at his watch a couple of hours before Katie, his sister, would arrive for dinner, so a cup of coffee was in order. He filled the kettle, closing the lid and placing it on its stand before turning the power on.

Jack was a thirty-year-old aspiring entrepreneur and businessman, fit with an athletic appearance of six-feet-one, medium build with dark brown hair and blue eyes, what every young girl was looking for, (Well, that is what Jack liked to think) vain, good-looking, handsome even (That is what girls had told him). He was full of life and enjoying every minute of it.

He switched on the power, a loud cracking noise was heard, followed by flashes of coloured light and a short puff of smoke from the wall socket, throwing Jack headfirst against the pantry door, his head smashing into the stainless-steel door handle, blood spurting everywhere as his body writhed on the floor, his face blue, agony stretching from ear to ear. He lay there on the floor, his eyes closed.

"Hi, Jack, it's me. I thought I would come and give you a hand cooking dinner. I finished my lecture early today and I couldn't see the point in going home first. Where are you?" she said, her eyes searching the kitchen as she opened the door.

Not seeing Jack in the kitchen, Katie walked over towards the door leading to the sitting room, passing the island unit before she saw Jack's body, frozen, laying on the floor, his arms bent tight at the elbows, his head and knees in the foetal position, his face and hands blue, his clothes and face covered in blood, a pool of congealed blood on the floor touching his head, matting his hair. She felt sick seeing him lying there, panic filling her eyes.

"Oh my God! Jack, Jack!" she screamed. "What have you done?" She was shouting at the body lying in front of her, the blood draining from her face, a cold sweat gripping her body. She knelt by his side, cradling his head in her arms, her hands and dress covered in blood, tears streaming down her cheeks. "It can't be, Jack. Talk to me please." She screamed and screamed, frightened and alone.

*****

Chapter 3
Doctor Doogood

The door opened to the consulting room of Dr Doogood at the Skepton General Hospital A&E, Katie taking the chair offered to her by the doctor.

He looked at his notes. "Sister to Jack. Is that correct?" he asked warmly, a smile offering her his support.

"Yes," she replied nervously, not wanting to hear what he had to say, frightened at what he would tell her.

Katie, a twenty-three-year-old student at Leeds University, was studying BA (Hons) History & Politics. She was tall like her brother, Jack, with long dark brown hair styled with a waterfall plait, with sparkling brown eyes, stunningly attractive and a figure to match, a good catch for someone; that is only if Jack approved of course.

He smiled again, "Let me see you smile. There is some good news. Jack will recover. That is the good news. The burns caused by the explosion are luckily only superficial rather than everlasting, and with care and the proper treatment, his own body will repair his scars over time." He looked down at his notes again. "The gash to his forehead caused by the fall will however leave a scar but I would add that skin grafting and cosmetic surgery could reduce that significantly. He will still be your handsome brother, Jack."

Katie burst into tears. "Is he alive? Will he recover?" she struggled to say the words, confused, holding her head in her hands. Doctor Doogood rang the buzzer on the wall behind him, summoning a nurse to come and sit with her to lessen the experience. She was obviously having trouble listening carefully to what he was telling her.

Nurse Edmonds entered the room and took a chair beside Katie, taking her hand in hers, offering her comfort and support.

"Would you like a cup of tea or coffee? Perhaps that would help. There is no rush. Jack is alright. He is sedated right now. His body needs time to recover. You should be able to sit with him after we have finished our chat."

Katie smiled, albeit a small one. "Jack owes you his life. If it was not for your emergency call, he would not have survived his injuries. They always look worse than they are most times. He's going to be fine but I need to tell you that after his brain scan, we found something's not quite right and making it worse. We do not understand the information the scan is giving us. In fact, we have never seen anything like it before, so we will have to conduct further specialised tests to give us the answers we require before he will be able to come home." He frowned. "Sorry but it could have been a lot, lot worse. He's young. He's strong and healthy, so there is no reason why he should not live a normal life. So let's take it from there. Bit by bit, you will see everything will be fine." He smiled reassuringly. Nurse Edmonds squeezed her hand in support.

"Thank you, Doctor. Sorry, I just couldn't handle losing him. He is all I have got left. Both my parents were killed in a car crash last year. It would finish me if I lost Jack as well." She burst into tears again, sobbing uncontrollably. Nurse Edmonds pulled her closer, putting her arm around her shoulders, comforting her.

"I will leave you for a short time, Katie, with Nurse Edmonds, give you time to understand the reality of the situation. I will come back shortly."

"Thank you, Doctor. She will be fine. I will take care of her." He left the room.

Katie played with Jack's wristband, reading the details.

JACK CAMEBRIDGE 09121988: trauma… comforted by the fact that the label was not attached to his big toe, morgue style.

Like a parcel in lost property, she said to herself. She looked up as Dr Doogood arrived.

"Feeling a little better? Nurse told me I would find you here," he smiled.

"Yes, thank you, Doctor. I am sorry for my bad manners earlier; I just panicked." She stared into his eyes.

"Not to worry. That is understandable under the circumstances. I would like you to see Nurse Edmonds and she can arrange to have a bed put up for you, so you can stay if you wish. Perhaps you need to go home and collect some night clothes?"

"No, I am not leaving his side. I will call my best friend. She will bring what I need. I must stay here by Jack's side."

The tears began to flow again.

"That will be okay. Don't upset yourself. We can talk tomorrow. I will ask Nurse Edmonds to come and sit with you."

*****

Chapter 4
69, Ponsbury Close

"We should call the police. Let them sort this mess out. Pass me your phone please. I've left mine in my car."
"Are you mad? 'Call the police.' You are sometimes just too fucking stupid for words. Do you think I want the embarrassment of telling a police officer some strange dog has shit in my bath? You are kidding me. You are a fucking idiot." Her face was bright red. She was screaming like he had never heard her before.
"Call the police and you can fetch a bin liner because you won't be here much longer than that, you Pratt." Neville's eyes scanned the geometric shapes made in the carpet, avoiding her violence. The words would not come to him.

"You are fucking useless. Take the bloody dog and yourself off to the RSPCA. You are not wanted here right now. Leave your fucking mess to me. I will sort it out, find a way, something you obviously cannot achieve. Off you go before I throw something your way." She pulled at her rubber gloves, making sure they were secure. Her eyes hated him.

The front door slammed shut.

She scooped up the pile from the carpet in the lounge and sprayed it with *Dettol* and a stain-remover before heading upstairs to the bathroom to clean away pile-two.

She threw the flannel and hand towel into a bin liner ready for the dustbin. She turned the hot tap to full on, hoping it would wash the bath clean, at the same time emptying the bottle of *Dettol* and most of the contents of the stain-remover aerosol, then taking care of washing every inch of the bath clean several times. She would be using the shower from now on. She would not chance another pile of crap.

She took the bin liner and empty aerosol downstairs, putting them both in the dustbin, ready for collection. She paused. *No, if he dares to come back, that will be his first job, the council tip; that will teach him. All this must be his fault. I will get to the bloody bottom of it if it kills me.*

She went back to the lounge carpet and a final inspection. "Mm, mm, that will do," she said to herself before pushing the sofa over the place where the dog had crapped, hiding the evidence. *Fetch the police.* Those words played on her mind time after time as she returned to the kitchen and the fridge, pouring herself a large glass on Pinot Grigio left over from their meal last night. *Stupid man, fetch the police.*

Her office thought she was suffering from a migraine attack. She wished that was the case as she finished her glass of wine. She returned to the fridge, emptying the remains of the wine bottle into her glass. *May as well get pissed, never had a headache, so let's have a hangover. Fuck everything. What a mess life can become in the blink of an eye!* She threw herself into a chair, putting her feet up on the island unit. *He will pay for this. I was supposed to be meeting Bill for lunch and a quick fondle in his car afterwards. Now he will have the hump and knowing him possibly a wank, convincing his imagination that it is my hand around his prick.*

The door slammed behind him. No sign of Jasper. He had the common sense to leave him with his best mate, David. Knowing the kind of mood she was in, that was certainly the right choice to make.

He stuck his head through the kitchen door, keeping well clear of any missiles that may come his way. "Can I join you?"

"Ha! Bloody Ha! Where's crapper?" her voice slurred. Anger shone in her eyes, evil or hurt – what was the difference? Her face and neck red from the wine. Neville saw the empty bottle and glass sitting on top of the black granite work surface. Hoping that was where the bottle would be staying, he walked towards her.

"Look, none of this mess is my doing. I was out when all this happened. Are you sure all the doors were closed? You hadn't left one open?"

"Get out before I do you some harm. I just knew it wouldn't be long before you put the blame at my door. He's your dog, so it was your crap. Get out!" she screamed, hurtling her slipper at him as she continued her abuse. "Get out, I tell you. Get out and don't ever come back."

*****

Chapter 5
Where to Next?

Two weeks passed. Neville was still in the doghouse, toe sucking and sex off the menu. In fact, almost everything was off the menu. His bunches of flowers found the bin and the lead crystal vases remained empty. He was even cooking for himself. Belinda was eating out, shagging at the Premium Inn on the outskirts of Skepton, telling Neville she was spending time with her friends. He would have to wait. She was still considering whether she needed him or not. She kept the black bin liners handy in a kitchen drawer just in case; that would be his first indication of her intentions.

A snob, yes, vindictive and cruel, yes. Lies came easy to her. She had no guilt about shagging Bill, her line manager. She may need to use him yet. Who knows how it all will end?

Bill, in a timeless marriage to Jill which was going nowhere, was a senior manager for a large international company specialising in industrial ceramics and enjoying mid-life at the age of fifty-five. Overweight by more than a few pounds now, hair thinning with grey streaks and brown eyes, quite handsome but now beginning to show his age, overworked and stress leaving their mark, he had learned how to stay cheerful with his lot, enjoyed flirting with women eighteen and above, although he preferred the more mature and sophisticated woman nearer his own age, his comfort zone. Belinda was a good match and balanced his egos with the hustle and bustle of his busy lifestyle.

Neville was comfort-eating and losing weight at the same time, obviously doing more fretting than eating, wondering where he would live if she carried out her threats. Jasper had gone to a good home. There was no point in hanging on to him. It was her or him; at least that's what she insisted on. Jasper had gone. He was still waiting for her.

For the first time in their relationship, he began to turn things over in his mind, hatching a strategy. A plan would be useless. He closed his Building Society Account. 'Just in case,' he told himself. He began to save for that rainy day, should it ever come along. He poured himself another beer.

She was late again. He peered at his watch, just gone midnight, wondering what she was doing and who she was doing it with. He finished his beer and went to the spare room, pissed off for another night, knowing he wouldn't sleep. He heard the back door close, the clatter of her house keys as she threw them on the marble worktop in the kitchen. He turned out the bedside table lamp, rolling over, pretending to be asleep.

*****

"I will not be home this evening. I will be out with Janice. We will be staying overnight in a hotel in Birmingham. We are going to a show at the NEC, grab a meal before the show that should take my mind off things and make me feel better." They were just about polite to each other nowadays, although Neville had an inkling it wasn't Janice she was seeing but her man friend. He had suspected something was going on. The way she dressed, her underwear, all those silly tell-tale signs you ignore usually until it is too late.

'I will nip to the bank at lunchtime and withdraw as much cash as possible,' he said to himself as he sat, watching her drinking her orange juice, his mind ogling her breasts. She was attractive, sexy and good fun until the shit hit the lounge carpet and the bath tub. Now it was all but over. He was a realist and he certainly wasn't going to sit around letting her command the high ground. He had ideas of his own and he was determined she would not get the better of him. He even considered going to the solicitors to find out how much the whole thing was going to cost him. He would give it a few days. She will want to break free if that is her plan.

Bill, no. He is convenience, a distraction from the inevitable he had read the letter from Simpson & Smith, her company's main rival. She had applied for an account manager's position and had been accepted. He would like to be a fly on the wall when she gave Bill her notice.

No, No. Neville, you would wish you hadn't been a fly.

*****

The bank told him he could collect his withdrawal in three days' time, i.e. Thursday, £14,000 pounds plus a bit. It had been easier than he thought. All above board, she would want to know what had happened to the money. She would demand her share. She can fuck off – that's what he would tell her. She would get nothing. She would threaten him with a solicitor's letter and kick him out. He had laid awake these last few nights, rehearsing his words.

You can fuck off to your fancy man.
You are getting nothing from me.
You can threaten me as much as you like.

It is amazing what a pile of dog shit can achieve within a marriage in two short weeks. He knew as soon as he held the cash in his hand that it was over between them. 'Time for the Warden's WW2 helmet,' he chuckled to himself, relieved in his mind now that he knew what he had to do.

Five sealed bags stamped £2.500 in twenty-pound notes, the remainder in various denominations counted out at the counter and placed in a manila envelope with an elastic band holding it all together. He looked at the receipt, mentally adding to what he had scraped together, already giving him a grand total of almost £21,700. He smiled, pleased with himself. It wasn't the money. It was the fact that it was his, all his and not hers.

He was beginning to enjoy himself having come to terms with the fact he would soon be single and that she would be pleading with him for a divorce inside six months and handing him a cheque for his half of the house, mortgage-free, certainly more than enough to start his life over again.

He came home with a Chinese takeaway. He opened a bottle of Chablis to celebrate his pending victory when he saw the note.

Pay the window cleaner.

No, he would not. He put it in the empty rice container. Sitting at the table, he switched the TV on. Manchester United were at home to Chelsea.

*****

Chapter 6
Welcome Home

They drove away from the hospital, leaving a chapter of their life tucked under Dr Doogood's arm, there in a file titled:

JACK CAMBRIDGE 34 34 NP 45 Z Dr Doogood Consultant Case Number: 235678/890/2018.

They shook hands, saying their goodbyes and thank-yous.

"Let's stop for lunch, Katie. I know I shouldn't, but I fancy a Kentucky fried chicken meal. Do you mind? It's either that or a pub meal. We can go to the Star and Garter on the High Street if you would prefer that."

"No, Kentucky's fine. You know I like that. That is why you suggested it." She gave him a big smile. She loved him so much and was glad he was coming home.

Katie parked the car, took Jack's hand and headed for the High Street and Kentucky. Jack found a table near the window overlooking the High Street. Katie took her place in the queue. *Two chicken meals, a glass of milk for Jack and a raspberry milkshake for me.* She was rehearsing her order ready for when her turn came. She turned around searching for Jack. There he was near the window. She smiled. He waved back, returning her smile.

"Are you enjoying that? It's like you're in a race or something," she laughed.

"Not exactly. I am bloody starving. You could never get fat on three NHS meals a day and that's supposing you didn't miss one or couldn't face the choice. Sorry am I being a little piggy."

She touched his hand. "No, don't be silly. I could see how much you were enjoying it. That's all."

He smiled. "I need feeding up a little, but I will get there. Do you want me to stay over at yours for a few days or do you want to come and stay with me?"

She frowned, not sure that she had said the right thing. "That is a definite 'no'. This is something I need to face on my own. Just give it a few days and then if I am okay, why don't we go off to the East Coast for a few days? I will pay." It was his turn to laugh.

"Yes, I would like that but let's wait and see how you get on. I will be popping in to check on you at every opportunity, so make sure you are dressed properly in case I bring Tina when it's her turn to drive."

"In that case, I will be naked." He gave her a mischievous grin.

"No, you won't do that, Jack. You know she is engaged to Ron, your second-best friend. Ron, remember him?" she frowned.

"That doesn't mean I can't fancy her," he laughed.

"No, but it does mean you will do as I say, doesn't it, Jack?" she stared at him.

"Yes, I suppose so. I was only pulling your leg."

"Hmm. If you say so, but we both know that is not altogether true."

The car pulled into the drive.

"Let me have a look at your appointment card so I know when to make myself available. I just hope they are on days when I have not got a lecture. I don't want bad attendance marks, do I?" she smiled.

"I take it that means you will be coming with me to my appointments. That's not necessary. I will be fine on my own."

"Forget it, Jack. I'm coming with you. I want to know what is going on. The consultant's version of events, not one of your made-up fairy stories, so don't say another word and that's final. I'm coming. In fact, I will keep the card and copy it so there will be no misunderstanding between us." She put the appointment card into her pocket, giving him a smile.

"Do you know, Katie, you can be worse than mother used to be sometimes."

"That well may be true but I can tell you now I am not washing your socks or boxers like mother used to. That's your job. I will help you with the shopping and cleaning and that is about all. Everything else will be down to you, so come on jump out and let's organise supper. I suppose we will have to shop after we empty the fridge and throw everything away, not the wine though." She took his hand as they walked up the drive to the front door.

Jack was lucky. He bought this house with money left to him by his grandfather when he was twenty-five, a grand Victorian detached house. 'HIDE AND SEEK HOLLOW' it was called. It had a large garden, large rooms and high ceilings. Katie loved this house and often wished it was hers, a husband and two daughters, a dog and several cats. All she had right now was her own bedroom, four more to go; the house excited her.

Jack pushed open the door, sweeping up the loose mail as the door opened. "Crickey, you would think I had been abroad for months on Missionary work. Just look at this lot. You can help me sort it out if you like over a glass of wine or two."

"In that case," she said, taking the mail away from him, "we will leave all of this on the kitchen table, empty the fridge, then off to the supermarket because we need to drive there and back."

"Is there anything else, madam?"

"No, but you are not driving, and I am not drink-driving. Does that explain things?"

"Okay, I get the point. What do you want for supper anyway? I will let you decide. It's how you oversee everything else," he laughed. She laughed too.

"Phew, Blimey! We will need to wash the fridge drawers and everything, and to be on the safe side, we will throw the whole stinking lot away." She held her nose in a gesture to emphasise the smell. "God, where are the bin liners?"

"Top drawer on the left."

"Okay, I will collect the rubbish and dump it in the bin whist you concentrate on cleaning that bloody mess-up."

"Short end of the stick, you mean? Sorry," he smiled.

"Thanks. I am glad you are here with me. I will cook your favourite dish if you like." She gave him a hug. "I love you so much. I am just thankful God saved your life and yes, beef stroganoff will be great. Thank you. I will buy you a nice bottle of Merlot in return."

"Put the heating on, Jack, just to take the damp chill out of the air. It smells a little and it's beginning to turn cold again," she pretended to shiver.

"Yes, I will light a fire in the sitting room. We can eat in there if you like. It will be cosier and easier for us to keep warm."

"Well, that feels better. Let me just make a list of what we need at the supermarket. Have you a pencil, Jack?"

"Yes, in the top drawer over there at the end of the island unit," he pointed towards it.

"Oh my God! How do you find anything in this jumble, Jack? It's a right mess in here," she held up the pencil. "A bit bloody grubby reminds me to bring you a new one," she laughed.

"That's one Mum bought for me years ago, sorry," he laughed.

"Let's go, come on," she held out her hand.

*****

Chapter 7
Indications

It had started to rain. "Get as near as you can. The last thing I need right now is a soaking in this bloody rain."

"That's not as easy as it sounds. Everybody has got the same idea," she replied. They drove around for the second time.

"Just there, over there," he said, pointing. "Look, they are just leaving."

"Well done! That's as near as damn it. Thanks," she replied, smiling.

"I will grab a trolley and meet you inside," he ran off, pulling his coat over his head. She parked the car and dashed inside to join him. "You pick. I push. You pay. How's that?"

"Not quite. I'll push. You pick. You pay. This is supposed to be you buying dinner. My treat from you to me, remember?"

"Okay, you win."

Vegetables, dairy, the Butcher's counter, wine, not too big a shop, just the essentials. "We need bread, Jack." She pulled the front of the shopping trolley, guiding him towards the bakery, down by the tinned food bays, beans, peas and tinned fruit. In a tin; they had it on a shelf.

Jack stopped in his tracks, just managing to grab a shelf, holding baked beans he dropped down, kneeling, gasping for breath. She panicked, "Jack, what's the matter?" Her voice almost a shriek, she looked down at him. His face was pale, his eyes closed shut and his body limp. "Oh my God, Jack! Jack! Talk to me." She slapped his face, wanting him to open his eyes and talk to her. She smacked his cheek again, desperation showing in her eyes. "Jack, please talk to me."

He stirred, lifting his head. "What's happened?"

"You just collapsed. Don't you remember anything?"

"No, everything went blank. I just felt so weak."

"Can I help you?" asked the tall gentleman peering down at Jack's slumped body, searching the fear in Katie's eyes. "Would you like me to call for an assistant? They are bound to have qualified staff to hand."

"Jack, do you need help? This gentleman will fetch a first-aider."

"No, that won't be necessary. I'm okay. I just slipped. Thanks, but I will be fine."

"Are you sure? It's no trouble."

"Thank you. It is very thoughtful of you, but I think I can manage him now," she gave him a friendly smile. He turned away, passing a woman pretending to shop for sliced peaches on the opposite bay, holding the can in her hands, nosing at what was happening with Jack and blocking the aisle. Within two minutes, there was almost a crowd gathering, exchanging gossip. "We are going straight home and I am going to call Dr Doogood. There is something wrong and we need to know what it is. Are you okay to walk or shall I get some help?"

"No, don't do that. I am okay. Let's finish shopping and get back home. A cup of tea and a sit by the fire should put things right. I'm okay." He stroked her arm, giving her a smile.

"You had better be. I couldn't handle it if anything was wrong with you. Oh, Jack." She pulled him closer to her.

*****

"Look, it's silly, thinking you are fit enough to cook, so let's be realistic about this. I am going to order us both a takeaway. Chinese or Indian, you choose. Okay?"

"Tomorrow I will cook the stroganoff, tomorrow." His mind was still a little confused. "Sorry, I couldn't help it. You are not angry with me, are you?" There was a sadness in his voice.

"No, silly boy. Tomorrow will be fine. Choose, otherwise we will be here all night," she replied, giving him a comforting smile, waving her mobile in her hand, ready to order. "Indian is that okay with you?"

"Yes, fine. I will just order a few dishes, some rice and some garlic nans that should keep us happy. You can open a bottle of wine if you like. The Chiraz would be fine," she shouted as she made for the door.

She ran back. "What am I thinking of your coming with me, until I know what's wrong with you? You are not leaving my side. Come on," she held out her hand.

"All this is not necessary. You know that I will be fine."

"No, you won't. You are coming with me even if I have to drag you there. Come on now."

"Can't they deliver?" he asked in desperation.

"No, not at this time of night. It will be quicker to go and fetch it. Now come on. Stop dawdling."

*****

It seemed to take ages. It always does – phone ringing, people collecting their orders, you sit there watching the traffic out of the window or you sit and stare looking at a silk picture of a Buddha or a twelve-inch television screen recycled from car boot sales and only available for takeaway outlets. Jack was quiet, watching the passing traffic through the window.

She sat watching him. 'I think he is worried about the incident at the supermarket. It frightened him, although he will not admit it. It scared me too. I will call Dr Doogood first thing tomorrow morning,' she said to herself.

"Number 13."

"That's us, Jack. Come on, let's get back home and in the warm by the fire. I'm hungry, are you?"

"A little," he sounded strange, not interested.

"Are you okay? You're not feeling funny again, are you?"

"No, I am not feeling funny. I was never funny. Why do you keep going on at me?" he snapped, pulling the door open for her, all eyes on them as they left with their meal.

She gave him the carrier bag. "You take these," she replied, hurt, a little angry with him. It will keep until they got home; she told herself. She was worrying now. 'Perhaps it is something serious.'

"Right. Let's get home. We can chat over dinner with a glass of wine."

Jack offered no reply, daydreaming, looking out of the side window, keeping his thoughts to himself.

Katie organised the plates and dishes. Jack corked the wine and made the fire up in the sitting room. She put the main dishes and the rice on a large tray ready for Jack to take into the sitting room. "It's ready, Jack. Can you come and give me a hand please?" she called.

"Here, you take this tray and I will bring the *naan* breads and spices with the cutlery. Thanks. I'm starving." She followed him into the sitting room, closing the door behind them.

"This is cosy. It reminds me of the times we did this with Mum and Dad, doesn't it you?" Silence. "Did you hear me, Jack?" She prodded his arm.

"Sorry, I'm miles away. What did you say?"

"Never mind. It is not important. Are you hungry? Help yourself. There's plenty to go around," she grinned.

"I think you bought enough for the week. What's left should keep us going for at least a couple of days," he replied, returning her smile.

She watched him. Something wasn't quite right. She could sense it. Then it happened. Jack keeled over at the side of the table, his body shaking uncontrollably. She was frightened. "Oh my God! Jack! Jack! What's wrong? Don't leave me, Jack," the tears stifling her words as she struggled to stop the shaking, holding both of his arms, hurting him. She could see it in his eyes sunk back into their sockets, almost ghoulish. Then as suddenly as it happened, the shaking stopped. Jack opened his eyes, staring at her like a stranger to him as if he had woken from a bad dream. He was slobbering and lying in a puddle of pee on the carpet. Her hand could feel the warmth of it.

"Jack, it's alright. I am here. Look at me," she screamed. "Look at me. Tell me you are okay." She was shivering with fear. He stood up, offering her his hand. Now it was Jack's turn to comfort her.

"Come here, Katie. Let me hold you. I'm okay, just a little shaken but I am alright. I just know everything is okay, so there is nothing for you to worry about." Jack cuddled her, holding her tightly against him, wanting to protect her.

She stared at him, frightened, concerned by it all, and yes, he did look alright, but she wasn't convinced that it was over and things would get back to normal. "We should call the hospital and have them send somebody to give you a check-up. Something is wrong, Jack. Let me call them."

"No, I will not. Let's clear this mess up and get to bed. I will be fine after a good night's sleep in my own bed. We can talk to Dr Doogood tomorrow if that will make you happy, alright?"

He gave her a hug. "Okay. Tomorrow we talk to the doctor, you get off to bed and I will clear this lot away and do whatever is necessary. Then I will come and say goodnight. Now leave this to me. You go upstairs and shower and then get into bed."

"Okay," he kissed her cheek.

Twenty minutes, and she was on her way upstairs to say goodnight to Jack. She pushed his door open. He was asleep. She checked he was breathing and kissed him on the cheek, removing the wet towel from his hand and pulling the duvet up around his shoulders. She put the light out before going to her room across the hallway. She paused, glancing at the wristband, her mind busily turning the words over in her head. 'TRAUMA!'

She turned around, listening for any noise or movement from his room. She had purposely left his door open. It was all peaceful and quite. She opened the door to her room, leaving her door open before she got into bed

She lay there listening all night. She got out of bed twice to check on him. He was fast asleep, a heavy sleep. Satisfied he would be okay, she finally closed her eyes.

*****

Chapter 8
Time for Change

April would soon be drawing to a close and the situation with Belinda and Neville had not improved. She was concerned about putting an end to their marriage, so she raised the stakes, leaving metaphors for Neville at every opportunity. *I may be away for the weekend with Janice, or why don't you take that holiday to Corsica you have always promised yourself?* She had no intention of their break-up interfering with her new job as Account Manager at Simpson & Smith. She had bought new clothes for the big occasion, day one in two weeks' time. She needed to get a move on; she told herself, doing her morning make-up in front of the mirror, sitting at her dressing table. She could see more of herself, having removed photos of Neville and Jasper that had been blue tacked to one side of the mirror. Satisfied that they were heading for the local tip by now, suffocated inside a heavy-duty black bin liner, she grinned. She liked that thought. They would be there for another hundred years or more and serve them right. It was all their fault, a large grin satisfying her ego.

She had finally come to terms with the apportionment of blame resting clearly on Neville's shoulders. Jasper was just an innocent victim. Now it is pay-back time; she would tell him when she came home from work this evening, perhaps cook him dinner, a glass or two of Merlot, his favourite wine. 'I shall wear a sexy dress, no bras, raise my nipples, plenty of cleavage exciting his lust, raising his expectations, build up his hopes, tease his prick and then burn him.' She grinned. She could already feel the excitement running through her body. She pouted her breast like a pigeon during mating. All she needed to do now was to contain her thoughts and get through the day. 'This evening will come soon enough.'

Then it would be Bill's turn. He would fare no better than Neville. Like him, he could lay no blame on her. He was a middle-aged nobody, going nowhere and certainly not with her. She had used and abused him these last few weeks, expensive restaurants, nights away, a gold necklace and the odd couple of hundred pounds to tide her over until next month's pay day. Devious bitch! No, just settling a score after all he had more than his monies worth, let's face it a shag a week for the last fifteen months and lots more. Besides, God, he is getting off lightly. 'Has it really been that long?' she asked herself. It made her feel like a whore. Perhaps just dumping him wasn't payment enough. She would think about it during the next few days, 'Perhaps take him for a couple of grand. I know he's got that much. He always enjoyed bragging rights about his savings that she, staying indoors, knew nothing about, his little secret, perhaps a bit more even,' she grinned to herself. She was enjoying it now, showing her true colours.

It was the grunting during their lovemaking that finally did it for her. Well, that was her excuse. Even she had to justify plunging the knife in his back. There was certainly no feeling of guilt. In fact, she found it difficult to think of anything that was good about their relationship. It had become boring, although on reflection it was never really any good from the start. She used him as a distraction, allowing complacency to take over their relationship from her going-nowhere marriage to Neville. It was easy now to have all of these bad thoughts convincing herself that life would treat her better. She would have to wait and see. She had gone too far to turn back now. Neville knew someone was screwing her and he probably knew it was Bill.

She finished her make-up, tapped her fringe one final look of approval in the dressing-table mirror and then stood up with both feet inside her dress, pulling it upwards, slipping her arms in the short sleeves and zipping the back, no chance of spoiling her hair, the first summer dress this year. She turned towards the full-length mirror on the wall next to her dressing table, adjusting herself from her shoulders, past her breasts and finishing just above the knee. She smiled, pleased with the result. She looked good; she told herself as she collected a linen jacket from its hanger inside the wardrobe, checked her watch, grabbed her handbag and made for the stairs, ready to face another day at the office. She smiled, knowing that Bill was on the early morning train to London.

It was a good day to take copies of client accounts, copy lists of addresses and contact details from the master file, telling Beryl to fill the paper tray in the photocopier. Perhaps that was what made her decision to dump them both before she started work at Simpson & Smith. It seemed so easy now, with nothing to hold her back.

I will phone the solicitors as soon as I get to the office and get the ball rolling, tell Neville to leave and screw him for every penny he has got. Idiot, fetch the police. Those words would stay with her forever. After all, that was the first and last nail in his coffin. She smirked and then laughed as she locked the front door behind her, a smile stretching from ear to ear. *Single again. God!* The thought of that excited her. That warm feeling inside would see her through the day. She wanted to sing.

Morning has broken…

*****

She stopped at the kerb in front of the drive checking for traffic when he called her.

"Hi Petal, and how are you today? Feeling horny I hope."

"No, I am not horny. Don't you ever consider it's about time you thought of better things to think about rather than sex all the while, something more important, like how are you feeling darling? Good I hope. That would be a start. You just don't turn me on anymore with your dirty talk. Don't you think at your age, we should get past that?" she deliberately paused, waiting for his response.

"What's the matter with you? For God's sake, I thought you liked talking dirty."

"Well, your thoughts are wrong this morning as usual, especially this morning. I haven't got time for all this. Oh, and by the way I am handing in my notice. I am leaving in two weeks' time. I will leave my resignation letter on your desk just in case you get back to the office tonight."

"You are fucking joking, bitch. Where did that come from? I—"

She hung up.

'That just cost you a couple of grand more, Bill. *Bitch!* You will pay for that,' she smiled. '*Easy, bloody easy.*'

Knowing she would have to lie on her back a few more times, ten grand sounded better. 'I could live with that, one last grunt.' She smiled to herself, accelerating down the main road into town. She had plans to rid herself of. 'Neville first. Get that out of the way and then that condescending bastard Bill. I'll make him pay.'

*****

Chapter 9
Daisie

Doreen Breathshott was a sixteen-year-old thug. She wasn't born that way but that is where her short life had taken her, robbing school kids in the playground during school time and anybody that took her fancy at night time, usually middle-aged or old, vulnerable people, male or female. That did not bother her. She could handle a man of her own size with no problem. She grew up with three hard-nosed brothers who funnily enough took after their mother, not their father. He spent most of his life at his Majesty's pleasure.

Standing at five feet ten inches tall, with broad shoulders and a bulldog face complete with short-length auburn hair, with matching brown eyes, you couldn't call her attractive by any stretch of your imagination, fearsome-looking rather than attractive, leaning towards the build and looks of her three brothers. Ugly.

Seeing his offspring, you would think he would be built like a brick-built shithouse doing time for GBH or robbery. On the contrary, he had the body of a weasel, looked like a weasel, weighed in lighter than a jockey, with not a violent bone in his body – laughable but that is life. His grubby appearance, his short brown hair and blue eyes did nothing to enhance his appearance. In short, he was a bloody scruff.

Most of his Majesty's service was for fraud or embezzlement. In fact, his first term inside was for stealing a lorry load of toilet rolls from his employer. The judge sentenced him to three years in Wakefield Prison. Ever since that first sentence, he has gone under the nickname Shitty Breathshott, Shitty for short, to anyone who knows him. I would have said 'mates' but you don't make many of those inside. In short, he was a dipstick. He liked being inside. The best he could hope for on release was soggy beans on toast and a couple of beers down the Bad Neighbours Public House. Sex was off the menu. His missus was Vera, a tall blue-eyed leggy but attractive blonde-haired woman, and at the age of forty-five, she looked in pretty good shape. Unfortunately, her looks disguised her lifestyle. She was always too busy shagging everything else on the estate, poxed up to her eyebrows or pissed most of the time. She enjoyed putting it about that went with a cough like a horse, *and God knows what that looked like.* You dare not think; Shitty was best out of it.

He was never far away from his next stint inside. In fact, it was only the lengthy drawn-out prosecution service that gave him a respite between sentencing and parole. Otherwise, he would be in and out like Vera.

Considering his first term inside was at the tender age of eighteen and he is now fifty-one, you would think he would have learnt a valuable lesson. Was he too thick to realise or did he enjoy the company at her Majesty's pleasure, in thirty-three years? He had only been on the outside a little under seven years. That gave him seventeen outings, each with a free train ticket home and whatever he earned inside in his pocket.

He spent most of his time on the outside with her, his daughter Doreen. God knows how she got that name. He was inside when she was born. He only knew her name when the officer gave him a letter announcing the birth. She was seven months old when the letter arrived. He could never bother to work the dates out but probability would tell you that her real dad lived somewhere on the estate.

In between school and the odd weekend thrown in, unless of course, she had better things to do, which generally was the case, he would spend time with her

In between the Bad Neighbours Public House and watching TV, he would clean the house. What a nightmare that was! In fact, he spent most of his spare money on bus fares to the Job Centre, signing on for benefits and buying black bin bags.

What he should have done was to put the bin liner over his head, rob the local Post Office because he had no chance of getting a job. As soon as you gave your address and your last place of work to the silly sod behind the counter at the job centre, you knew you were wasting your time and that your application form would probably find its way to the bottom of the pile before you left the centre. At least being sent down for robbery, he could go back inside with a bit of credibility instead of having to blush when some rotten piss-taker goaded by someone who knew him from past visits asked him what he was sent down for. He always felt a right Pratt when he told them. *Stealing church funds.* That was his last sentence. No disgrace in that. He was well past any sense of remorse, but the lag would make the most of it, two weeks fag ration probably.

*****

The estate was quiet. It was Friday, piss up night in town or nearer home at the Bad Neighbours Pub.

Doreen left the pub around nine o'clock. She had something set up, an old biddy coming home from the Bingo Hall in Dorrit Street, a ten-minute walk for her. She was carrying too much weight to hurry. She would wait at the end of the lane, a fag in her gob or chatting on her cell phone.

The lane separated the back-to-back gardens of Dennis Street on one side and Belmont Street on the other, with rows of terraced housing dating back to 1890, a mixture of good and bad, neglected and cared for, depends whether you worked or not, just short of being classified as a benefit street, care and don't-care residents.

Doreen threw her fag down on to the pavement, heeling it. She made off to the alleyway further down the lane. Her victim had no choice but to pass at the junction.

Daisie had left the Bingo Hall with her friend, and neighbour Ilene. They had been lifelong friends, now in their eighties, but living life to the full Bingo night was something they looked forward to. They made a night of it, with fish and chips, sharing a pot of tea and a plate of bread and butter, playing, catching up on the week's events at the small family-run restaurant around the corner from the Bingo Hall. They said their goodbyes as Ilene turned down the jitty, leading to her back gate and home. Daisie walked the last fifty yards on her own.

It was quick all over in a flash. The old lady approached the junction, a fist in her face, knocking her to the ground, followed by a boot in her ribs. Doreen wrenched the handbag from her hand and made off down the lane, heading back towards the estate. The contents of the bag stuffed into her pocket, the bag sailed over a garden wall, ready to become part of an on-going investigation. She paused, turning around, looking back at her victim lying where she left her on the ground, motionless, a blur in her evil mind. She lit a fag almost routine for her after a violent assault, robbery, in that order, then back where she came from the Bad Neighbours Pub, drinking with her dad.

There were drinks all around when she returned from the ladies, not a bad haul, a gold watch, credit cards complete with pin numbers written on the back of a tattered notebook that had seen better days, ninety quid and a polythene sleeve with five gold sovereigns in it.

"Where did you get to? I thought you had buggered off home," her dad asked her.

"Don't ask. It won't help you. Let's just say I had a bit of business to take care of," she grinned. A greedy smile filled her cheeks. She didn't give a shit.

*****

The ambulance arrived at Dennis Street and Daisie was taken away, lights flashing, siren sounding, her injuries unknown.

*****

Chapter 10
Skepton General Hospital

"Are you okay, Jack? Not feeling poorly or anything, any pain?"

"Just how many times are you going to ask the same stupid questions? Ever since you woke me up this morning, you have gone on about it. Leave me alone. I'm okay, alright?" He was a little angry. She could see it in his eyes. She was only trying to be nice. It was just as difficult for her as it was for him, but he knew that he just wasn't thinking straight. She convinced herself. Something was worrying him and that was her only concern right now.

"Please don't be angry, Jack. I am only trying to help." Tears formed in her eyes as she spoke.

He took her hand. "I know, of course. I know. Don't feel sad. Everything will turn out okay. I just know it will. Please be patient with me, please." He kissed her gently on her lips. She smiled, knowing he meant every word he said. She gave him a warm smile, wanting to hug him as the duty nurse approached them.

"Jack Cambridge."

"Yes, that's me. This is my sister, Katie."

"Good morning. If you would both like to follow me please." She pointed with her hand to a door just down the corridor, her other hand holding the manila folder, Jack's case file, consulting room 3.

"Good morning. Please take a seat."

"Thank you, nurse. I will call you if I need anything further."

Just being polite, Katie thought, frightened. She hated situations like this. They both replied 'good morning, doctor Doogood'.

He opened Jack's file. "Let's talk about yesterday, Jack. Your collapse in the supermarket and again later at home. Tell me your version of events, Jack. Tell me everything. Even things that you feel are unimportant. I need you to tell me as much as possible. Then I can decide what is the best course of action to take." He smiled, "And you, Katie. Then I would like you to tell me your version of events, everything, no matter how silly they sound. Every detail is important." He paused, giving them both time to reflect on his words. "Just relax. This is a consulting room, not the dentist's surgery." He grinned. They both smiled, beginning to feel a little more comfortable, not so frightened.

"Jack, you start with your version of events. What happened in the supermarket first?" he spoke softly, reassuringly, offering him a generous smile.

"I am not too sure how it happened in the supermarket. We were just walking to the bread counter when I came over all dizzy. My mind went blank and all I remember was sliding down the side of the shelving in the canned food section and everything around me went dark. There was no pain. My body just seemed as though it wanted to relax and I could no longer support myself. Then all I remember after that was Katie slapping me and shouting at me and a tall gentleman looking down at me, speaking to Katie, and that's about all I remember."

"Good. Thank you, Jack. Now you, Katie. You tell me what you saw." He smiled, wanting her to relax. He could see she was still nervous.

"I was walking behind Jack, following him. We were holding hands when it happened. Jack just suddenly released his grip on my hand and slumped to the floor, his eyes wide open, staring at me, frightening me. I panicked, slapping his face. It was a reaction not what I intended. I just did it. I had to slap his cheek twice before he responded, opening his eyes, and then a man was offering me help. Jack was alert by then as though nothing had happened, shouting – 'No, I am alright. I'm fine. I just slipped. That's all.' I thanked the gentleman and we carried on with shopping. Jack seemed okay after that and we finished our shopping and left the store. That's all I remember. It was over just as quickly as it had begun. It just frightened me, frightened us both." She glanced over at Jack. Doctor Doogood was making a mental note.

"Nothing either of you can add?" He looked from his desk. He was writing up his case notes. "Are you sure there's nothing more? Anything. It could be important."

"Okay, let's talk about what happened at home. That I think is the most worrying of the two events, so please think carefully before you say anything because it is what you don't tell me that could be become important."

He turned over the page, ready to make fresh notes. Jack and Katie both looked a little concerned. He would give them time to relax a little, before they talked about it. "Just tell me how you are feeling right now? Are you feeling much better after a night's sleep or are you feeling more tense right now?" Jack paused, wondering why he asked that question.

"I am feeling fine as though none of this has happened. I can't explain it. I just know that everything is alright. There's nothing wrong with me apart from this scar on my cheek and even that will heal up over time. I am convinced of that as well." He frowned, wanting them both to believe him.

"Okay, let's move on. Tell me about what happened at home over dinner, Jack, but before you answer though, had you been drinking wine?"

"No, definitely not. I had poured the wine but never really had time to drink any. My glass was just as I left it."

"Good. Now tell me what happened in your own words in your own time please."

"We had just started the meal. We sat in the sitting room by the fireside. It was warmer there, with the house being empty for a couple of weeks. I was just beginning to enjoy the meal, an Indian takeaway, when I just rolled over onto my side, collapsing at the side of the table and that is all I remember. When I came around and stood up, I just felt fine.

I couldn't explain it. Katie was in tears, screaming at me. We hugged and it was over. We ended things there. I went to shower and got into bed exhausted by it all. That is all I remember until Katie woke me this morning."

He avoided mentioning the slobbering and wetting himself. That was the bit he found difficult to come to terms with, although he was sensible enough to realise that it would not go away and the doctor was sure to question him and Katie about it. He looked down at the floor, avoiding the doctor's eyes. He was embarrassed and he hated that feeling. His face and neck began to colour.

"Thank you, Jack. Please don't feel embarrassed by it all. I'm a doctor. You can trust me," he laughed. There was a pause. Then Jack and Katie joined in with the laughter, big smiles before the doctor's eyes turned towards her.

"Katie, you now please tell me what happened in your own words. Take all the time you need. There is no hurry."

Her faced had coloured. She too was embarrassed about Jack peeing himself and slobbering like a small child. She looked down, talking to her shoes.

"It is as Jack said. He just keeled over, collapsed to the floor, shaking uncontrollably. I had to hold his hands down. I hurt him. I know I did. Then I slapped his cheek, shouting at him, scared out of my wits, afraid that it was all over. He was dead for one minute. Then, as quickly as it had happened, it was all over. He stood up as though nothing had happened, taking me in his arms and comforting me. I wiped his mouth. He had slobbered during his shaking and he had wet himself. I could see the puddle on the floor. I touched it when I knelt beside him. He showered and went to bed. I checked on him and he was in a deep sleep. He slept throughout the night. I woke him, taking him a cup of coffee." She looked at them both, confused. Had she told him everything? She struggled to think clearly. She found the whole thing overwhelming. And just wanted it to end.

"Thank you, Katie. Let's take five minutes and go and have a cup of coffee in the restaurant. We can talk there. Perhaps you will find that more relaxing. You are both tensed.

I can see it in your eyes," he gestured with his hand, pointing to the door.

They chatted in the queue at the restaurant, pushing there trays along as if they were just passing through at a service station on some motorway. Jack took a packet of biscuits. Doctor Doogood had a cheese and tomato sandwich and Katie couldn't quite make up her mind that was too busy worrying about jack. She settled for a cup of Ceylon tea.

They took a table away from customers already having a late breakfast or a mid-morning coffee. It was hard to tell but the table they chose seemed to be as private as one would expect in a public place. They took their places at the table, Jack collecting the trays, taking them back to the counter. Katie sat next to Doctor Doogood. She would find it easier to talk that way instead of facing him, not needing to look at him face to face. She would let Jack do that although she did feel a little guilty. After all, they were there because of Jack, not her.

"Well, your stories seem to blend well. I cannot see from what you have told me any serious change in your condition, Jack. The symptoms you have described could be put down to tension and stress rather than trauma but I cannot give you an accurate diagnosis based on our discussion here today. I will write up my notes and discuss it with Professor Martin. He's the man. We need to take a good look at your case, Jack. He is the leading UK Specialist in this field of neurology. He has written several books on the subject and knows what he is talking about but I will have to let you know after I have discussed your case with him. I will write to you and confirm your appointment. In the meantime, I will arrange for you to have a second MRI scan that should help establish the best diagnosis of your condition although I have to repeat what I have said earlier. It could just be a simple case brought about by stress. Let's just hope that is what we find. So, don't worry. We will get to the bottom of it. I am sure we will. I will be in touch."

*****

"Do you want to wait here in reception whilst I bring the car around?" They were on the third floor, waiting for the lift.

Jack frowned. "I thought we had agreed that we would just let things get back to normal. Is that what we agreed?" He seemed a little annoyed.

She touched his arm, giving him a sorry-smile. "Yes. Sorry, Jack, not thinking."

The door's opening sound alerted Jack. It was followed by the dragging, sliding sound of the bed being pushed and pulled by the two hospital porters. "Mind your backs please," the one doing the pushing shouted.

Jack turned around and stared at the patient lying on the bed, a drip bubbling on its stand, the pipes feeding the fluids to her arm somewhere beneath the blanket. As the porter guided the bed past Jack, he looked down again at the patient's bruised face, her eyes closed from the swelling. Her grey hair matted with congealed blood colouring one side of her face, all kind of images flashing in front of his eyes. He squeezed Katie's hand.

"Ouch!" She looked up, staring into his eyes and saw the sadness in them. It frightened her. "Are you okay, Jack? Are you feeling alright?" He turned, facing her. They stopped walking. The trolley turned the corner and was gone.

"Yes. That old lady, I am sure I have seen her before. That's all. Nothing for you to worry about. Let's get off home. We have a lot of talking to do."

She smiled, pulling him towards the main entrance and the car parks.

Home.

*****

Chapter 11
The Plan

As days go, today was busy, busy stealing, busy arranging, leaving nothing to chance. In fact, you would say 'sabotage' was her intention, files removed, key papers shredded, never to see the light of day again. All in all, she was satisfied. She smiled to herself, smug with her success. She felt horny, a feeling she hadn't shared for a few days, quite exciting. She had no problem convincing herself that she was wet and that excited her thoughts even more. She even visualised Neville sucking her toes, him spreading her legs flashed through her thoughts. *God! I hope I don't give in tonight, overcome by guilt or lust. Not fucking likely. What a thought!* No, she was stronger than that.

She decided the solution was to do it now. She made her way to the ladies' toilet, a guilty look around the office, wondering if anybody had seen her, the lock clicking into place. A hot flush flooded her body, her neck and cheek turning a cherry red, lust in her eyes. She lifted her dress, her hand reaching down between her legs, stroking her excitement. She closed her eyes and drifted into another world, her dirty world.

Her desk phone was ringing. "Hi, it's me. Sorry about earlier."

"Shush, I can't talk now. Let me call you back." She was lying to him of course. She slammed the phone down. *Bugger it*, she said to herself, frustrated, annoyed. Why did he have to spoil it? She was on a high from her orgasm and he just killed all of that. Twenty grand flashed through her thoughts. Her eyes spun like the drums on a slot machine, with bells and dollar signs. She needed to give herself time to think.

'Give him some bullshit. Don't let that phone call change your plans. Dinner with Neville. That is the priority right now.' She needed a fag.

She stood with the storeroom door open, overlooking the car park, smoking, drawing heavily on her filter tip, her mind confused. She paced two steps, turned around and repeated it all over again and again.

It's twenty grand, in cash, she said to herself. She busied her mind on that rather than facing the immediate problem demanding her attention. She needed to calm down from her high, relax and start thinking clearly. She stood on the cigarette butt and stared out into the clouds blowing over the skyline. It was going to rain. That's all she needed right now. Her desk phone rang again.

"Hi, it's me again. Is it alright to talk now?"

"No. I told you no. I will not call you back. Stop pushing me. I'm upset, or don't you think I should be?" The phone danced on her desk as she slammed it down again. A colleague mimed the words, "Are you okay?" She grinned and then laughed as though nothing had happened. She waved to her colleague in response to her concern and then went about her own business.

She wanted another fag. She didn't want another fag. Her mind was so confused. She just wanted to run away from the whole bloody mess. She bit her thumb. Then she walked down the office to play catch up with Beryl, to take her mind away from the confusion. Her face flushed with annoyance. She sighed.

"Have you seen the Bilger file? I seem to have misplaced it?" she lied, avoiding her eyes. "I'm sure I left it on your desk earlier. Can't you find it? You haven't filed it by any chance, have you?" She grinned knowingly.

"I'm not sure," she touched her arm. "Did you manage to finish that copying for me? I'll take it back with me if you have and have another look for that Bilger file. You are probably right, and I have filed it," she smiled.

"It's all there. Look on the table," she pointed with her hand at the pile of photocopying. "I've put the files you wanted me to copy on the top of the pile. Let me know if you have everything else you need please?"

"Yes, I will. Thanks. You're an angel." She returned to her desk, satisfied, pleased something had gone right at last.

She managed to cram all the photocopies into her briefcase and a single carrier bag, both brought into the office with her for this singular assignment. She even felt like a spy. She wasn't sure whether it was touch of guilt or fear that made her feel nervous. She passed it off with ease. In fact, she felt thrilled that she had planned it and pulled it off under his nose. If he ever finds out, he will be well pissed off. That's for sure.

She had an insurance policy tucked away in her garage filing system just in case, a video of Bill and the office bike Norah shagging in the boardroom at last year's Christmas party. It was more of a comedy than a pornographic portrayal of office sex, Norah lying on top of the boardroom table, naked from the waist down her legs up in the air, spread as wide as she could possibly get them and held into position by her hands. That is when comedy takes over with Bill, his bare arse smiling in the half light of the office, with his trousers around his ankles as he heaved up and down, grunting and panting like a wild boar, both hands anchored to her tits. Norah was screaming her delights each time he banged into her. Now that is something she was sure he did not want to share with his wife or Norah's boyfriend, Felix. Shuddering at the thought, she grinned. *Go on show Felix.* No, that won't be necessary. He's fucked either way. She enjoyed the thought though, grinning now from ear to ear.

"Did you find it?"

"Oh, hi Linda. Sorry, yes, I did. Thanks. What are you up to?"

"Routine, boring routine. What else… Bill left me a shit load. I should finish it before I go home. I fancy a cigarette, do you?"

"Yes, I could do with a breath of fresh air," she laughed. "I get bored as well, you know. It's not all fun doing my job either. Anyway, you will find out soon enough."

"What does that mean?" She looked confused.

"Well, you may as well know now. I was going to leave it until Wednesday, but I don't see the point anymore." She stared straight at her. "I am leaving in two weeks' time. I have taken a better position at Simpson & Smith, better prospects, more money and I get a company car." She blurted it out almost out of breath, waiting for Linda's response.

"Oh my God! What did Bill say?" she asked, investigating her eyes. Belinda turned away, embarrassed.

"Fuck, you haven't told him, have you? You haven't." She struggled to get the words out. She was laughing. She couldn't hide her emotions. "He'll kill you. In fact, I don't believe you." She was laughing again.

"Oh, but you should because I have put your name forward to take over my job when I have gone. Now do you see?"

Her face lit up with the excitement on hearing her words. She touched her arm. "Please tell me you are not joking," she said, excited, grinning with pleasure. "It is true, isn't it? I just know it is." She flung her arms around her, pulling her close to her. "Thank you. Thank you. My God! I am so happy."

"Wow, you haven't got it yet. He will have the last say. Surely, you know that I have only recommended you for the job."

Linda frowned. "He will say yes though, won't he? You can twist his arm. I know what you two get up to. Everybody in the office does."

"Okay, I will convince him that you are his only option and then you and I will be all square. Agreed?"

"Agreed," she smiled. "Thanks. When will you tell him?"

"I have left a note on his desk. He should be back this evening. I have told him about it but he won't believe it until he sees it in writing with his own eyes. He'll be back here tonight to collect it. Then he will scream a wobbly, kick the wastepaper basket. Well, you know the score. He's had more than his fair share of Wobblys since I have worked here, so stop worrying. Just let things take their course. He is not to know that I have told you. Is that clear?"

"Yes, very clear. Thanks, Belinda. I mean that. Can I tell Felix?"

"Just leave it a couple of days just to be on the safe side. It will happen. I can at least assure you of that much," she smiled. "Now let's finish our smoke and get back to work."

*****

69, Ponsbury Close:

She took her briefcase and the carrier bag into the garage, returning five minutes later to the kitchen, brushing her dress down, searching her clothing for dirty marks.

She opened the fridge, took out the half empty bottle of Chiraz, closing the door and then searched for a clean glass from the wall cupboard above her head. She poured herself a drink. Gagging they call it. She took a large gulp and then filled the glass to the top. *That feels better*, she said to herself. She kicked her shoes off, took a chair from the table and put her feet up on the work surface.

She looked concerned, something nagging in the back of her mind. She took a sip from the glass, stood up and walked over to the hallway, collecting her shoes as she did so. "He won't be home until late. He has taken to popping into the Pied Bull, for a couple of pints on his way home," she said, talking to herself. She took the stairs, put her glass down on her dressing table and stroked her breasts. She still felt horny, stroking between her legs, finding a rhythm, forcing her to position one leg on the stool facing the mirror. She felt good. She paused, pulling down her thong, exposing herself in the mirror. That got her going. Just looking at herself raised the tempo twofold. She began stroking herself again, pushing her fingers between the swollen lips of her vagina, getting her rhythm back. She slipped her fingers inside her vagina. She gasped, thrusting herself onto her hand in a forcing motion to maximise her pleasure. She teased her clitoris with her free hand, bringing herself to a climax before collapsing on to the pleasure bed, her legs wide apart, dangling down, almost touching the floor. She desperately wanted a man inside her. No, not Bill or Neville, somebody new. She wanted sexual excitement back in her life again and she realised that frigging herself was not the answer, just a short-term remedy.

*****

It was time to get back to reality. She began pulling her tracksuit bottoms on whilst grabbing a top from the bedside chair as she hopped one-legged, pulling her bottoms up as she headed for the landing, slipping her top on and dancing her way back down the stairs to the kitchen and Neville's farewell dinner.

She glanced at the wall clock and smiled to herself. *I can't believe I am doing this, except for the fact I'll get excitement and a great deal of pleasure from fucking up their lives like they have fucked with mine. Well, not anymore. Payback time has come, and I am determined to enjoy it to the full. Neville, you are done. Bill, twenty grand, you bastard.* She even gestured, holding out her hand, folding stuff. *This time not his prick. Those days have gone. Well, after I get the cash that is, perhaps one last shag. I haven't really made my mind up yet.*

She gulped her wine, excited by her thoughts, her face flushing, no, not embarrassed, that feeling of pleasure that ran through her body, her lips still tingling from her orgasm. She was enjoying her thoughts.

She took the salmon fillets out of the fridge, and unwrapped them. They were straight from the fish market at lunchtime. She lay them on tin foil, deciding how to prepare them before sticking them in the oven. She washed and trimmed the asparagus, placing them in the kettle, filling it with water and putting it in the saucepan of water, leaving it on the gas ring ready to cook.

Salad, I think, with new potatoes, vine tomatoes from the market. A lemon dill to flavour, French rolls with butter and his wine. He can cork that, give him something to do, let have

a feeling of intimacy with the meal. He will more than likely be busy ogling my breasts, wanting to grope me, she laughed. 'If only he knew the truth, he would be hiding a dagger up his jumper.
I'll lead him on, get him all worked up and feeling horny before I rip his balls off, not just tell him politely to fuck off. It's all over between us.'

She spent the next hour preparing the meal, laying the table. 'I'll leave the candles until I hear his car in the drive. I had better text him and let him know dinner will be at eight o'clock and I guarantee he will have a hard-on during the journey home. He will probably roll up with a bottle of wine and a bunch of flowers past their sell-by-date. It wouldn't be the first time. That's what used to piss me off,' she grinned. 'It will all be over soon. I will wake up a single woman, Neville-free. We can argue the detail afterwards.'

Single. That sounded good. She repeated the word *single* as she made her way to the shower, a makeover, a sexy dress for show only and I will be ready.

*****

Chapter 12
Dinner for Two

Belinda took one last look in the mirror. *That looks good,* she said to herself, running her hands down over her breasts, exciting her nipples, a smile that disguised her innermost thoughts, butterflies in her tummy. She felt horny. She had that first-date feeling. 'God! I knew this would happen.' She walked to the door, put out the light and raced down the stairs to her glass of wine.

'Well, I suppose I need to act and look the part I am supposed to be playing.' She stroked herself, hoping her lust would turn to anger, but no such luck. That made it even worse.

She heard the car pull up on the pea gravel in the drive. She quickly lit the candles, then ran upstairs and hid herself behind the door in the bedroom. 'Let him see the table before he sees me. I want him to take one last look because this will be the last time for him. I need to make room for the new man in my life.' Her mind immediately turned to sex. Doggy-fashion exploded in her mind. She shut her eyes, gripping the door handle to regain her composure. She opened the door and walked down the stairs to the kitchen.

"Hi, Belinda," he said, nervously handing her the bunch of flowers. "Shall I open the wine?" He was struggling to find the right words. His eyes and his lustful thoughts were too busy consuming her body, his face flushed with excitement. Could this be a change of heart? He was confused. He paused and walked towards her. "You look absolutely stunning." His smile, no, his lust struggled to fit his face. She walked away from him, avoiding the obvious another mistake that just added to her excitement of feeling horny again.

"Yes, that would be nice. I'll just put these in water. I will put them in a vase later." She forced a smile, pouting her breasts. His eyes pounced on her cleavage, with wanting in his eyes, lust no doubt stirring in his boxer. She grinned, a little embarrassed by the occasion. Was she having second thoughts? Definitely not. That was a no. She was already thinking about Bill. He's next.

"Sit down and finish opening the wine. I've cooked your favourite, fresh river salmon with asparagus spears, new potatoes and vine tomatoes," she smiled.

Neville looked down, concentrating on opening the wine. He couldn't believe his luck. *Perhaps she will apologise. I hope so. I could certainly fuck her right now, at the table.* His thoughts were racing from him, his face and neck coloured. He was scared not knowing. *I suppose*, he told himself, still struggling opening the wine, his nerves on edge. He panicked, not wanting to fuck things up, hoping she would be the pudding.

"This looks nice. When you said dinner at eight, I thought you meant fish and chips from the village. I'm surprised. Thank you. Not what I expected. How are you? You look stunning, sexy." Repeating himself, his voice stalled, wishing he hadn't used the word sexy. Play it cool. That is what he told himself driving home from the Pied Bull. 'Fuck it.' She sensed his embarrassment.

"How's work these days, still as busy as ever?" that was the best she could do, her mind clouded with dirty thoughts, toe sucking, shagging doggy fashion over the end of the table. *This is becoming a mess.* "Are you ready to eat? Pour the wine. I'll serve it up now." Again, it was the best she could come up with. She was nervous, a lot more than she expected to be.

She wanted to change gear, back pedal if necessary. This was becoming unbearable. Her sex drive was telling her to let him fuck her. His dirty mind agreed with that but all she wanted to do was scream: "Get me out of here. Your bed. You lie in it. Okay?" Then she followed Neville's eyes, lips, cleavage and then up her skirt and instead of moving closer to the table and closing the picture, she was tempted to pull back in her chair, allowing her short skirt to ride up her thighs, showing all.

Her excuse was to build him up and then chop him down hard – the truth. She was so horny, very horny and was hurting. She was wet by now and that meant her willpower had all but gone. She wriggled down the chair, her skirt going in the opposite direction, Neville's eyes popping, the bulge in his trousers hard by now. Knowing him, she knew he was big and that is what she craved for right now.

She stood up, offering him her hand. They made it to the third step before he was inside her, like a bull. She groaned and screamed, "Harder, harder. Fuck me harder. Ah, ah, you bastard. I'm coming. Don't stop. Keep fucking me."

They both orgasmed, sweaty with lust. Neville pulled her upstairs and that is where it ended. She ran to her bedroom, slamming the door shut and pressing her back against it. Neville stood there like the loser he was, bewildered. He kicked his shoes down the stairs in anger, picked his trousers up and headed back downstairs.

He took a serviette from the table to clean himself. He dipped it in her wine, no longer caring. He couldn't care less. He hated her for all she was now and all she would ever be was a fucking bitch.

He went to bed pissed and full of hate, kicking his toe on the top step in a hurry to make to the bathroom. "Fuck you. Ah, you bastard," he shouted, wanting her to hear as he raced to her door, trying the lock. He turned it a few times, cursing under his breath. Belinda was frightened, wishing he had fallen down the stairs. Her only thought, as she lay there after he had finally gone to the spare room, was collecting on the insurance policy, adding it all up in her head, the house, insurance, savings. She smiled. 'If only.'

*****

Breakfast at Tiffany's did not come next. She was sitting at the table waiting for him, covered head to toe in her dressing gown. There was no cleavage or leg on offer this morning. It wasn't business as usual.

He was the first to speak. "Now you are going to tell me it's over I suppose." He ran his fingers through his hair, disgust written all over his face.

She hesitated. You could see the anger in her eyes. "I should have told you last night. That was my plan but things didn't work out that way, did they? We are better off without each other. I don't want to sit here day after day with the both of us hating each other because that's how all this will end. Believe me. Let's go our separate ways and call it a day." She looked away from him, drawing heavily on her cigarette. Yes, in the kitchen, unheard of.

There were no apologies on either side. They just exchanged angry looks, each blaming the other. "I may as well tell you now that you will be hearing from my solicitor, Brahms, on the High Street next to the bank. And you what are your plans?" Her eyes were demanding an answer.

"I'm not sure," he lied. "I will wait for his letter. That's the normal procedure, isn't it? Fuck me off, pay the bill. Sounds good to me." With defiance now he was bitter, the injured party. He picked up a wineglass and hurtled it the length of the room, finally smashing it against the back door, shards of glass splinters going everywhere. "Fuck you, bitch," he grabbed his car keys and left through the side door to the garage. She didn't even look up. She heard him kick something in anger at the garage door, and was relieved he had gone.

It was all but over. She couldn't handle the crap from now on. She was ready for Bill. He doesn't know it yet, but his hard time is coming sooner than he thinks. Her eyes could already see the bundles of £20 notes in the cardboard box, there on the kitchen table, open just like her legs had been half an hour before. His last grunts made her feel sick. It was not what she wanted right now but tongue in cheek. She would be giving him his weekly wank in the supermarket car park at lunchtime as though nothing had happened. She would dress for the occasion, swallow her pride, so to speak, pretend to be nice, lie, cheat and steal. She had got it all worked out. 'Would it be that simple? That is up to you,' she grinned to herself.

She laughed aloud. *Another dollar, another day.* That wasn't that hard.

*****

Chapter 13
Notice

Belinda got to work early, a fag and a chat with Linda started her day, the second day of her notice.

"Have you heard anything yet? Has he called you?"

"What do you think?"

"I don't fucking care. I'll play along with him for a couple of weeks, make sure your position is confirmed and I get what I want," she smiled to herself. *What I want*. She dared not tell her that she blew her smoke into the car park, her eyes searching the empty spaces, expecting his car to pull up. He was late. 'Why?'

"You don't hate him that much surely. Tell me what's the real story? Has Neville found out about you and Bill?" she grinned. She knew she had struck a chord.

She threw her cigarette into the car park, blowing her smoke up in the air as she turned to face her. "You may as well know," she paused. "Me and Neville are old hat. It's over between us apart from the shitty mess that will surely follow us, so don't expect any detail. You know me better than that. All I ask is that you keep what I have just told to yourself and that includes Felix until after I have gone. That is if you value your new position. Can I rely on that?" She gave her a stare that would frighten the devil. She was angry because she had been forced her to tell all.

"I think I value my new position more than you think. So yes, my gobs shut. Happy now?" She threw her fag out through the open door. Angry, she turned brushing past Belinda to get out of her way.

Why is the world full of bitches like her? she asked herself. She walked towards her office, brushing herself down, pulling her fingers through her hair in an attempt to regain her composure, ready to start the new day all over again. *Day two*, she smiled. *Life isn't all bad.* The dollar signs tumbled through her thoughts. She had been forced to tell her all, greed was keeping her company giving her the courage to go through with her plans.

Bill was waiting for her. He had just had words with Linda. 'He had been hoping to catch me on my own in the storeroom. I'll bet, and I am glad he hasn't. Just smile; that will beat him.'

"Hi, good morning. I got here early hoping we could talk. I think I owe you an apology of sorts," she gave him a smile, a leery smile. His eyes responded.

"Let's talk in your office out of ear shot of that lot. We are already the gossip of the day."

"What did you tell her?"

She paused, adding to the drama. He was angry, hurt not being in control and that really pissed him off.

"I told her what I am about to tell you. It's over between Neville and me. Perhaps now you will understand how I was feeling yesterday?" His eyes sparkled like a schoolboy holding his prize. In Bill's thoughts, that was her tits.

"You're joking. You should have told me first. I could have said anything to her just now."

"You weren't here, were you? And you didn't tell her anything either, did you?"

He looked passed her, his eyes searching the skyline from the fifth floor, embarrassed by her anger.

"No, I didn't tell her anything. What would you have done? You put me in this position. I just wanted to talk to you. That's all."

"Firstly, I did not put you in any position and you weren't here when I expected you to be, hoping you would be nice, a cuddle perhaps in the stockroom. Don't you think I care or something?" *The robbery had started.*

He walked towards her and then reminded himself where they were. "Sorry, I should have known it was more than just going off at each other yesterday. It's my fault. I will make it up to you if you will let me, will you?"

God! Talk about playing into her hands. He is as good as being implicit in his own robbery. She couldn't hold the laughter back. Her heart was pounding in her breasts. Her face and neck had turned a blush pink from the excitement of their conversation, from blazing guns to horny. *You can grunt as much as you like. I will take what I want.*

"You know I am yours, although you don't deserve me sometimes, supermarket for pleasure, not lunch?"

She could see the bulge in his trousers, the sweat on his forehead and the relief in his eyes. *I think I won that round. He never even mentioned my leaving in two weeks' time, his cock obviously throbbing in anticipation along with his expectations.*

"I will see you there at twelve, usual place?"

*****

The car park was a little fuller than usual for this time of the week, Tuesday. She found a space of six rows down from him and walked over to where he was parked. He was smoking, the smoke billowing from the open window. That means his breath will stink. That pissed her off. She always brushed her teeth before they met up. He tasted better that way.

He pushed the door open, throwing his cigarette butt out at the same time, a smile from ear to ear on his face like a lunchtime schoolboy let out to play.

"Hi, have you been waiting long?" These were the only words she could come up with, although she had told herself that this lunchtime had to be convincing or the game was up.

"Five minutes, there about. How are you? Okay I hope. You're looking good." His eyes focused on her cleavage. He loved tits which is why she chose that jumper this morning. She even purposely left the bra at home on the bathroom chair. That was a big decision.

I hope I have made a good choice, she said to herself, smiling, encouraging his lust.

"Hi. I'm fine. Thanks," she replied.

It was her nipples that did it. He was struggling to concentrate with his words. His eyes were in total control.

"Come and give me a kiss. I could do with one right now. It has been a miserable day all round so far, a bad time at home with Jill complaining. I am spending too much time away from home. Then Linda and then head office giving me a hard time over that Newbridge contract, the one you have been working on. Apart from that, what have you got to tell me? There's something. I can sense it and I don't mean your new job at Simpson & Smith." He stared into her eyes, waiting for her response. Her face dropped, surprised by the Simpson & Smith comment. She was struggling now, thinking.

She threw her arms around him, her lips searching his mouth, her tongue inside his mouth before he could say Jack Robinson; that should work. He pulled away from her gasping for breath, his face colouring as he stared back at her. "My God! We should have more falling out if that is your idea of an apology."

His hands brushed her raised nipples, exciting her. It showed in her eyes. She felt disgusted by it but sexually wanting it at the same time, letting him know she enjoyed it. His reaction was immediate, lips over her right nipple, his slobber staining her jumper. She wanted to slow things down, explain to him in her own way exactly what he was paying for, to make him face the reality of the situation.

She whispered in his ear. "Later, Bill. Let's talk then. I will let you play, you naughty boy!" The words excited his thoughts. *You naughty boy.* Those words made him hard in the right place and there was no disguising his pleasure.

"Sorry, I just need you right now." A sweat covered his neck and forehead.

"At this rate, Bill, you will come before you start and that's not good for either of us, is it?"

"Okay, tell me about Simpson & Smith. What happened there? I thought you were happy doing what you are doing, so it came as a shock when your future boss rang me giving me his good news. In fact, he was fucking enjoying himself at my expense. How do you think I feel about that?"

"Bill, I was in a job going nowhere. Surely you want me to be a success like yourself, respected, looked up to, don't you?" She chose the bullshit carefully. His face lit up. A small child came to mind. He was gloating in her words.

"Well, I suppose put like that, yes, but that doesn't mean it is all over for me and you, is it?"

Those were the words she wanted to hear, music to her ears. She could not have put it better herself. "Don't be silly." *Sign here.* "Of course it's not all over. Why you should think that, I will prove it to you." She leant over him, stroking his prick. "Take it out. Let me see you." Those were the words he loved to hear.

'Fumbling' wasn't the word. She offered her help by undoing his belt, pulling him free and then taking it in her hand, wanking him off, its head polished and reddened by his erection. It spurted all over his trousers. He had lost control. "Ah, shit, fancy that happening. I didn't even have time to enjoy it. Too bloody excited. That was the trouble."

He looked down at the mess, spunk everywhere. She pulled out tissue after tissue from the box in the door pocket kept there for such an occasion. She laughed. She could not help herself. "No, it's my fault, Bill. I should have given you a blowjob instead and saved all this palaver."

The bullshit kept coming. She could not help herself, but she soon realised she had committed herself to taking his disgusting organ into her mouth the next time they had sex. *Never mind. I'll just have to keep my eyes shut, I suppose. Twenty grand.* That thought took away the pain.

"I think we best call it a day. I will just nip and buy a sandwich. We can have a few words later at the office if you like." She leant over, kissing his lips.

"See you there then okay, later."

"Yes, that will be fine if I can get this mess sorted out. See you there then," he smiled, satisfied with the mess. He was faced with no other choice.

*****

Not the best lunchtime I have ever had. Say a couple of hundred quid at the most, but at least the ball is rolling in her direction, a lot more suffering to come, but she could handle that disappointment and the disgust that would come with it.

Cheese and tomato, she settled for, a bottle of fresh orange juice and some horseradish kettle chip crunchies from Gloucestershire. She smiled. Whatever next, she had eaten others in their selection and they had all been good. "Nothing ventured, nothing gained," she said as she approached the checkout.

"Hi," she heard the voice but could not see who was calling her. She turned the other way. It was Linda. Her immediate thought was that she had followed her here. She was certainly devious enough. She waited for her in the foyer.

"I thought I saw you in the sandwich bar. I turned around to call you and you had gone." She held up her carrier bag. "Lunch."

"I have just met with Bill, had a grilling about my new job. Apparently he has known about my move since last week. He knows my new boss from way back and apparently he couldn't wait to rub his nose in it."

"Oh God! That sounds a little boring, them knowing each other. I mean I wasn't inferring you had made a mistake with leaving or anything like that," she smiled. "Do I believe that? She could not be happier. I wonder if she will be thinking the same way when I dump Bill and he's after putting his hand up her skirt. It was her time to smirk."

"Let them make the most of it. These things won't last forever, will they?"

"No, I suppose not, first one back puts the kettle on," she grinned and walked away to her car.

She wanted to get back and sort things out with Bill. She had already been working on her plan but she would have to soften him up first. That was not going to be easy. 'He was worldly and tight-fisted but if he wants me to keep opening my legs, then he will need to open his wallet.' That little bit she had worked out. The reason for wanting so much from him was much harder and it needed to be credible and stand up to scrutiny. Bill was not the kind of person that would rush into anything, apart from her knickers as this lunchtime had proved.

Linda was waiting for her in the staff dining room, a cup of tea waiting for her. "Thanks, I knew you would beat me back here. My car was at the far end of the car park. I watched you pull away before. I even reached my car. Has he been around?" she frowned, waiting for an answer.

"He's down the other end of the office, talking to somebody in technical support. I don't know his name. He's a big guy with matching ears. Remember him? He asked you for a dance at the works party last year," she laughed.

"Yes, it was funny, I admit. Poor sod!"

"What did he have to say then? Come on, give me the gossip please."

"There's no gossip. Remember what we agreed?" She nodded her head and smiled. "Nothing heavy. He just said I hope I know what I am doing. That sort of crap you always get when you tell them you want to leave. Actually he has been a bit too good about it, hoping I will change my mind, I think."

Linda's face flushed as she said the words, "You are not changing your mind, are you?" She looked desperate, touching her arm.

"No, don't be silly, and don't do anything to harm your chances. Remember what I have told you. If anybody walks into his office telling him that you have taken my job, you will be out the door sooner than you think. I am telling you that for your own good." A veiled threat more likely, but she did not need to know that.

"Oh, I won't say a word. I promise you. I give you my word. You will tell me that I have got it when he tells you, won't you?"

"Yes, don't panic. He's going nowhere and I know that for certain." She touched her arm, frowned and walked out the door back to her own office. He was there waiting for her.

"I thought you might be here. You wouldn't notice a thing." She looked down at his trousers as she spoke to him. "Yes, we need to talk but I can't make tonight. I'm in the doghouse. Can it wait until tomorrow night? She goes off to her sisters, so I will have the all clear. Can we say straight after work at the Belmont?"

"Yes, that suits me really. I have some things to do at home, black bin bags. I'm sure you know what I mean," he grinned.

"You've really done it. God! I can hardly believe it."

He had 'cock' written over his face. His grin gave him away. He will have a hard-on by the time he gets back to his office, his dirty mind doing overtime. She could see it in his eyes, read him like a dirty book.

"Tomorrow then."

*****

Chapter 14
Room 166

Room 166
Dr Neville Scrudge
Head of European Research
A room in a converted Victorian Workhouse situated on the Outskirts of Skepton Town Centre, home to Dr Neville Scrudge and his Co-directors in the offices of SICUP Inc. was a research facility for who knows what? It was a secretive organisation working on government contracts, unspecified.

Neville was a routine man and at forty six years old, he looked good for his age, not handsome or attractive and at six foot two and of slim build, with dark brown hair and grey eyes, he looked exactly as he should, rimless glasses giving him that academic appearance, a nerd really, and what Belinda saw in him, it's difficult to say. They drifted into it, probably for his position, DIRECTOR. I think that's what converted her to being a snob but those kinds of relationships never seem to blossom. They just muddle along until something shouts, STOP. Now they were drifting out of their relationship, all because of a pile of dog shit.

I suppose to everyone else. It's just beggar's belief but the truth of it is, there in the black bin bags he was putting into the boot of his car were his worldly possessions.

He had found a room in a boarding house. It was clean, tidy and offered him a car parking space in the large rear car park. It would tide him over. He had applied for a transfer to the Milan Office. He had included a very extensive portfolio of achievements with his application. Now he was just waiting for confirmation from head office. The grapevine had told him the position was his, just a matter now of completing the red tape and all the crap that goes with internal transfers.

He would lie to her, telling her he was on transfer duties in Milan. The move was only temporary. He would come clean the day the money from his share of the house hit his bank account. He had plans for that day.

*****

Belinda arrived home early for her. She would normally arrive home much later. No stopping off for incidentals unless she needed them, of course. She almost stopped at the village shop. Then as she slowed down, she reminded herself of her new status in life – single. She smiled to herself and accelerated away, heading for home.

She slowed down as she approached the house, making sure Neville was not at home. She wanted to avoid another confrontation like this morning's episode. That frightened her, surprised her what effect a sudden change can have on an individual. Neville was no different but this morning was the first time he showed a violent side. Normally, he was kind and considerate, placid even. Perhaps she ought to make a mental note of that outburst.

The drive was empty, all clear. She parked the car, went into the house and engaged the safety chain. 'Precautionary,' she told herself.

She threw her jacket over the back of a chair, then kicked her heels off and making for the fridge, a half bottle of Chiraz, she poured herself a glass and switched on the TV, her feet up on the granite work surface. She clicked through the channels. Nothing took her fancy. She thought about what to cook, and then decided she couldn't make her mind up and went upstairs with her glass of wine to shower. She idled on the third step. Lust told her to hurry up and put last night's episode behind her. She already had enough on her plate with Bill and his demands on her body. That did not add pleasure to her thoughts.

She stood under the shower. Without a thought, she looked down searching for pooh. *That's dog shit to you and me.* She just did not want to say the words. 'Nothing,' she sighed with relief, washing the thoughts away – Neville, Jasper and the old firm. She laughed out loud. Even she could not believe her situation.

She went to the bedroom, pulled on a pair of tracksuit bottoms and a t-shirt and skipped down the stairs. Mushroom omelette for dinner with salad she had decided.

The house phone rang. She hesitated before picking it up. 'No, it wouldn't be Neville. He would use her mobile number. Perhaps it's mother. I promised I would ring her today.' But with everything happening in her life right now, she had forgotten to call.

"Hi, Belinda."

"Hi, it's me. Jill's just nipped down to the village, so I thought I should ring and make sure you are alright, are you?"

"Yes, I'm fine. Thank you. Just showered about to cook my supper, so I can't talk. See you tomorrow at the office. Goodnight." She hung up as he was about to reply. Now she would wait for him to call back.

She poured her second glass of wine, her thoughts teasing her mind. *What to think about first? How far I should take it with Bill? How much?* Can she settle with Neville quickly? She realised that she would have to give him half of the house. All she wanted now was how much and how quick.

'I will call the estate agent first thing in the morning and see what they have to say pretending to put the house up for sale.' That didn't happen very often in Ponsbury Close, so any agent would be keen to offer her a free valuation, the emphasis on free of course. Then there will be the Solicitors. That won't be free. Don't go there. She would make sure that was down to Neville. After all, it was his fault.

That only left Bill and then she would have to tell her mother when she had sorted things out. Her dad, she would call him. No hurry. There he was, enjoying a new life with his second wife down in Surrey.

New life. Those words excited her thoughts. *My house, new boyfriend,* she smiled to herself. Then she saw the letter on the dresser.
Belinda.
That's what the envelope said.

Hi, there is no need for fancy talk. Just to let you know I will be collecting the rest my belongings from the house tomorrow, should you wish to be away from the house, that's fine. You have my number if you need to contact me. Neville

She smiled, a long swig of wine followed by a cigarette. She blew the smoke away from her face with her hand. Well, that seems simple enough or was it her mind that was chasing her thoughts? *Is he up to something? Have I missed something? Maybe.* She closed her eyes. No, that didn't work. All she could see when she did that was dollars and bell reels. She tried again, this time with her eyes wide open. A cold shiver ran down her back. Her thoughts were already telling her to backpedal and make it up with Neville. She took another long swig of wine. 'Fuck it. This always happens when I think I have made my mind up about something. My inner voice tells me to stop, think and think again.' She raised her glass above her head, intending to do what Neville did at breakfast. Then she stopped dead in her tracks. *No, no. Don't let them win. You have a plan. Remember? You can't just throw it all away because that is what you are doing. Neville will not want to know you. Bill will say, 'Fuck off, you bitch,' and then where will you be? Ay, in the shit.*

She did not sleep well.

*****

Chapter 15
Fate Takes a Hand

"Goodnight."

It was well past closing time. Doreen Breathshott made her way out of the car park, turning left on to Gumby Road which would take her to Dorrit Street and then down to the town centre. There would be more going on down in the town at this time of night. She fancied another victim. A young kid pretending he's eighteen would do nicely, only what's left of his pocket money and his iPhone if she was lucky. Perhaps that would probably cover her night's expenses. Anyway, she had to weigh in on two cards at the ATM.

She had no pity for her victims. She took after her mother. She had left her dad pissed up in the Bad Neighbours Pub, dropped him a tenner in the top pocket of his jacket to buy himself a burger from Eric's hotdog van when they threw him out later, which was generally the case.

Vera was nowhere to be seen, probably shacked up with some divvy no doubt. She wouldn't be alone. That costs money. She learnt that lesson a long time ago and has practised it ever since.

It had started to rain and the cobbles on Dorrit Street were sloping away from her, slippery, getting slippier as the rain fell more heavily now, and then it happened.

Her feet were taken from underneath her. She hurtled forward, her arm snapping as she hit the railings at the bottom of the garden of 26, Dorrit Street. Then her face hit the gravelled wall, snapping her neck backwards.

No noise, the only sound was a cracking sound, the sound of her neck breaking. It was all over for her. Fate had taken her and she would lie where she fell probably until the early morning. Only the brave ventured out at night in that neighbourhood and tonight's rain made it almost certain that would be the case.

The following morning, the ambulance came to take her away. The incident had been reported by Dave Swift, an early morning shift worker. An investigation into her death was put down to misadventure and not until her belongings were being carefully logged and placed inside a plastic bag would the truth unfold, not that it would help her latest victim, *Daisie*. She was still in intensive care at Skepton General Hospital.

*****

The police knocked the door at 53, Brent Road, Newton Housing Estate. "Mr Breathshott," shouted Sergeant Smythe, a head could be seen behind the safety chain as the door creaked open slightly. He stood there in a shirt that was long overdue for a hot swim in the washing machine, his trousers held up by an equally scruffy tie, egg drip on his filthy shirt; where they came from was anybody's guess.

"Can't you give me a break? What am I supposed to have done now?"

"Nothing like that. We are not here to arrest you. We have come about your daughter, Doreen, is it?"

"Why, what's she been up to? You just can't leave us alone, can you? She's ain't here, so fuck off." He pulled the door shut and put the hall light off to hide himself. He had done it many times before. So in his present state, half-pissed, you could forgive him for thinking, *no, not again*.

The officer knocked on the door again. "Come on, Mr Breathshott. Open the door. We have something important to tell you about your daughter, Doreen."

The door opened this time. He had managed to pull his shoes on. "I've already told you. I ain't seen her. She's nor 'ere. Have a look for yourself and then you can fuck off and leave me alone."

"I'm afraid it is more serious than that, Malcolm. I am Sergeant Smythe from Blisset Road Station and this is PC Donce. We need to come in and talk to you. You know the form, so don't make things difficult. You know it won't help you in the long run."

He stood to one side as they came into the hallway. He wobbled like an alchy, belched as he walked away from them. They followed him inside. A mess – that was an understatement, filthy mess that would be nearer the mark. There were more stains on the sofa than there were patches on Joseph's Technicolour coat and that was only the beginning of the mess. A book of betting slips and a pencil sat on one arm of the sofa, a disgusting looking mug on the other arm, folded pages of racing papers and what looked like a porno magazine, which had seen better days, were scattered amongst the cushions.

All rooms have a focal point. This one was not the utility oak, dining table and chairs showing its years, shoved up against the opposite wall, littered with dirty plates and cutlery and an empty brown sauce bottle laying on its side, welded to the table in a brown crust of dried sauce near to a heap of screwed-up betting slips. Next to them was a chipped glass ashtray brimming with fag ends peppered in ash. The only other item of importance in the room was a fifty-inch flat screen TV complete with crack in the left-hand corner, the victim of a drunken missile no doubt fixed to the wall, taking prime position. Daddy Long Leg cobwebs climbed up to the ceiling complete with dust attached like jungle vines but even this was not the focal point. It was in fact the enormous pyramid of dirty clothes heaped up against the wall below the television. There were three piles. The one to the left had the looks of a compost heap. The clothes had sunk over time and were welded together as one lump now. You would have to peel the clothes off one at a time. This was obviously the not-wanted pile.

The other two piles, like the twin peaks Nun & Kun in the Himalayas, were in constant use, a colourful display despite their filthy state of y-fronts, boxers, shirts, jumpers and t-shirts, all XL the property of Malcolm's three brick-built shithouses. Malcolm's clothing existed of what he stood up in or what he managed to cram into an ex-army shoulder bag, not a hint of any of Vera's clothing. They were probably under lock and key in her bedroom. Malcolm's were hiding under the settee where he slept at night. Sofa rates, that's all he paid.

Ignoring the rest of the room, you could forgive yourself for thinking you were in a slum dwelling which about summed up Malcolm's part-time family home, which he visited from time to time.

That was it, complete with peeling wallpaper, a shit-brown ceiling caused by endless heavy smoking. A sorry site to come home to if that is what it was – your home.

Sergeant Smythe turned as he neared the pile of dirty clothes. His image caught in the half mirror in a square frame hanging on the opposite wall. He closed his eyes in disgust. He turned. "Perhaps it would be better to get this over with at the station."

"No, tell me or I'll keep my gob shut. Take it or leave it," the words stuttering from his mouth. He was obviously having trouble focusing his mind properly. Smythe gestured with his hand to PC Donce to make towards the door.

"What ya fucking mean? She can't be dead. She went to the ATM in town how could she be dead?" He fell backwards on the settee rolling to one side, raising his head as he wobbled to his feet. "Dead, it can't be. You're just winding me, you bastard. You never did like me or my kids. You shagged the missus though, so she tells everybody."

Smythe grimaced. He wanted to hang one on him but hesitated. What's the fucking use? That would only delay things and all he wanted right now was a mug of tea and a fry-up in the station canteen. That was his focal point down at the station. 'So let's get it over with,' his inner voice was telling him. Donce looked away, his eyes looking for a clean piece of carpet. He wanted to snigger. No doubt his boss would tell him in no uncertain terms to keep his gob shut. "Malcom, let's make this simple so you understand. We are going to take you to the station now, where we can offer you a nice hot mug of tea and you can listen to what I have got to tell you or you can sleep it off in a cell. The choice is yours. You're going with us and that's that."

"Fuck you." His stare was full of hate, knowing it wasn't Smythe's fault. He was just doing his job. "Okay, lead the way and pull the fucking door shut or the tele will be gone long before I get back."

The door slammed shut against the stiff latch and they made for the stairs. Malcolm just wanted to fall headfirst over the stair railings to the bottom. He could not focus on anything, his mind a complete blur. Life had taken its toll, and right now it was beginning to show. Hate rolled in his eyes but he always found it easier to cope on the inside. The rules and regulations wrapped around him like a blanket providing him with some comfort, at least, three meals a day and somewhere to hang his head. Out here on the outside living on the estates, it was dog-eat-dog and the bigger the dog, the more the bite hurt. He never uttered another word during the journey to the station.

"Let's go to the morgue first, Malcom, and get that over with and then we can take your statement."

"Statement, what about?"

"Come on, you know the routine. Where were you? Who were you with, witnesses because we can't believe you, can we now? We learnt that lesson a long time ago." He turned, facing PC Donce. "Take him down and get the formalities over with. I will... I will call the Coroner's office and get the low down on what happened. I need to find out the details from the Forensic report and what has to say about her death. I will catch up with you later. Oh, and by the way they have found his missus, Vera, and they are bringing her in, so deal with that as well."

Donce and Malcom left the interview room and went to the morgue to identify the body.

*****

"Have you finished your statement, Malcom?" It was his attempt to being nice and getting things over with. Malcolm looked up from the table where he was sitting next to PC Donce.

"We're about there, Sarge. Just reading it through. It's not complicated. Nothing suspicious, just routine."

"Right. Well, his missus is here to make a statement and identify the body, so the sooner the better. Do you want to see her Malcolm, the missus?"

"'Av' I gorra choice? She'll find me anyway, so let her in if you like. I don't care." He carried on reading his statement. He wanted to get back home and get his head down.

"They got you here then," Vera, his wife, shouted. She looked refreshingly decent for a change. "Were you with her?" She looked at the mess and called her husband sitting at the table trying to hide himself. "Just look at you. What a fucking a mess you are! You were never a father to her, never here for me or any of your kids. Fucking disgrace. That's what you are." She walked towards him, raising her clenched fist, with rage in her eyes.

PC Donce stood up, ready to intervene. "No Violence. Keep that for use at home, okay? Not here. Or I will bang you up, both of you." She turned to walk away.

"I'll tell her dad. He will want to be at the funeral, so the best place for you will be back inside, out of his way. Go and snatch a handbag or summat, you bastard."

He did not look up. He got the message loud and clear, his mind making plans already, a bottle of vodka nicked from the co-op. That was favourite. He could be back here within the hour. Vera glanced at him, her eyes full of hate. It was the last time she ever wanted to see him. She followed Sergeant Smythe to the morgue. It was all over for him.

*****

Chapter 16
A Breath of Fresh Air

'Brancaster Staithe,' the signpost said.

"Shall we stop here? This is where we used to come with Mum and Dad, remember?" Jack pointed to the signpost. "And we always used to lose you, hiding in the reed beds. That was your favourite game. I remember that too," Jack laughed, "It was fun though, wasn't it? You used to do it with me sometimes."

"Hmm. Well, we won't be playing that game today. Let's just walk to some of the old places we used to visit."

She took his arm and snuggled up to him. There was a slight wind that felt quite chilly on her cheeks. She had dressed sensibly, a large white fisherman's cable knit sweater miles too big for her, one of her father's but warm and comfortable, like her walking boots. She felt safe inside it, although it was two, perhaps three feet too long that it almost hung around her knees. She let go of Jack's arm and attempted to shorten it, holding both sides between two fingers at the waist and pulling the body up almost to her shoulders, then letting it fall. Now it sat at waist-level but she now looked pregnant and suddenly the two of them became a married couple. Jack laughed. "If only we had a mirror, a click and a flash." He handed her his phone.

She laughed, "Oh, my God! What do I look like! Promise me, Jack, you won't show this picture to anybody. I couldn't face the embarrassment. This is just between the two of us, will you?"

"Pregnant mum?" They both laughed. They were enjoying each other. It was just what they both needed after the last two weeks of hell.

She gave the phone back to him. Smiling, Jack forwarded the picture to her phone and then clicked 'delete'. "There you are. All done. You have the only copy, okay?" She jumped up at his shoulder and kissed his cheek, gripping his arm. "You are so sweet to me sometimes, my big brother. Do you know how good that makes me feel? I'll tell you, shall I? I love you so much. That's how I feel," she said, squeezing his arm again. He looked down at her face, smiling.

"I love you too, sis. Let's race each other to the Angler Pub. Winner buys lunch?" They both dashed off laughing and giggling and suddenly the pregnant mum was no more.

Katie ordered their food and Jack paid. He let her win. She deserved it for putting up with him, but he would not tell her that.

There was whitebait, a shared starter, then ham and eggs for the pair of them and a stack of railway sleeper chips to share.

"This is fun. I know you let me win. Thanks," she smiled.

"Well, just fancy the gossip if anyone found out I had won a race against my pregnant sister." She reached over, slapping his hand.

"But I'm not pregnant. At least I hope I'm not."

"Excuse me. What did you just say? Because if I heard you correctly, I will be very angry."

"Angry why?"

"My sister having casual sex. Don't let me catch him." He was angry.

"Jack, it's nothing like that, you know. I would never do something like that. I was just winding you, silly boy." She smiled, grinning at him. It was contagious. "You devil."

He reached over, tapping her nose. They both laughed aloud. Everyone in the bar turned their eyes towards them. Some grinned, some laughed and suddenly life felt good again for both of them.

After lunch, a glass of beer and a visit to the pub toilet, they wandered off, holding hands up the road back to their car.

"Tell me what the letter said from the Consultant?"

Jack paused, "Have you been reading my mail?" He stared into her eyes, waiting for her reply.

She looked away from him. "Sorry, it was there on the kitchen table. I thought you had left it there for me to read. That's all. I wasn't prying. I thought you wanted me to look, didn't you?"

"I have no secrets from you, Katie. You know that we have always been able to talk about everything and anything. So no, I know you're not prying but that was not the reason for my mentioning it now. Let's say I am just surprised. That's all."

"I do not understand, Jack. Tell me, please, will you?" she looked straight into his eyes, wanting him to respond.

"I should have thought that was obvious. Two whole days and you haven't even mentioned it. Not one word from you. I waited until lunch today, giving you every opportunity to ask me about it, but nothing. You amaze me sometimes. So why haven't you mentioned it?"

"My thoughts were the same as yours. I have been waiting for you to tell me about it. After all, it is you we are talking about and, not me," he laughed. "Bloody typical they are, the only words to describe it. Both of us thinking the same thing. So now we are talking about it, is there anything you want to ask me?"

"I just found it difficult to get past all those tests. They want to perform on you an EEG, a PET and another MRI scan. I thought I was reading a script for *Star Wars* film or something similar, not your health check. What have you decided? Are you going to have the tests?" She looked at him, concern in her eyes, almost in tears.

"Katie, please don't upset yourself if I don't go. I will never know and I could not live in that state of mind. So yes, I am going next Wednesday. Will you come with me? Lecture or not, I want you by my side. Mother would have been there. Dad would have just waited by his phone, worrying about me.

I don't want you in that situation. I want you to hear what they have to say to me. Help me through this. Please say you will come with me?" They both stopped. Katie threw her arms around him, pulling him close, wanting to feel safe. Jack squeezed her, gently kissing her cheek.

"I'll take that as a 'yes' then," he replied, pulling his face away from her, smiling at her, happy with the thought that she would be coming with him. It will be a big day for both of them.

Jack had a secret. When he lay in bed and closed his eyes at night in the darkness, that's when it all began. That's when his mind was in control of his thoughts and emotions. He closed his eyes, wanting those thoughts to go away. He couldn't tell her. She would only worry herself sick if she found out. "Jack, are you okay?"

"Yes, just happy daydreaming. You know me. My head is always full of rubbish. Let's drive over to Holt. See if I can't buy you a small present in one of those chic shops you like to go looking around in."

"You mean boutiques, Jack, and yes, I would love to go. We could finish the day there with tea or supper. Let's just see how we get on. Is that all right with you?" She squeezed his hand, pulling him along to the car. She was still doing the driving.

"Okay. That's that sorted. Remember that little tea shop in the High Street next to the King's Arms, where we used to go for a cream tea with Mum and Dad? Let's go there after we have shopped and then perhaps we can find somewhere to eat supper on the way back to our hotel. That sounds better to me."

"You win. Jump in. We will be there in half an hour and you can keep your promise to me. My present, remember?" They both laughed.

Parking the car was always a nightmare in Holt but after several circuits of one of the larger car parks, they managed to find a space just as someone was leaving, their shopping all done.

*****

"Will you buy me this, Jack?" Katie held up a soft toy, a small puppy dog with a large smile, waving it above her head at Jack further down the aisle.

Jack returned her smile. "You choose. If that is what you want, let's pay for it. I would like to look around in that bookshop next door," he replied.

"Okay, thank you. Let's go." She offered him her hand and she followed him to the till to pay. The assistant wrapped it for her and she left the shop, a happy girl following Jack into the book shop next door.

"How many times have you been in this shop? A thousand. Dad always brought you here. That's where you get it from, browsing, buying. You just love nosing around especially second-hand books, yes?"

"Alright. It pleases me like that cuddly toy you don't really need pleases you." He raised his eyebrows, staring at her. She smiled back, happy that they were enjoying themselves.

Tea at Daisies' Tea Parlour, based on a Victorian theme: now it had changed hands after Mrs Bettinson passed away a couple of years back. The waitress told Katie as she took their order for cream teas. The new owners were younger, more aggressive in some pleasant way; hence cream teas were available all year round. Forget summertime tourists. This is 2018 and tourists travel all year round nowadays, so why not cream teas to have if they are asked for? "Oh yes, we sell cream teas. All the while you would be surprised like last week, for instance we sold out twice. Amazing what a couple of buses can do," she smiled. "It won't take long."

"Did what she say surprise you, Jack? She's right. Why not? We are the proof."

"Hmm, yes, we are." His eyes drifted down to the floor as though his mind was occupied. His body became listless. He slumped down in his chair.

Her body almost went into a state of shock. A cold chill ran down her back. She could see something was wrong. She grabbed his hand as she stood up. "Jack, talk to me. There's something wrong. Tell me what's wrong. Please, Jack, talk to me." There was desperation in her voice. Fear showed in her eyes. It's all happening over again.

Jack began to shake his head from side to side, his eye struggling to open as though he was drunk, but she knew that was not the case. "It's his mind again," she said, "taking over his body. It's not Jack."

Eyes began to look towards them, a few nudges. Don't look. Now that kind of talk made her feel scared and insecure. Then as suddenly as it had happened, Jack opened his eyes and stopped moving from side to side, sitting there as though nothing had happened. "Oh my God, Jack! It happened again. You are frightening me. We must go back home. I will take you to the hospital to see Dr Doogood. We can't keep going on like this. I can't bear it anymore." She was crying by now. Her face had reddened and a slight sweat had broken out on her forehead; panic had overtaken her.

Jack stood up. "It's nothing, Katie. I'm just tired. That's all. Let's skip tea and get back to the hotel. I will be okay after a good night's sleep. I have just overdone things today. That's all. Can we go?" His eyes looked sad. He hated not wanting to tell her about his dreams, but it would not help things now even if he wanted to. She must never know. Nobody should know. It would always remain his secret.

Jack paid the bill. Katie offered the girl their apologies, leaving the shop, collecting their car and driving back to their hotel. Their holiday to the East coast was over. Another sleepless night for Katie lay ahead.

*****

Chapter 17
Beryl Heatherley

She had turned it over in her mind a thousand times during the last two days. Bill was away from the office today, giving her time to sort out her thoughts for him – Neville, her new job at Simpson & Smith and making room in her life for a new lover. Would she be able to make it a new life all round? She hoped so. Her plan did just that, but paper thoughts and the real world were very often poles apart.

She had left the office early. She wanted to look her best for Bill at their meeting later that evening at the Belmont Hotel, her new beginning, promises and lies all wrapped in a blanket of greed and deceit.

She sat at her dressing table. A skimpy silk dressing gown hung from her shoulders. The glass of cold Prosecco wine straight from the refrigerator felt good bubbling in her hand, her mind floating away on holiday clouds, enjoying sex games and sunshine with her new lover. *Tall, dark and handsome, fit and sexy*. Those thoughts brought a smile to her face and raised her nipples pushing through the flimsy silk robe as her thoughts drifted back to married life with Neville.

It hadn't been all bad. He was a good lover, well-endowed and she enjoyed him inside her. He could make sex last a long time, satisfying her selfish greed. She could feel him inside her, now his warm fluids dripping from her vagina, as he pulled himself free, she wanting more, insatiable or greedy. Did it matter? She always felt good. That is what mattered. None of her lovers could give her that level of satisfaction.

There had been lovers during their marriage, many lovers, but Neville never needed to know that.

She took another sip of her Prosecco.

You can't just write off twenty years of marriage, roll it up like a brown paper ball and throw it down the road as trash, watching as it runs away from you until it was out of sight. Neville meant more to her than that. He just did not fit into her plans for the future. She would give him a divorce and let him go forever. She no longer needed him. Functional thoughts, yes, but she had learnt over the years that life can be cruel. He would survive and be happy with someone else in his life. She smiled, finding comfort in her thoughts.

Eye shadow is the bane of a woman's life. Get it right and it will make you feel good. Get it wrong. You may as well go to bed and wash it off in the morning, look good and please your lover. That is what she needed to do this evening. 'Please Bill, well, his twenty-five grand. That sum sounded better than twenty. Where would it end?' She finished her wine and laughed at life. She stood up and let her robe fall away from her shoulders. She turned to the wall mirror, raising her glass in satisfaction. *If you want me Bill, there will be a price to pay, without guarantees of course I might add.*

She cupped her breasts in her hands, teasing her nipples. She wanted sex right now. She could feel the wetness between her legs. Her excitement raced through her body, butterflies in her stomach, a blushing to her face and neck, a slight sweat bathing her body. She wanted dirty sex now.

The house phone rang. *Fuck it. I was enjoying that.* She picked up her robe and headed for the stairs. *Who could that be? Neville. Not sure,* she said to herself.

"Hi, you're through to Belinda." It was the solicitor's office.

"Hello Mrs Scrudge." *That name grated. That will have to go, de-pol,*' she smiled.

"Yes, how can I help you?"

"I just wanted to tell you that Mr Bryant, the solicitor that will be handling your case, can fit you in tomorrow afternoon at 4 pm if that is convenient for you. I understand it is such short notice, but it is all he has available for at least the next two weeks. Could you make that appointment?"

She paused, "Okay. That will be fine. See you tomorrow then. Thank you."

"Thank you, Mrs Scrudge."

*Ahh! There goes that name again, s*he said to herself. "I will put it in Mr Bryant's diary. See you tomorrow. Good evening."

*****

Beryl Heatherley was tall and scrawny, and it looked like a tin of beans would do her the world of good, with a beaky nose, large dark eyes heavily shadowed like a koala bear's. Her hair was a double helping of Shirley-Temple curls hanging down to her shoulders which made her head look out-of-proportion to her body.

She came from a very good and respectable family but opted out of that kind of life in her fourth year at Kingstone High School. Now she led a wandering life, a drop out from conventional society, a free loader is what they call it, druggie, yes. Unfortunately, she defied several attempts over the last couple of years by her father to take her back home. She didn't hate them her parents, yet she could give no sound reason why she had chosen her present way of life.

She stood watching as her grandmother made her way out into the yard. Part of her still lived in Victorian times I'm afraid, a ledged and braced lavvy door with the customary nine-inch gap at the bottom, reason unknown a bit rotten in places but serviceable, an elongated keyhole which substituted for a spy hole nowadays, the key lost years ago and the old-fashioned latch, a nail on the back door holding the lavvy paper on a the end of a length of looped sisal string, whitewashed walls. Some things never changed. The inside lav, that was for visitors. At eighty-five years old, she preferred not to climb the stairs anymore. She used a pot during the night under her bed in the downstairs parlour.

She waited for the latch to click into place and then crept close enough to look through the keyhole. She had a few minutes with which to rifle her grans purse. She was there on the wooden seat, her knickers rolled down to her knees, doing her business, busy her hands shuffling a strip of loo paper.

"I'll be going then, Gran. Got to rush. I have to sign on at university by 11 o'clock. You don't want me to fail, do you?" She stuffed the two twenty-pound notes into the pocket of her jeans.

"Don't be silly. You get off, my dear; will I see you tomorrow?"

"Yes, I'll pop back tonight probably. See you then, Gran," she shouted.

"Bye, Beryl. Take care me duck and watch the roads as you go." She was gone before her gran got the words out of her mouth, a smile on her face.

University, they had never met. She dropped out of school and as far as the authorities were concerned, she was still a long-term truant. She would turn up one day. That was for certain. She could not avoid that even if she did not realise it.

*****

She was loitering under the gaze of the clock tower on the Square in the centre of the town, waiting, fidgeting for her next fix, Jed, who was her dealer, another Kingston High School dropout wanting to make a quick buck. Sometimes he would accept a quick shag in the back alley, running off High Street if she couldn't pay but not today. It was market day and there were lots of drops to make, outsiders coming to town needing a fix, better takings on market day. He held out his hand grabbing the money, offered to him and handed her a fix in return.

She gave him a time for her next fix – tomorrow, Friday, 4 o'clock, same place, a pleading in her eyes. Jed was gone as soon as he had taken her money. As he left, a blind man and his dog stopped beside her, the dog nudging her leg as he passed her. She looked down and for no reason kicked the dog and shouted abuse at the bewildered and frightened man.

The dog yelped. People passed by them saying nothing, just watching as she continued her abuse screaming, raising her hands to add effect to her anger, finally walking away her hands deep in her pockets, clutching the small plastic bag containing her powder, her daily fix. She was heading for an alley further down the High Street, seeking comfort in her world of torment and make believe, safe for a few hours more.

In a blink of the eye, she had gone. The blind man comforted by an onlooker now feeling safe to intervene, driven by his guilt for not having helped the blind man earlier.

Daily life carried on as normal in the Square, a passing incident that would remain unreported to the authorities, but who cared? This is the way of life these days and we even call it progress.

*****

Chapter 18
How Far Should I Go?

She got out of the taxi. She had made her mind up not to drive. She wanted to drink to help lubricate her performance, make it more forceful. She had certainly dressed for the occasion. She knew Bill's eyes would be rolling in their sockets as soon as he sets eyes on her. He would struggle to contain his lust and it would take a high degree of difficulty keeping his hands to himself.

Belinda was playing her game. He was the unknowing victim and that is the way she wanted it to stay. Neville would be a pawn and the bad guy as far as Bill was concerned. Let him get his teeth into him not her. She realised of course that she would have to allow for a certain degree of flexibility within the outline approach to the crime because surely that is what it would be. Her goal was to use his shame to end the affair, allowing her to walk away with his gift into the sunset, the beginning of her new life.

"Wow! Stunning, absolutely stunning," he moved closer, whispering, a grin stretching across his face. "Sexy."

"Behave. I've only just arrived. A gin and tonic would help. I want cooling down. This dress makes me feel horny," she whispered, her reply dragging on the word 'horny'. Bill's face began to flush, not believing his luck.

"New, is it?"

"Yes, I bought it especially for you. Why not? Neville's time's up. He's gone, so I can spoil you now, give you more of my time. I just hope you are ready for it," she lied, dishing out the bullshit big time, but that had been her tactic from the very beginning. Her eyes seemed to sparkle. Cloud nine they call it. She half expected him to ask her to put it in writing.

He passed her drink. "Did you book a table, darling?" she asked, her eyes purposely searching his crutch area, knowing that would excite him, something he would not let pass.

"Tell me then. How much did your dress cost? How much do you need? I know you're a little short right now." *Got him,* her inner voice said to her.

"Really?" She sounded surprised, an inner grin to herself, another lie.

"Yes, come on. Tell me. Then I will see if I can afford to buy you dinner this evening as well."

"Dinner is on expenses. You know that," she laughed, smiling, pulling on his arm. "Anyway, it was nearer £350 a bit more than dinner." She laughed again. "Sorry." She squeezed his arm and stared into his eyes.

Surprisingly, he replied to her without thinking. "You're worth every penny. I will bring it to the office in the morning, you naughty girl." It was the words that made him feel horny. He just wanted to get dinner over with and get his hand up her skirt. He had been thinking about nothing else all day.

"Thank you." She leaned over closer to him, kissing his cheek. "You naughty boy, you've got me wet already." She watched as his eyes lit up like a schoolboy with a new toy to play with.

"Let's go through. Our table should be ready. We can eat and…"

She stopped him, putting her finger against his mouth. "Shush, you will only make things worse for yourself. Just be patient and you will get the best shag you have ever had," she whispered again. He took her arm, pulling her towards the restaurant, his dirty mind wanting to skip the first two courses and start with the pudding – her – wanting to get things over with. He was struggling to contain the bulge in his trousers.

*****

"Tell me about Neville. I want to know where that story started and will finish. You kept that quiet. Was that intentional?" She was surprised, not expecting that one, her face flushed. She had to think as she pulled her fork away from her mouth. She was enjoying the garlic mushroom starter, wishing she had kept the conversation dirty. That would have kept Bill happy and entertained, but it was inevitable that these kinds of questions would catch up with her.

"Yes, I did not want to tell you, not because of any reason. I just wanted to be sure it was over between us. That's all. I didn't want to get your hopes up and then decide to stay with Neville. Surely you understand that?" She took his hand, her eyes searching his face. *Did he believe me? Of course he must never know that the reason for the breakup of their marriage was a pile of dog shit because that would be an end to everything here and now Bill would cringe at the thought.* "We just drifted apart. It's as simple as that, and nothing more. Stop worrying. You have got me all to yourself. I thought that is what you wanted, isn't it?" she said, her eyes pleading with him.

"Of course, it is what I want. You know how much you mean to me. I would do anything for you. You know that. Don't you believe me?" It was his turn to plead.

"Of course, I do, you silly boy, but I will need your help. Will you give it to me?" He misinterpreted the words. He had already got her knickers down, ready to enter her when his inner voice slipped into gear.

"Yes, depending what help you need. If it's not money, of course," he laughed aloud.

Her heart almost stopped as she heard the word 'money'. Her heart was beating out of control. A heavy sweat bathed her body. She had misjudged it all. *Fuck. Fuck it,* she said to herself.

Bill noticed the heavy sweat and colouring to her face. He had upset her, and his dick did not like that. "Sorry, I did not mean that literally. Just kidding. How could I refuse you anything?" he smiled.

"I was just relieved I had told you. I wanted to, but I needed to be sure. That's all. You are not angry with me, are you?"

"Don't be silly. I just wanted to know. We need to talk about it if you want my help. That is all."

The conversation died a little. They were both weighing up their options, balancing their thoughts against their expectations.

I will lose him. He will get cold feet and I can wave goodbye to that twenty-five grand. She was sulking now at her thoughts, dreaming up lies in her head to pull him back into her plan and stop him drifting away from her.

Bill's thoughts swayed between sex and his chequebook, but he realised he was hooked, knowing fully well that he would milk her for as much sex as he could get before he gave her another penny. All he wanted right now was sex, dirty sex, and she was good at that, something that had never been on the menu at the marital home.

They managed to get through the meal with starts and stops of idle office chat. Then Bill hit her with another bombshell.

"Did you have to fuck him, that slimy toad at Simpson & Smith, your new boss, Brendon Rudd? I know what that bastard is capable of. You best be aware of it. He will have a plan. It's all a game with him. Just keep clear. Are you listening to me?" The words had jealousy written all over them. Even his eyes burnt with contempt for Rudd and it was a veiled warning to her.

My God! Where did that come from? I thought I was doing well. Perhaps I should just fuck off and leave him to it, slap his face, spit at him and create a scene. She was fucked.

He could see the anger and the hate in her eyes, wishing he had kept his mouth shut. She didn't give him time to apologise or offer her an explanation.

"Bill, you can think what you like, so take me home please. It's all over. I do not need your help, want your help or your dirty thoughts anymore. You have overstepped the mark this time. Now please." He could see the rage in her eyes. His dick hated him, and he hadn't got a clue how to get out of it.

I best keep my gob shut and let her sleep on it. A bunch of flowers in the morning. He was annoyed with himself.

Not a word was spoken between the two of them after that. He paid the bill and said goodnight to the manager and then drove her home. "Goodnight. Sorry. Talk to me?" he pleaded, but she was not listening. The front door slammed shut and he was one pissed-off person.

She checked the alarm, kicked her shoes off in the hall and threw her keys onto the work surface in the kitchen.

The bathroom, a pee, she brushed her teeth, taking a good look at herself in the mirror. *The bastard!* Where did that ending come from? She burst into tears, her plan in tatters. 'Serves you right for being greedy,' she said to herself.

She did not sleep, just wanting the morning to arrive.

*****

Chapter 19
The Journey Home

It was drizzling, not too hard, just annoying. It was accompanied by a stiff breeze blowing in from the North Sea. It would be all blown over by lunchtime and the sun would come out from beneath the low cloud cover.

Jack put their bags in the boot of the car. He raised his hand to pull the boot lid down when suddenly his body froze, his arms unable to move as darkness closed his mind. There was nothing. His thoughts were a complete blank, a slight sweat creeping over his upper body. He was afraid and then the images and faces began to dance inside his mind. Loud screaming could be heard. Thunder and lightning rolled away into the distance as the faces began to fade and the screaming stopped, the sound of clanking chains bringing it to an end.

They had decided to skip breakfast at the hotel and just head for home, snatch something on the way if that is what they both wanted to do. Otherwise it would be a straight journey home. Jack only wanted himself right now, time to think, make his excuses, no lies to Katie. He hated lying but felt he had no choice, deciding that was the way to handle the situation from now on. He could justify the lies he told her to himself, so that gave him a little comfort knowing that was not the final solution.

Katie closed her door. "Here, I have got this blanket for you. Just keep warm and take nap if you want to. I know the way home," she laughed, giving him a warm smile. "Come on, let me see you smile," she frowned.

"I'm okay. There is no need to treat me like a pensioner who feels the cold around his legs. Just don't fuss, okay. Promise?" There was a touch of anger in his voice.

"Sorry, I should have known better. Close your eyes and go to sleep. If you need anything, just ask. Okay? Let's go." The car pulled away from the kerb. Jack closed his eyes and Katie took the road north, heading home.

She decided to take the A47 as far as Kings Lynn and then head north towards Leeds following the A1 before turning off for Skepton and home. She would have at least one pee stop on the way, perhaps a meal if Jack was up to it. He would come first. It was in situations like this. That is when she realised just how much she needed him. She pulled the blanket up around his chin with her free hand, slowing down as she did so. She smiled. She loved him so much.

The A1 was busy, the main artery to the north and Scotland. She kept to a steady speed of 60 mph. That should bring her to Grantham before lunchtime. She could stop there for a pit stop, toilet, fuel and a meal. She did not want to cook when they reached home. That is of course if Jack feels the same way.

They had travelled about twenty miles up the A1 Motorway when Jack opened his eyes, pulling the blanket away from his chest, pushing downwards towards his feet, allowing him to sit up in his seat. "Where are we?" he asked.

"Hi, we are heading north on the A1 towards Grantham. I thought we could take a pit stop there and grab a meal if you are up to it." Jack yawned. "Yes, that sounds good. Sorry, I was a little grumpy at the hotel. I feel much better after that nap. Thanks." He gave her a smile and stroked her arm. "You're too good to me and I don't show the respect you deserve, do I?" he pleaded with his puppy-dog eyes, wanting her forgiveness.

"You do not have to apologise. I realise you are under a great deal of stress after your accident, so I can live with it. I just wish you would talk to me about it. That's all. I'm concerned for you. Surely you understand that, don't you?" There was a little sadness in her words.

"I do, really I do. It's just that I get these weird dreams that don't really make any sense and I am missing Mum and Dad. Brancaster brought it all home to me." His voice began to break up. He stuttered the words. Katie panicked and Jack sensed that. "I'm okay, just upset by it all. Sorry. I can't help the way I feel." A tear rolled down his cheek. "My life is shitty right now, but I just know that everything will be okay, and I will be back to normal quicker than you think."

"Good. I am glad to hear it. Tell me about your dreams, will you?" she asked, ignoring the tears.

"I don't know where to start really. It all began just after I had my first MRI scan. I dreamt about..." his voice stalled. "The best way to describe it would be something like looking through a kaleidoscope but they were not colours I was seeing but people, faces. I could hear voices shouting, young girls screaming but there was no connection to each other. It was scary really. Then there was the incident in the supermarket when I just collapsed. They started all over again, different faces and voices this time. Again nothing connected. They were just jumbled images and voices. That's the best description I can give you." He gave her a confused look.

"Well, tell me about collapsing when we were having our takeaway. Was that the same sort of dream?"

"No, that was about the hospital, an old woman on the... Don't you remember? She was on a trolley being wheeled away somewhere. Again nothing made sense."

"Oh dear, well, you had better explain it all again to Dr Doogood when we see him. I will call him in the morning and make an appointment." She tapped his arm. "You will be alright. You have got me on your side," she laughed.

"Thank God. I need you more and more just lately. I will make it up to you, promise," he smiled.

It wasn't too long before they reached Grantham, a quick meal of Ramsey's fish and chips with mushy peas and bread and butter Northern style. *Beautiful* as Pa Larkin would say.

They continued their journey home, both avoiding questions about his state of mind. Let the doctors sort that out. They both agreed that would be the best solution. They would concentrate on looking after each other. Jack would be dad and Katie would be mother. That was the solution they could agree on and it suited them both.

"We need to get some shopping, milk and bread. Otherwise no breakfast or a hot chocolate for us both before bedtime," she grinned.

"Okay, where?"

"Well, if you haven't forgotten, we need to collect your prescription at the chemist in town. There's a Tesco Extra around the corner from the chemist, so I will park up and we can walk to the Square and get your prescription and some bits of shopping. Okay?"

"Yes, mother, you're in charge." They both laughed. She nudged his arm.

Katie found a space on the High Street. "Twenty minutes, that will do," she said, "unless we have to queue in the chemist, although the prescription should be ready for us to collect. We best hurry just in case."

They walked to the Square. "Do you want to come with me?"

"Can I wait here? I don't like chemists. They always remind me of the time I went with mother to collect my chicken pox cream. Ahh, do you mind?" He shrugged his shoulders and then grinned.

"No, okay, you wait here and don't wander off," she smiled, nodding her head. "I will be as quick as I can. If I am late, you wait by the car here. Take the car keys. We have got until quarter past," she pointed to the clock tower.

"Thanks, I will stand here, promise."

Katie walked across the Square to the chemist's to collect his prescription. Jack walked away from her towards where the blind man and his dog were standing. "Hello, what's your name?" he asked, stroking the dog's back, showing him a friendly smile. The dog looked up into his eyes, wagging his tail. "It's Biba. Thank you for asking," the dog's owner replied, smiling.

"How long have you two been together then? You seem a good match," Jack asked.

"Just over a year. He's fantastic and makes my life liveable again. Every blind person should have one, shouldn't they, Biba?" He patted the dog's back. Biba wagged his tail.

"I agree. Yes, they should. Let's hope it happens one day," As he spoke, Jack looked over towards the railing protecting the base of the clock tower and access to it. A strong padlock secured the gate in the railings. He smiled at the plastic cup sitting on top of one of the rails. Somebody thought they were being clever or a spy had left a signal for his contact. That annoyed him. He glanced up at the clock, almost ten minutes past four. 'Better look for Katie,' he told himself.

"Well, glad to meet you. Take care both of you and enjoy your day. I must go to meet my sister. Goodbye."

"Goodbye and thank you," the blind man replied.

He heard Katie calling his name. He looked over towards the chemist. She shouted again and then Jack saw her walking from the side street holding the shopping. He walked over to join her and walk back with her to the car.

"The prescription was ready then?"

"Yes, I just had to pay for it and then I dashed to Tesco. I saw you talking to the blind man under the clock. Don't move, I said," she reminded him. She offered him her hand. He took the shopping from her and gave her the car keys back.

"Sorry, I'll take that, and you need these," he laughed. "Let's go and get home and light a fire, have a glass of wine and get warm, even watch TV," he grinned. She squeezed his hand.

"Hot toast and Brussels Pate for supper. We can have that with the wine but as soon as we get home, I am making that appointment with Dr Doogood at the hospital. No arguments." He laughed, 'Just like mother.' She really was.

*****

Chapter 20
The George & Dragon

Belinda leaned over, one hand on the steering wheel, dropping her overnight bag on the passenger-seat, pulling the door shut. She started the engine and set off on her trip to Bolton. There would be no work today. She hadn't even bothered to call in sick. She left explanations for her absence to Bill and let him dish out the lies. After all, it was his mess.

By the time she reached Leeds and picked up the M62 to Bolton, a two-hour drive, she told herself there would be no turning back. She even turned her mobile off. She wasn't taking calls today. She had already ignored three calls from Bill and one call from Linda.

Today, Friday and over the weekend, she would play the biggest gamble of her life. Then she would return to work on Monday as though nothing had happened. She would accept any excuse for her absence that Bill had given without question. She decided after her fallout with Bill that he would either be all in or all out of her life, no dilly dallying or in-between arrangements. She still intended to take him for a ride but now she had upped the ante. She would relieve him of fifty thousand pounds and nothing less or nothing at all. That was her gamble.

She came to that decision whilst in a pissed-up state after she got home from the Belmont Hotel incident and by the time she had pulled herself together with a cup of coffee in the early hours of the morning, she was relying on an old saying, *Nothing ventured, nothing gained.* She had decided to gamble and play it cool. She cringed at her own thoughts. Her stomach lurched into panic mode. She was frightened. *Play-*

it-cool was nothing like she had ever done before. What she wanted right now was a large gin and tonic in her hand that would help.

She was heading south to spend the weekend with an old school friend, Julie Peawood, a divorcee with no children and no mortgage but more importantly, she was satisfied with her life. Two or three holidays each year and several weekends away, some paid for, some not and obviously there were good weekends and bad weekends. Life came as a package of work, fun and commitment, take out what you put in and so far, she had been very lucky. She wasn't greedy or avaricious but sensible, reasonable, with a sense of humour and a positive outlook on life. Belinda was hoping that she could point her in the right direction. She wasn't seeking a soft shoulder to cry on. No, she was much too hard for that, neither did she want sympathy, but she did want company away from her immediate problems. She knew what she wanted, and she knew how to get it. This weekend away, ignoring Bill's calls was a punishment, a hard lesson for him. He would be shouting and swearing by now pulling his hair out. His dick would be telling him what a fucking idiot he has been. She laughed to herself.

The further she got away from her problems, the happier she felt. She pulled into Birch Services to buy cigarettes, use the ladies and fill the tank. All done. That made her feel much better. She checked her phone – two missed calls again from Bill, then a text message.

"Just let me know you are okay. I've told the office you have had to visit your dad in Surrey taken ill. That's all I could think of. Come home. I'm sorry. Call me, please."

She smiled. He's coming back regretting his arrogance and stupidity last night but she had no intention of calling him. 'Let him worry himself to death thinking I have finished with him. What a joke!' She was angry with herself. This morning, she wanted to go around to his house and tell Jill the whole story, but greed told her to keep her calm. The situation was not lost, just pushed back a little, nothing that could not be resolved.

Julie was her second choice. Sylvia Ransome, of same school and same age, was away on holiday in Lake Garda, the jewel of the Italian Lakes. At least that is what the answer machine was telling her, so she called her second choice, Julie. No harm done. She need never know.

*****

Number fourteen, the Rushes B3 9DP. Her sat-nav put her near but not quite there. She called Julie.

"Hi, you're through to," Julie picked up the phone, "Belinda. I recognised your number. Where are you?"

"Well, my sat-nav is telling me I am here but I can't see the house," she replied.

"Ha, can you see a drive to the left of the post box? That's where you need to come down that drive. Sorry, I should have mentioned it when you called this morning. My fault but you're here. That is all that matters."

"Okay, I see it. Thanks."

Julie was waiting at end of the drive for her, a period Georgian house in the background, very nice, landscaped gardens, mature trees, with manicured lawns sweeping away on both sides down the length of the drive and beyond, a large imposing Cedar of Lebanon tree spreading its magnificence in front of the house, a private location,. It reminded her of a scene from an Agatha Christie novel. She was already jealous. You could see it in her eyes.

Belinda pulled up on the drive behind a sports car, this year's model, a Mercedes-Benz E Class Cabriolet. *God,* she thought to herself. *What I have got myself into? I can't bear it.*

"Hi, you made it then. Good to see you. A good trip down?"

"Yes. Quite pleasant and thank God for sat-nav," she laughed.

"How are you?" They hugged and kissed each other. Belinda followed her into the house, and yes, the jealousy kept coming. The house was fabulous, Beverley-Hills style. Amazing.

"We'll go through to the kitchen. I've made coffee. Is that okay for you?"

"Wow, what can I say? This is what you call a kitchen? Fabulous. You have done very well for yourself."

Julie pointed to a sofa near the window looking out across the sweeping lawns. Belinda couldn't believe her eyes. She was speechless, wishing she hadn't come.

"Do you take sugar?" she asked, passing her a cup of coffee from the tray spoon in her hand.

"Yes, one please. That's wonderful. Thank you."

"How on earth do you manage to look after all this?"

"Gerald, my ex, I have a daily and a gardener two days a week and before you ask, he's in his sixties. He's not one of those young sexy Italian migrants with rippling muscles and a six pack with dark curly hair and sparkling brown eyes I'm afraid," she laughed.

"Well, you can't have it all I suppose, but I see where you are coming from." She joined in the laughter, her eyes busy taking everything in and funnily enough, she was not jealous anymore. She couldn't compete, so why not embrace Julie's success and enjoy the weekend? She was already feeling much better, securer and safer in her temporary surroundings.

"So, what brings you down from the West Ridings? It's been a long time, 2016 at Harrogate, wasn't it?"

"Yes, I feel so guilty now you have said that."

"No, need to apologise on my account. You are welcome anytime. I have booked us a table at the 'The George & Dragon' pub for lunch, well, in half an hour actually," she said, looking at her watch, a gold Rolex. That didn't go unnoticed.

"Thank you. That sounds good," she replied, smiling.

"Well, if we finish up here and get off to the pub, it's only a short walk and we can have a drink before lunch." She stood up. "I will just grab a jacket and if you finished your coffee, we'll be off, shall we?"

"Yes, fine. Sounds good to me," she smiled warmly, a slight grin. She was feeling spoilt, beginning to relax. She had to if she was going to tell her about Neville and Bill. She wouldn't of course be mentioning Jasper and the shit pile. She told herself. Her mind shuddered at that thought, a slight shiver running down her back. *Courage girl,* that's what her mother would say.

The front door shut behind them.

*****

"This is nice. You're local. That's handy, especially if you do not want to drive. Is the food good?"

"The best around this area. There are more expensive restaurants in town of course, but Friday is market day and all the best places will be full and car spaces, well, I've no need to tell you about those," she smiled.

"Good afternoon, Julie. Madame, I've saved your usual table."

"Thanks, Rubin. You're a darling. We will go into the bar and have a drink first. Bring us a menu please," she replied, touching his arm in a friendly gesture.

He smiled back at her. "Certainly, Miss Julie. The special dish for today, ladies, are fresh Loch salmon with asparagus spears and Jersey Royal potatoes with a Rhubarb jus. The pudding today will be home-made apple pie served with custard or fresh cream with coffee to follow."

"Amazing, Rubin. I'm hungry already," she smiled.

"Welcome to the bar at The George & Dragon. What will you have? A gin and tonic if I remember correctly."

"Yes, thanks. I have a feeling I shall enjoy myself here," she said, her eyes searching the décor. She looked around at the faces, a mixture of men young and old. No doubt Julie will point out the ones of interest. She spotted a Bill down the far end of the bar. He will be one to avoid. She could see his mind working. *Dirty thoughts no doubt,* she told herself.

"Two large gin and tonics please, Andy. Ice, Belinda?"

"Yes, please."

"With ice then, Andy. You are busy today. Any special reason?"

"No, there's never an explanation. Fridays just happen. I have never really thought about it. Mostly regulars, the usual crowd." He pointed over to the dominoes players at the table near the fire. "And who is your guest? Aren't you going to introduce me?" he replied with a broad grin, and a Lear. He obviously fancied Belinda.

"Andy, this is Belinda, an old school chum of mine. We were at boarding school down in Cheltenham together," she smiled.

"Hi, Belinda. Nice to meet you." She gave him a frown as he stared at her cleavage. "And this is Peter, my neighbour." He held out his hand, his eyes down the top of her dress. She accepted it with a smile. Thank God, he's overweight and married. That pleased her. She would find her own man. They were just wasting their time. Stunning she may be, hard she is, desperate never. You wouldn't be getting between her legs in a hurry. She smiled in control. That's what pleased her.

"Shall we sit over there and give the undesirables reason to gossip about us? They are already nudging and whispering amongst themselves. They will have your clothes off before we sit down for lunch I'll bet."

"Well, that's the norm. I get every time I go into pub or restaurant, you're just as pretty as me, desirable, single," she replied, smiling.

"I have a definite advantage over you, Belinda. I have already told the dirty buggers that they haven't a chance. You, unfortunately, are the new girl on the block," she grinned. "Cigarette?"

"Yes, please. Are we allowed to smoke in here?"

"Out, in the garden." They went through the bar and out into the garden, choosing a table bathed in sunshine, facing south and overlooking the open countryside.

"You still smoke then?"

"I'm not what you call a smoker. I can leave them alone for weeks at a time. It's when I'm stressed, they help me pull myself together."

"I know exactly what you mean. I was there in that place when me and Gerald agreed to split up. It was the divorce that took its toll on me and these helped me through all the crap," she replied, holding up her cigarette, her free arm supporting her elbow, the smoke swirling its way to the clouds.,

"So, are you going to tell me all about it or do you need time to think it over?"

"Perhaps another one of these will help, my round."

She waved to Andy, pointing to her glass, miming the words *two more*. She knew exactly where to find him, at the bar window ogling Belinda. 'He's gone. No shame at all,' she grinned.

"He'll just stick them on the bill. Well, young lady from Skepton," she laughed searching her eyes for a hint of what was to come. Belinda frowned, a certain fear showing in her eyes.

"I don't really know where to start. You already know what there is to tell you about Neville. It's over between us after twenty years and to be honest, now that we have agreed on the divorce, it just feels like we should have done it years ago, put it down to complacency, boredom, but the point was we were going nowhere, what with his work, my work and no kids. It was becoming a marriage of convenience for the both of us." She had a little sadness in her eyes. It wasn't all bad.

"Now tell me what you missed out, the other man, men. You tell me or am I supposed to drag it out of you like in one of those cheap American love stories," she grinned mischievously.

"I should have known better. Sorry. I just find the whole thing messy, not with Neville but with Bill." She looked down at the table, embarrassed with her own words.

"How long has this been going on? I assume that it is still going on, isn't it?"

Andy arrived with the drinks. "Stick them on the bill, Andy, please, will you?"

"Sure." He cleared the empty glasses and changed the ashtray, turning around and giving Belinda a smile, a fancy-you smile, as he walked back to the bar. *No chance, you dirty sod,* she said to herself, grinning.

"Look, don't feel bad about it or embarrassed. You can tell as much or as little as you like, but knowing you, we'll get the whole story off your chest and I suggest that would be the best option." *Well, not quite all of it.* She cringed at the thought. She took a deep breath.

"When I split with Gerald, we were living in a three bedroomed detached house in Trotney in North Cheshire, a hamlet in the stockbroker belt on a small plot of around fifteen houses, nice, private and everything that goes with it and like your marriage, ours was the same and I thought like you did once and I had made my mind up. It would be best for both of us, so from the sale of the house and our investments and savings, I bought the house I live in now *Cedars* out of my share from the proceeds of the sale and like I told you, Gerald has been as good as his word and I now have an independent and good way of life. Gerald now lives a playboy lifestyle in the Bahamas. So, I am sure I can offer you a few words of wisdom. So, let's order lunch here, have another drink and if you think that will help and then afterwards we can go through to the restaurant for lunch and then you can tell me the real story."

She smiled, touching her arm. "Thanks. That makes me feel a lot better. Do you mind if I have a white wine? Otherwise heavens know what stories I will be telling you if I stay with the gin."

"That sounds a good idea. I will join you. What do you fancy for lunch?"

"I don't know. I haven't even looked at the menu. I think I will go for the special. The salmon looks inviting. What about you?"

"Great. Well, that simplifies things. I'll join you with the special." She waved to Andy as he passed their table serving drinks for guests waiting for a table for lunch. "Two house white wines please, Andy, if you will."

"There now all we need is Rubin to come and take our order."

Andy returned to the table with their drinks. "Thanks, Andy. Could you please tell Rubin two specials and a bottle of Chilean Merlot and tell him we have decided on the garlic mushrooms for our starter. Are you okay with that, Belinda?"

"Yes, that's fine. Thank you."

"We had better give Rubin five minutes before we go through cigarette?"

"Thanks. I haven't relaxed this much in months. Now I regret not visiting you more often."

"Well, you're here now, so tell me all about Bill. How did that come about?" Julie grinned. She walked right into that question.

"Well, it's like this," she burst out laughing.

"I know you are going to tell me it was a day trip to Blackpool or an office Jolly, was it?" She joined in the laughter. Andy wondered what the hell they were laughing about.

"Enjoy your wine, girls," he smiled, leaving them to enjoy their drinks, back to the bar gossip for him. "We've all heard that before." *She got a good body on her. I wouldn't mind giving her one. Nor would I. And so on and on it went.*

"We best go through poor old Rubin will be coming to find us wondering where we have got to. Are you hungry?"

"Yes, starving in fact. I skipped breakfast this morning a heavy night. Well, you know all about those kinds of things I am sure."

"Shall I serve the wine now, Miss Julie, with your starter or would you prefer to wait until your main course and have it then?" she smiled.

"Rubin, you know me better than that. It's called another bottle," he grinned. "Yes, miss, quite right. I will open another bottle when you are ready. Enjoy your starter."

"Well, let's get back to the storyline, shall we?"

"I forgot where I was."

"Bill, was it?" she grinned.

"I hate telling stories. Its where to start. That's the problem."

"Tell me about Bill. Perhaps if you start with him, the story will begin to tell itself hopefully."

"We were working late one evening, a difficult contract, and Bill asked me as a favour if I would work with him on it until it was finished and that is where it all started.

He suggested we grab a sandwich and a drink afterwards at the pub around the corner from the office. We took his car – my first mistake. Caught last orders and the last two sweaty cheese sandwiches, grated cheese, you know, pub grub. We ate those and managed to get a second drink. Bill knew the barman and then we drove back to the office car park to collect my car. You can guess the rest. Thank you for helping me. I owe you one, a snog and before I knew where I was, his hand was up my skirt. I will admit it surprised me. It surprised me even more because I did not want him to stop. I was excited, enjoying the roughness of it. Somehow it turned me on. We didn't shag but we both enjoyed the snogging and the foreplay and from then on, it was a grope at the supermarket car park twice a week, an after-hours shag in the stockroom and the occasional weekend away when Neville was visiting the head office in Milan. It started as cheap, dirty sex and that's pretty much it. It's still dirty sex, but now Neville is out of the picture. I'm no longer sure. It's better than nothing I suppose, and it will tide me over until something better turns up, Mr right even," she frowned.

"Unfortunately for Bill, that is not what I want. He's married which doesn't help. So, there you have it."

They finished their starter and drank most of the wine.

"That was very nice," she smiled. "How was yours?"

"Lovely. Couldn't have been better. Thank you," she said, returning her smile.

"Now whilst we are waiting for our main course, tell me what you have missed out. I am pretty sure you have not told me everything, have you?" she asked, a mischievous smile on her face. Belinda paused, wondering what she should tell her. She would change tactics. That seemed the softer option, less intrusive. She would give it a try.

"Tell me about you and Gerald. When you began to drift apart, did you have affairs or lovers, casual I suppose?"

Julie grinned. "Not that easy, Belinda. Moving the goal posts. This chat should be all about you, shouldn't it?" Belinda was embarrassed and looked down, avoiding her stare. Julie felt her embarrassment, but it told her there was more to follow – motive, intent. *Let's play her game*, she told herself.

"We will come back to you," she laughed. "Sorry. I did not mean to be rude," she replied, touching her hand.

"Let me tell you about my affairs. That would help I think, and then I expect you to tell me the whole story and the truth, mind you. Don't leave the dirty bits out. I'm a grown girl," she smiled, reaching over and squeezing her hand.

"Ready?" she grinned. Julie returned her smile.

"Yes. I can't wait." She grinned back at her.

"Although Gerald and I had a normal marriage, good times, bad times, we could never somehow make it right between us. Sex wasn't as good as it could have been and with Gerald always away on business trips, that wasn't enough for me, so it was not difficult for me to let my guard down and sleep with men I knew. It started quite easily, a friend's party, drinks, idle chat and sometimes dirty talk, then in bed, shagging each other for all it's worth. Sounds crude but that is how it was. That got me into a habit almost until one night I nearly got caught. Gerald came home unexpectedly and then things began to change. I wanted it to stop, the cheating that is not the sex. I enjoyed that too much, but I did like Gerald a lot and my good side told me to split up with Gerald. That was the only fair thing to do in the circumstances."

"Believe me that wasn't easy but as things turned out, he felt the same way. I never asked if he was playing around. No point, so we agreed on the divorce and the rest you know, so there you have a history of my sordid sex life and my broken marriage." She took a large gulp of wine, her face flushed, glad it was all over for her. She can relax a little, perhaps enjoy herself at Belinda's expense.

"Now it's your turn." She grinned.

As she spoke, Rubin served the main course, opened the second bottle of wine, filling their glasses. "Enjoy your meal, ladies," he smiled, returning to the kitchen.

Julie's face flushed and not from drinking too much wine, embarrassed more the reason. Now for the bit she was dreading, she sighed, looked Julie in the eye, ignoring her heartbeat which was racing away, pounding in her breast, a slight sweat on her neck, her face flushed. 'Here goes,' she said to herself.

She turned her head slightly, avoiding direct eye contact with Julie. She had decided to avoid telling lies, that is, apart from Jasper's misdemeanour and just tell it as it was. *Perhaps it will work out better than I think it will.* She would begin by offering suggestions and avoid making bold statements about ripping Bill's balls off. That would come later. Neville will become her conscience and show her soft side, a total lie, of course, but Julie need never know that.

"This all blew up out of all proportion from a jealous outburst from Bill a few evenings ago, supposedly a romantic dinner for two, followed by some serious shagging. That was until he accused me of shagging myself into my new job basically and calling me a bitch. I just told him it was all over there and then and demanded he take me home. I had enough with Neville calling me a bitch, but I could handle that, knowing that he did not really mean it. More of a show of anger at himself, so that was not difficult to put to the back of my mind. Bill's words, however, I can't forgive. You could argue that they were brought about through jealousy and spoken in a fit of anger, but nevertheless it hurt me just the same."

Julie took her hand, "Goodness, me luckily I didn't have to go through any of that. Anger yes, but not in a bad way. A few shouts some, heated arguments, but nothing as serious as you are telling me. Sorry, I can see it is still hurting."

"Uh, I will get over it." The first lie was coming up. "I just wanted to get my own back. In fact I almost went to see his wife, Jill, and make a clean breast of it all, tell her everything but that would hurt her and not him, the bastard."

"I just wanted to forgive him the next morning, but I quickly changed my mind and then my only thoughts were of getting back at him somehow and that is where I am right now."

"Let's talk about something else, take your mind off it for a while. We can always come back to it if you wish." Now she was lying. She wanted to be part of the get-back-at-him plan.

"How's the rest of the family, good I hope?" Julie could see through her tactics but welcomed the change of conversation. 'Let her think about her story. Perhaps that could work in my favour.'

"I heard from my mother last night and I had a call from my Solicitors office, my appointment to get the ball rolling with my divorce from Neville. I've already told him about my arrangements and he seems fine about it, so that helps."

"Have you agreed terms with him?"

"Yes. In an around-about way. Luckily, we don't have a mortgage. We paid that off a few years ago. The benefit of a childless marriage I suppose, so we have agreed a straight split down the middle, half each."

"What loose ends? Are there any because it is usually those small things that you feel are unimportant at the time that can end up bogging you down? And believe me, you want to avoid those circumstances at all costs. I learnt that at my own expense."

"Mm, he keeps his and I keep mine. He has already emptied his Building Society Account and his bank account. He doesn't know I know that, so I will leave it there. Any advice to give me?" There was a pleading in her voice, a forced smile.

"It sounds good to me as long as neither of you change your mind. Yes, it looks fine."

"Anyway, he's thinking of moving away. He has applied for a move to Head Office in Milan, so hopefully that should happen soon after all his application is just a formality, so I think he will want to close the deal as soon as possible so he can leave everything behind with a clean sheet. As for me, I need to get my mortgage application approved in the next two weeks or I will have to declare my new employment, so I want to hurry things along as well and that is in my own interest of course and should not affect the terms of the settlement we have both agreed upon and hopefully that will be the end of it, our marriage I mean."

Rubin was heading towards their table. Julia raised her eyebrows indicating his arrival. Their conversation ended there.

"How was your main course? Up to the Dragon's standard I hope, Miss Julie?" he asked, smiling.

"Yes, of course Rubin. I knew you would not let me down. We both enjoyed it very much. Ah, gives ten minutes before we finish with the pudding please."

"Certainly. Are you both having custard or cream, or one of each?" he grinned.

Julie looked at Belinda. "Custard?"

"Oh, yes please," she smiled.

"Thank you, ladies. I'll just pour the last of the wine."

"Well, shall we nip into the garden and have a cigarette? I'm gagging."

"You don't mean that, do you?" She touched her arm with a laugh.

"Not that gagging. Perhaps tomorrow night when we go into town, I have booked a table for the two of us at Annabelle's, a small family owned and run Italian Restaurant and believe me if you like Italian food, that is the place to go."

"Crickey, you are spoiling me."

"Not tonight. It will be a bottle of Prosecco and a movie, perhaps pate and salad for supper. Will that do?"

"Yes, that will definitely do," she replied, smiling.

They left the table and walked through the bar out into the back garden watched by drooling eyes. The usual nudges and the words would follow them until the bar door to the garden closed shut behind them.

"Thanks. We ought to have sat out here in the garden. It's quite warm I'm surprised."

"Yes. It is quite warm, isn't it?" replied Julie. "All we don't need right now is one of those wannabes joining us from the bar. Let them stay where they are and keep themselves to themselves."

"I agree. We will finish smoking our cigarettes and go back and finish our lunch and the wine of course. Then we can settle up with Rubin get back home crash out and relax for a couple of hours if you like," she smiled.

"Yes. I'll go along with that." She grinned, returning her smile.

Lunch was finished. They were happy. Rubin was happy. The sun was shining, and Belinda was relaxed for the first time in months. They held hands back to the house.

*****

Chapter 21
Mother

HIDE AND SEEK HOLLOW:
"I thought I could hear you. How long have you been up?" asked Jack, stretching his arms and rubbing his eyes, yawning.

"Good morning, Jack. Not long. Did you sleep well? I laid awake most of the night listening, in case you had another one of your dreams," she smiled.

"Fits you mean. Go on, say it." There was anger in his eyes. He was shouting at her.

"Jack, Jack, let us start the day again and stop shouting at me. It will not help you being angry at me. Good morning, Jack. How are you this morning?" She frowned at him, staring him in the eyes. His face was flushed. His eyes looked down at the floor in shame. He could see the tears in her eyes.

"Katie, I'm sorry, so sorry. I can't help it and I don't know why you know I would never want to hurt you. Please forgive me, will you?" he pleaded with her.

"Sit down and don't say a word. Just listen to me. I am going to call Dr Doogood at nine o'clock and then I am dragging you, if necessary, to that bloody hospital and we are staying there until we sort out what is wrong with you and you will tell him about your dreams, your state of mind and whatever else is worrying you. Do you understand what I am saying?" She stared at him, waiting for his reply.

"Yes, I have said I'm sorry and I mean it. Now can we put an end to this falling out?"

"Stay where you are don't move. What would you like for breakfast? All I can rustle up I'm afraid is what we have in the fridge and the cupboards which, believe me, is not a lot, so on today's menu we have cereals with milk, tea or coffee and I suppose I can manage egg and mushrooms but I suppose you have a choice of, boiled, fried or scrambled for your eggs, so what would you like?" She was being assertive, not rude or showing any signs of temper, just letting him know what his options were and that she was not in the mood for his attitude. He smiled at her. She took his hand and kissed his cheek.

"Throw in a couple of fried tomatoes and I will have the lot, cereals and the fry up. Oh, and Good morning."

"You make me smile. The sooner you are back to normal, the better, and you will be cooking breakfast tomorrow and no argument, alright? And we need to shop by the way. Will you be okay with that?"

"Yes," he smiled, thinking how lucky he was to have a sister like her.

*****

Breakfast was over. Jack helped with the washing up. "You are not going to leave them there, are you? Put them away, lazy boy." She pointed to the dishes on the work surface. "Now Jack, not later."

"Okay, don't panic. I heard you." Cupboard doors were shutting, cutlery chatting to each other as he placed them in the drawer tidy. He smiled at her. "There you are then." He kissed her cheek. "Can I go and take a shower now?"

"Yes, I suppose so, and don't leave a mess behind you because I will shower when you have finished and don't leave a heap of wet towels on the floor for me either please. Now go, shoo." She clapped her hands. He laughed as he dashed upstairs.

Katie grabbed Jack's hospital file and searched for the contact details for Dr Doogood. She glanced at the kitchen clock, half an hour. *That should give me time to shower and dress by 9 am.*

"Jack, Jack," she shouted from the bottom of the stairs. "Have you finished yet?"

"Yes," a voice said, coming from behind her. "I'm here."

"How did you manage that? I never heard you come downstairs. Are you a magician or something?" Jack laughed. She did not realise how right she was. Jack had no idea either, but he knew he wasn't a magician nor did he know how it could have happened.

"Right. I am going to shower and dress and when I come down, I will phone Dr Doogood, so don't go wandering off. Put the TV on and watch the news. Or tidy up." He grabbed the TV remote and put the TV on. *Tidy up*, he laughed to himself.

"Good morning. I wondered if you could put me through to Dr Doogood's surgery please."

"Do you have an appointment?"

"No, I just need to talk to him. He told me to ring this number at any time day or night. My name is Katie Cambridge."

"One moment please. I will see if he is available."

"She's just checking if he is free." Jack smiled back at her.

"Just putting you through now, Miss Cambridge."

"Thanks."

"Miss Cambridge, good morning. I expect this is a call regarding your brother, Jack, isn't it?"

"Yes, good morning, doctor."

"Please tell me about your concerns. Has he had a relapse or is it something more serious than that?"

"Dreams, doctor. Vivid dreams and voices. Jack's been having them whilst we were away on the East coast. I thought a break and the fresh air would do us both good. He had another attack and now he's telling me he keeps having the same dreams and flashbacks. Could they be serious, doctor?"

"That is hard to say. You had better bring him to the hospital. He's not to drive, you understand. Just come to reception and ask for Nurse Edmonds. She will be expecting you. Is that alright? Can you manage that?"

"Yes, doctor. We will leave straight away now."

"You may have to wait quite some time. I will try and fit you in between appointments. I don't want to take any chances. It may be more serious than you think, but don't worry. He is in safe hands."

"Thank you, doctor. Goodbye." She hung up.

"Did you hear all that or do you want me to tell you what he had to say?"

"Loud and clear. We better do as he says. Let's go," he replied, taking her hand.

*****

Skepton General Hospital:

"Nurse Edmonds, please. It's Miss Katie Cambridge to see Dr Doogood," she smiled.

"One moment please." She picked up the phone and spoke with Nurse Edmonds. "She will be with you shortly. Please take a seat." She pointed to a row of chairs by the window overlooking the gardens.

"Let's hope we do not have to wait all day. You've heard the stories about patients waiting on trolleys and all that."

"Jack, don't be petty. It is very good of the doctor to see us at such short notice, so stop being disrespectful. That's rude." There was anger in her voice.

"Sorry, it's nerves I suppose, not knowing. I hate that."

"Stop worrying. You heard what he said. Just be patient and sit still. You are making me angry," she frowned, disappointed with his behaviour.

It was thirty-five minutes before Nurse Edmonds came to collect them. "Good morning. Sorry to keep you waiting. The doctor will see you now." She gave them a warm smile and asked them both to follow her, a different room this time.

"Good morning, Jack. Katie, let's do the formalities first."

He took the file from Nurse Edmonds. "Thank you, nurse. I will call you if there is anything else."

"Thank you, doctor." She left, closing the door behind her.

He opened the file. "You are taking the medication prescribed for you, no driving, no alcohol. You look surprised, Jack. No alcohol?" Jack frowned. Katie closed her eyes and looked down at the floor. "I did have a glass of beer with my lunch but that was it."

"You are sure?"

"Yes, doctor. I am sure."

"Good. Well, that's the boring bit over with but not forgetting how important it is to establish the true circumstances, when I say 'no alcohol', that is exactly what I mean. Do you both understand that?"

"Yes, doctor," they both replied, frowning.

"Now then, Jack, Katie tells me that you had another relapse and that you have been having dreams and flashbacks. I want you to tell me about those and this time, do not leave anything out, otherwise I will not be able to help you. Is that quite clear?"

"Yes, doctor. I apologise."

The door opened, and another doctor entered the consulting room.

"Peter, glad you could make it," he stood up offering his hand. "Roger, just in time I hope?"

"Yes, we have just completed the preliminaries, so your timing's perfect."

"And you must be Jack and you are Katie. Good to meet you both. Dr Doogood has asked me to attend this surgery. I am head of the Neurology here at the hospital, so don't look so worried. I am here to help you, not eat you," he grinned.

"Good morning, doctor."

"Professor Martin I like to be called," he laughed. Katie's neck and face were a bright pink by this time and Jack had clammy hands and a cold sweat creeping over him, expecting the worst. *You have hours to live.*

Dr Doogood handed Jack's case notes to the professor.

"Hmm, tell me about your dreams and these memory flashbacks you have been getting, Jack. Take your time and tell me everything. Do not be short on detail. Then we can discuss your panic attacks. I think that is what they are but as yet, we are still undecided, so tell us all about it in your own words. Take your time." He repeated his words. "There is no need to rush."

Jack's face was flushed, and he looked concerned, not knowing what to expect. He looked over towards Katie. She looked as confused as he was.

Nervously, Jack began to talk about his experiences.

"I know I should have told you, doctor, when you first examined me, and I realise the gravity of my mistakes. So firstly, I would like to apologise for that, fear I suppose, nothing devious I can assure you. Just plain and simple fear." He took a deep breath, sighing before continuing with his version of events.

"The images and words first came to me after my MRI scan here at the hospital. At first, they were just blurred images and voices. That was the first time it happened. Then after that, they continued and became clearer and louder but still I am not able to see or hear anything I could understand. Nothing was linked together, no phrases or sentences, just jumbled up words that did not make any sense at all, then on the last occasion I could see the same blurred faces, but this time I could associate the faces and words with people I had seen in real life, still blurred faces and inaudible sounds but a great improvement on the first time. Perhaps next time everything will be explained. I hope so." Katie took his hand, smiling, encouraging him.

"Well, that makes the situation very much clearer. I only wished you had told me all this in the first place, Jack. Remember, we are here to help you and get your life back on track," he frowned. "What is your view having heard Jack's story, Peter?"

"Well, it certainly is on the surface. These revelations simplify things. That would be my immediate observation and changes my diagnosis significantly. I would suggest, from what I have heard, it is just a matter of short-term memory loss or memory lapse, even both and nothing more than that but being in the position as head of neurology at the hospital, I take caution and defer my prognosis until we have carried out the second series of tests. Would you agree with that, Roger?"

"Interestingly. My view entirely having determined that the blow to the head is surprisingly healing itself. There will be some scarring but we cannot find any internal injury, bleeding or the effects of concussion, so Jack, we need to fit you in as quickly as possible, so let me have a look at available dates. My diary is telling me this coming Friday or the Monday after that. Will you be free for either of those dates, Peter? Otherwise, we would have to postpone it until later in the month."

"That won't be necessary, Roger. I have Monday 14th free the week after," he said, putting his iPhone back into his pocket.

Jack and Katie both smiled, relieved. "Thank you, doctor – Professor."

"That's okay. I will write to you confirming time and place of your appointment. You should receive the confirmation within a couple of days, so cheer up. That's progress." He gave Katie a warm smile.

*****

"Happy, I hope so, are you?"

"Yes, of course I am, you silly girl, or should I say mother?"

"There's no need for that. I am your sister. Full stop, and don't you forget, nor your medication, no driving and no alcohol, just plenty of rest and fresh air."

"I haven't got any lectures on Thursday, so we will drive out into the Dales, perhaps Grassington for lunch. How does that sound?"

"Good, bloody good. Let's get home. I need to put my feet up."

"Well, the bad news is your feet will have to wait. We need to do a big shop and when we get back home, you need to call Christopher. He rang whilst you were in the shower this morning. And before you tell me off, I didn't mention it. You had enough on your plate with your appointment. He will still be there. I think it was only catch up. He certainly did not give me the impression it was anything urgent."

"Well, that's definitely a thank you, mother. So come on, let's get the shopping done and whatever you do miss, the bloody baked beans aisle," Katie laughed. He joined in, beginning to unwind a little. That pleased her.

*****

Chapter 22
Decadence?

HIDE AND SEEK HOLLOW:
Jack was enjoying the late morning sunshine in the garden thinking about the Consultant's Prognosis from his medical assessment session this morning with Professor Martin and Dr Doogood. Well, confession really. He didn't like giving up all of his secrets but he had told them enough and that was about as far as he was prepared to go. He smiled. He knew somehow that everything was good, and everything would be back to normal in no time, but he had to consider Katie's feelings. She was after all the most important person in his life.

Jack called, 'Chris Bell, General Manager of **Studentia,** a division of **jACKATIE Investments Limited,** Jack's own Company which specialised in Apparel, Footwear and Accessories for students. The company was well established with outlets and internet sales covering the whole of the EU, the USA, China, Japan and Australia.

"Good morning. How are you? Good I hope."
"Hi, thanks for calling me back, Jack, and more importantly, how are you?"
"Getting there I think. So, tell me what's going on? Give me an update. Don't overdo it, just the essentials will do. I will ask you for more specifics only if I think I need them, fire away."

"You need to call Yang Li (the CEO of the Pinky Corporation Inc. Shanghai, China). She's fuming and will not talk to me directly. She wants to talk to you. I presume you have your office mobile switched off?"

"Yes, I will talk to her later but I need you to tell her that she is required under the terms of our contracts to deliver any outstanding garments including accessories. We have on order with her."

"You know that she has stopped deliveries and that is giving us a lot of pain right now, so we need to resolve the impasse. Can we do that?"

"I checked their account this morning and she is in to us for a little under three quarters of a million, no deliveries, no money. I will make it quite clear to her when I talk to her that penalties for late delivery will be applied to her account if she continues to hold back her deliveries. Make her your priority and tell her I will call her later today, but first tell me what else is happening?"

Chris laughed, "Have you got all day?"

"It can't be that bad, Chris?"

"No, but there is a lot going on though right now."

"Then tell me what is worrying you?"

"There is nothing worrying me. We are about to launch the **'Decadence *Range*'** and we need you to pop into the office on Friday to watch the filming of the floor show. Hopefully with your approval, we can finalise the website for launch. You will have to agree the price range with Eric and his bunch but I have seen the draft figures and they are looking really good."

"Sounds brilliant. I'm quite excited, so yes, organise Friday's floor show but I want every employee involved, so arrange it around them and remember my briefing notes, heavy on the Art Nouveau image. Let them know how important they are to the success of the launch please. I know it is such short notice but it will be a good PR exercise and do you think we should invite Wendy and Ruben from the National Students Union and Gabrielle from the Skepton Gazette? He would arrange that anyway, but he encouraged Chris to make decisions."

"Yes, that would gain us some impetus for the launch because the sales forecast is heavy and if we achieve, it will set a new launch record. So I think under those circumstances, we had better involve the local Student Union guys as well. That will do us more good than harm, lay on a good spread with Champagne perhaps."

"Chris, you deal with the nitty-gritty. It's your budget, your show, not mine. You're good at that. Don't skimp on the hospitality, understand?"

"In that case, we ought to have the London crowd involved. I will arrange travel and hotels that should earn us a lot of PR, and if that works out good, we should go for a total international roll out."

"Great, just get on with it."

"You had better arrange a meeting that morning with Barry in Sales Marketing and Simon in Production along with Eric and his accounts guys. After all, he's the one that has got to fund it and anybody else you feel should attend. What I don't want is to approve the launch and the website only to find we have missed something very important. So, you had better make it a 6 am English breakfast start, and I will bring Katie along with me, so do not forget her Yogurt and Muesli. Is that it?"

"Not quite. You forgotten Ibis the UK manufacturer. Do you want them to attend?"

"Yes, I think we should, but they will come in the capacity of Consultants. No one is to know who they really are, apart from those already involved with them of course. Print up some phoney ID badges. That will help, and mail me their details. I do not want to be the one that puts my foot in it and I don't want anything getting back to the Chinese, understood?"

"Yes."

"We can make that quite clear at the breakfast meeting on Friday and could you please ask Barry to email me the Sales Projections, together with unit costs and mark ups so that I understand them fully and just what we are committing ourselves to, financially that is."

"Sure, no problem. You take care and I look forward to seeing you and Katie for breakfast on Friday."

"Good. Well, I am going to get a coffee and enjoy the sunshine…err…you better ask Barry to call me at home. I need to ask him a few questions. I will want to know exactly what I am talking about by Friday. Okay? That's it for now I think. I will call you if I need to ask you anything else before then."

"Something tells me that Chris has a sparkle in his eye for Katie and she likes him. I can tell from the way she talks about him. I wouldn't object, or would I?"

*****

Chapter 23
Temptation

Belinda stirred from her sleep, her mouth dry, her head pounding from her hangover. She felt dreadful. "Augh, my own bloody fault, too much too fast and too strong." They were drinking like a couple of teenage piss heads on a warm-up session before a binge down at the local nightclub.

Her eyes glazed. She tried to focus on the wallpaper pattern, not one she recognised. *Where the fuck am I?* she asked herself, panicking. She turned over on to her back, her leg touching someone else's leg. Her stomach jumped up to her mouth. Her heartbeat raced away with her thoughts, fear gripping her body. "Oh my God! What have I done?" she said, carefully pulling her leg away back to her side of the bed, her head and eyes facing the opposite wall.

Was it Neville, Bill or a complete stranger? She lay there, her body frozen, her left arm tucked in tightly against her body, ensuring there was space between them, whoever them was. She lay there for what seemed a lifetime, collecting her thoughts. Her courage seemed to have deserted her and there was no sign of life, no noise, no movement from the body lying next to her. She began to think that she had imagined it but that was not a rational thought. She had touched something or someone and it would do no good to pretend she hadn't. Fear gripping her body she was frightened, not in control. She moved her head slightly, building up enough courage to turn around and see who she had been sharing her bed with. Her whole body drenched in sweat now, fear in her eyes, her body frozen, her mind taking over, controlling her thoughts. *What would he look like?* Her face and neck burning with shame, she closed her eyes. *Who was it laying besides her? Did they shag?* Her memory was blank. She had to know.

She gritted her teeth, clenching her fists tight at the sides of her body. She turned her head, opening her eyes, not believing what she was seeing.

Oh, fuck. How did this happen? She closed her eyes wishing it wasn't true, although it exited her thoughts in a strange and unexpected way. *Did I?*

Julie stirred from her sleep, smiling at her as she opened her eyes. She froze, unable to move her body, her cheeks still warm and flushed with embarrassment. All she could think about was whether Julie had shagged her in her drunken stupor in the early hours of the morning and without thinking, she reached between her legs, feeling the wetness of her vaginal lips. She closed her eyes again, ashamed, wishing it was Neville or Bill sharing the bed with her.

"Hi, good morning. It's fine. Nothing happened and like you I have no idea how we came to be sleeping together in the same bed." She took her hand. "You look awful, about like how I feel, a bloody thumping head. I can definitely say we were well pissed last night and not a guy in sight," she laughed. Belinda laughed, allowing her emotions to gain control again.

Julie sat up. "Look at the time. I don't believe it," she frowned. Disappointment filled her eyes. Belinda's eyes were immediately attracted to her breasts and her large, raised nipples. They excited her. She wanted to expose herself. She slid her legs to the floor and stood up facing Julie. She wanted her to see her body. She wanted her to look at her nakedness, wanting her to share her desires.

"Don't go yet. Let's just relax for a while. There's no rush." She offered her hand, wanting her to lie beside her. She was already feeling horny. Belinda hesitated, slightly embarrassed by Julie's words, confused. She put one knee up onto the bed, exposing her vagina which immediately excited Julie. She wanted more. She could see it in her eyes searching her body.

"Come, give me a cuddle." She held out her hand again, this time inviting her to share her lust.

Belinda slipped under the sheets, covering her nakedness, unsure in which direction to go, home or sex quite simply put. *A one off you may enjoy it,* she told herself, her heartbeat racing again, butterflies in her stomach, her vaginal lips swelling, forcing them open. She loved that feeling and it excited her. It was obvious she was sexually aroused and she could not disguise her lust.

Julie pulled herself back down between the sheets next to her, feeling her warmth, her hand on Belinda's thigh, her desires wanting to caress her body, her own excitement causing a blushing to her neck and face. Her heartbeat increased. Her nipples stiffened as she leant over kissing her cheek. Her eyes filled with desire.

Belinda just deserted her inhibitions and before she realised it, she was laying on top of her, pushing her legs apart and kissing her lips, hungry for her sex. Julie responded, pushing her tongue deep inside Belinda's mouth. She began licking her tongue, exchanging saliva, raising each other's lust.

Julie pushed her hand down between Belinda's legs, teasing her clitoris with her fingers and in her innocence, Belinda immediately orgasmed, violently raising her bottom, arching her back, fighting her orgasm. "Oh, fuck! Stop, stop. I can't take anymore," she screamed, pushing her bottom up and down, wanting that tingling feeling inside her to stop. She lay there exhausted, turning her face away, feeling the guilt of her actions, ashamed.

Now Julie wanted her satisfaction and taking Belinda's hand in hers, guiding her between her own legs, wanting her fingers inside her. Belinda responded, reluctantly knowing she had to play her part, putting her finger inside her swollen lips, slurping as she increased her rhythm much to the pleasures of Julie. "Faster, faster. I'm coming. Don't stop. Ah, ah, oh, fuck. Keep going harder, harder. Ah, fucking hell. I can't take it," she cried, pulling Belinda's hand away and raising her knees to relieve the tingling sensation inside her vaginal lips, a burning sensation gripping her whole body now wet from each other's sweat, panting, exhausted, just wanting to hold her close, to feel safe in her arms. She collapsed beside her.

Nothing was said for quite some time. Then without warning, Julie jumped out of bed, raising her arms above her head. "Let's shower. We've just had breakfast, so we will have to settle for an early lunch. Come on, follow me." She had mischief in her eyes. She laughed, holding out her hand, wanting her to follow her to the shower.

*****

Belinda could hear the kettle whistling, *My God! I need a coffee right now*. Her mind was confused. Her lust fulfilled her, vaginal lips still swollen and wet inside from her orgasm. She needed a moment of calm to collect her thoughts.

"Coffee?"

"Yes, the best words I have heard since early this morning. I can't remember a bloody thing, can you?"

"That about sums me up all I can remember is paying the taxi driver. I think I may have even given him a kiss. I was that pissed. We both were, and I have no idea how we managed to get upstairs to bed."

"Thanks, I need this." Belinda took the mug of coffee from her, still embarrassed, her first lesbian affair and her quickest orgasm ever.

"It was great. I have never kissed a girl like that before. I didn't know I had it in me. It just seemed so easy."

"Well, it is easy. There is nothing complicated about it. I am not into sex toys but I do enjoy the kissing and the intimacy of your fingers inside me, so yes, it was great. Don't look so worried. I wanted you too. We both orgasmed, so that can't do any harm, can it? Come on, let me see you smile."

"Sorry, am I behaving like a silly schoolgirl?"

"No, not at all. I was worse than you the first time I kissed a girl."

"Really? Or are just saying that to make me feel better, are you?"

"No, now what do you fancy for lunch? I need to cook you at least one meal whilst you are here as my house guest. We've got meat, fish, pasta, salad and vegetables." Belinda looked confused. "I will let you think about it over coffee. I'm not sure what I fancy either, but I am sure we will decide between us."

"Hungry?"

"Yes, starving. I can't even remember what we ate last night for dinner."

"That was the problem and the reason we got shit-faced. We didn't eat. We were too busy on the Merlot and the vodka shots. You can drink well. I will give you that," she laughed.

"Were we that pissed. I know I felt like that this morning, but I can't remember anything about last night, perhaps a good job, ah?"

"Yes, definitely. What about grilled mackerel with a pepper salad and fresh crusty bread? I could rustle that up without much trouble. The mackerels are fresh from the fish market on Thursday. I had planned to cook them for my mother on Monday but I can cook something else for her."

"That will do nicely. Thank you. It's a long time since I had fresh mackerel. The last time was down in Devon, Paignton. I think it was caught by my own fair hand, well, some fishing line. That just happened to catch fish as if by magic, throw it in, pull it out loaded with fish," she giggled.

"That's lunch sorted then. You can set the table and I will cook, shouldn't take long. There is a fresh loaf in the bread bin over there. You can slice that up as well. Oh, and take some butter out of the fridge now please. Otherwise, we will never be able to spread it later," Belinda laughed. "We have all been there, haven't we?" she smiled.

"We can chat about you and Bill over lunch. You started telling me all about him, then I'm afraid the Vodka shots took over, but you did get as far as telling me he as good as called you a fucking whore shagging your new boss. Do you remember that far?"

"Yes, and it still gets my goat every time I hear those words, the bastard," she frowned. Her eyes were angry.

"As bad as that, I didn't realise you hated him that much. Do you hate him or are you just angry?"

Belinda wanted time to think, not about Bill or Neville but how much should she tell her, thinking this weekend was a complete mistake. *I just want to get home, shower in my own home and then face the music on Monday morning, Bill will certainly have a lot to get off his chest.* She could cope with all that but not this, a lesbian fling, with Julie wanting more. *I thought she might make a play for me in the shower. Luckily, it was just shower gel sharing and wanting looks. She even emphasised washing her vagina, stroking her lips, almost masturbating right there in front of me. No, not for me. I like men. So, I will go along with whatever pleases her right now, use her like she has used me.*

"No, I hate him, and I will draw a line under that part of my life. Neville will be in Milan. I will have a new job which I need to support my new mortgage, so life now is crap, but I am a survivor. I won't let him beat me; that's for sure," she replied, a little sadness in her voice.

Fifty grand with a little bit of luck, I will focus on that and not him. Let him have his sex. After all, he will be paying for it, she smiled.

"Thanks for listening. I do appreciate it," she replied, giving her a warm smile.

"You won't like me asking you this with you driving home later, but could you pour me a glass of wine? The one in the fridge will do. It's what we left before our taxi arrived last night. I remember that much," she laughed.

"I will have a small one with my lunch. That will be okay. I will still be under the limit." It was her turn to laugh.

"Yes. I bet you could really use one. I certainly need it, hair of the dog and all that crap. I just want one. I don't need any excuses."

She had washed the fish and put them in a deep-frying pan with a generous noggin of butter and lit the grill. *I had finished cutting up the loaf and sorting and washing the salad when she hit me with another dose of her lust.*

"You kiss well, and you pushed me past my comfort zone in bed this morning. Nobody has ever done that. Before I was coming from the moment, I pushed my tongue into your mouth, you naughty girl." She stared at her, a wanting-you look in her eyes, followed by a dirty smile.

Belinda wasn't sure what she had in mind. Was it a compliment or a suggestion of wanting more? Her stomach muscles tightened. She was almost scared on two counts. She did not want sex with her, neither did she want to hurt her feelings, but the words would not come to her. Her face flushed, and Julie could sense her mood.

She walked over to her. "It's okay. I wasn't flirting. It was just a compliment. Perhaps next time we meet up, we could be more adventurous," she smiled, touching her arm, catching her nipple as she took her hand away. Belinda could see the lust in her eyes but sighed with relief, knowing she wasn't making advances, although she guessed that she wanted more sex, dirtier sex.

"I'm about already here," she said, placing the plated Mackerel on the table.

"Come and sit down and help yourself before it goes cold."

Belinda was searching for words. She needed to be very careful what she said over dinner. Otherwise, she would have Julie's hand up her skirt. That much she had convinced herself of that but even though she was having second thoughts herself.

Julie's nipples were like beacons to her eyes and as she lifted her wine glass to her mouth staring at them, she wanted to suck them, taste her body. She could already feel that tingling sensation inside her swollen pussy lips, forcing her to open her legs wider in an effort to contain her excitement. She looked away, fighting her lust, hoping that Julie had not noticed.

Julie had noticed and wanted to take advantage of her weakness that excited her lust. She would give her encouragement. She wanted her.

"They look good." Belinda looked away from her as she spoke the words.

"Hungry, are you?" Julie's words were intimidating to her and she felt a little scared, frightened almost, not knowing how to reply.

"Yes." That was the only word she could manage and Julie, sensing her fear and her reluctance for more sex, let her word slip away. She did not want to push her away for good. *There would be a next time. Give her space and time to think*, she thought to herself.

Julie poured her a wine. "Let's get back to Bill. Tell me what you have in mind. I am sure you have a plan. He hurt you a lot and you want your revenge, don't you? Am I right?" She gave her a sympathetic smile, searching her eyes for any tell-tale signs.

Belinda was busy spreading butter on a slice of bread, busying her mind, attempting to cope with the situation, wanting to tell her but she just wasn't sure how much she should involve her. She wanted Julie to take the initiative. She found that a much easier way of reconciling her emotions and thoughts.

"Crickey, these Mackerel are tasty. How's yours?"

"Yes, beautiful. They bring back a lot of memories for me. Neville really. I shall miss him but he is not what I want. You are right. I want to get the better of Bill. His arrogance and selfishness has gone too far and like you have said, I want to bring him down to earth. I want to hurt him. Can you understand that?" she frowned, not knowing what to expect or even how she would react.

She chuckled. "I envy you. Do you know that I wish I could hurt him for you. I think he deserves everything that drops at his door. Do you think I can help you, become involved? I will if that is what you want, do you?" she replied with a mischievous grin. 'Was she playing a game? She must have a motive. Was it more sex?' she asked herself.

"I can't see how. Give me a clue. I just do not know what to do, except that I want to hurt him, get my own back," she smiled, a help-me smile.

"I was once told that there are two ways to hurt a man, his pride and his wallet. It really depends on how much hurt you want him to suffer. Which is it you have decided?"

"A lot, a fucking lot. I hate him and whichever way I choose, I know I will have to suffer having his dick inside me and that thought makes me want to be sick. The good times with him are over I'm afraid," she almost trembled with fear as she was telling her.

Julie took her hand. "Yes, I do understand how much you have been hurt, so let us try and work something out together. You will be okay. I am willing to help in any way I can." *At what cost?* Belinda asked herself. 'Will I be jumping out of the frying pan and in to the fire?' That was the bit that frightened her, but she had the resolve to carry it through, take his money. That is the way to hurt him the most. She grinned.

"Take his money. That is a good idea, but how?"

Julie paused. She took a sip of her wine and left the table, returning with a fresh bottle of Prosecco. "I will need this before lunch is over. I wish we could enjoy it between us. Do you have to go home? Couldn't you make an early start in the morning?" There was a hint of disappointment in her eyes, almost expecting her to say no.

"I can't. I have too much to do, too much to plan. The next few days will be the most important days in my life and if I want to destroy him, I must stay focused. We can share the victory together and enjoy ourselves, perhaps even shape our future together in some way." That should hold her attention and take her mind off sex. That is what she wanted. 'But I would not be able to cope right now, just keep her on my side, encourage her, give a little bit at a time.'

"Well, that would be my choice, so I must ask you how much he is worth apart from the obvious. You can't count his mortgage," she laughed.

"Has he got one?"

"Yes, but I know it is less than ten thousand pounds. I remember him boasting that once. I also know that he has several hundred thousand tucked away in various bank accounts and building societies. One thing he did enjoy was gloating about it to me once when he was pissed and that is something you are not likely to forget in a hurry," she replied.

"Several hundred thousand. Well, surely that has to be our starting point, doesn't it? Do you agree?"

"It is not where we start that worries me about your idea." *Give her praise. Let her think it is her idea. I can play humble for a few months. It will hurt but I will get there.* "It is the reason for the deceit that I am struggling with. Do you have an idea?"

"That is the simple bit. Neville, he's the reason. You have said yourself that you will have to get a mortgage, so we tell Bill you will need a short-term loan. It is as simple as that as I see it. Would you struggle with that? I will shag him for you if that would help," she laughed. Belinda joined in, seeing the funny side of that statement.

"You would not enjoy him. I can assure you. I drifted into the relationship. It would not have been a choice. I would have wanted if I am honest with myself but thank you for offering your loins." The laughter carried on for some time after that. Lunch was finished. They crashed out on the sofa, holding hands.

*****

Belinda stopped at Birches Service Station on the M62, heading back home just after 6 pm that evening.

I will just have to play it as it unfolds. She was not the kind of person who mapped out her own life. She spent every day planning other people and never actually made time for herself. Anyway, she enjoyed going through life on the seat of her pants. In fact the thrill of it all satisfied her ego. It made her feel good. She always wanted sex afterwards in a queer sort of way. It turned her on. Perhaps that is why she enjoyed dirty sex with Bill. She had never actually thought about it like that before, but could she cope without him tomorrow if Julie had her way.

She smiled to herself, her getaway from the Cedars.

Holding hands on the sofa and knowing what Julie was thinking frightened her somewhat. She made excuse after excuse to avoid any talk of sex, always bringing the conversation back to Bill and Julie soon realised that today her feelings for her would have to be put on hold.

They kissed goodbye. "I will call you" were her parting words.

A large gin and tonic with plenty of ice was all she could think about on her drive home. It was already getting dark when she pulled into the drive.

She looked for Neville and Jasper at the front door. Realising that they would not be there saddened her. She was almost tempted to call him, make things up, tell Bill to fuck off, start her new job but by the time the first gulp of her gin and tonic hit the back of her throat, she realised she had thrown the dice. They were still spinning as tears filled her eyes.

*****

Chapter 24
Fences and Forecasts

HIDE AND SEEK HOLLOW:

"You forgot your phone, so I thought I would make you a nice hot cup of coffee. I've brought it with me." She threw the mobile on to his lap, grinning.

"How are you feeling?"

"Good. I am just thinking through what I need to do this afternoon. I spoke with Chris earlier. I have got to do something now that I am beginning to feel better again," he frowned.

"So stop being cross with me please. I need your support right now. You know I do."

"Well, feeling better is one thing. Doing as the doctor says is another and I know which one is the most important and so should you too, do you?" There was a slight touch of anger in her voice. Her eyes said the rest.

"Katie please, I am just making a few important phone calls. That's all. I need to know what I am getting into by the time Friday comes around. We can have a day to ourselves on Thursday, I promise. I thought you wanted to go to Grassington. You still want to, don't you?"

"Yes, so let's compromise you make your calls and we will get away early tomorrow and spend the day together away from all this. Your recovery is more important to both of us. We can survive without all this if we have to. I will fetch my coffee and phone and join you out here, making sure you are doing what you told me and nothing more, understand?"

"It's worse than the workhouse," he laughed as she walked towards the house. The phone rang.

"Jack, it's Barry. Chris said you wanted me to call."

"Thanks, Barry. I just wanted to make sure you are happy with the way things are going for the Decadence launch. You understand how important it is I hope. I got your projections. Thanks. Very impressive. Now you have to convince me on Friday that they are realistic and not just fanciful estimates. I am asking you that question because we cannot afford to get it wrong. It literally is shit or bust, that is what I am telling you and I hope that is how you understand it to be."

"I most certainly do. We have been over the projections every day for the last three weeks until everybody hates me. That's why I have every confidence with my projections. I won't let you down, Jack. Believe me, I understand more than most of us just how important that this is for you and the rest of us. There will be no shit or bust. Everybody has done their homework on this one and you know what a hard taskmaster Eric can be. He's had my balls several times since you have been away from the office. It will be alright, Jack. I promise you." He sounded concerned, wanting some appreciation for all his hard work.

"That is exactly what I wanted to hear Barry. You have done an excellent job. Thank you, and I truly mean that. Thank your guys for all their hard work. Now all we need to do is pull it off. We will have to arrange a night out for everyone involved after the launch as a thank you."

"Thanks, Jack. Till Friday then. I'm glad you are on the mend. I can't wait for you to get back to the office. We have all missed you."

"Thanks, Barry. I want to be back. I've missed everything. I like to be involved. You know that and it's nice to know I still have a job there. See you Friday and thanks again for all your help."

He smiled to himself, feeling much better after that call.

"Well, that must have been good news. You're smiling. Who was it?"

"Barry. He was just giving me an update on the sales forecast. That's all. Are you okay?"

"Yes, I am always okay if you are. What about your Chinese lady, Pinky?"

"Katie, that is not appropriate. Her name is not Pinky. It's Yang Li and she is a very important piece of our jigsaw. Yes, she can shout and be obstinate at times, but she has been an asset to our success and I don't want to lose her. That is how important she is to us."

"Then what is the problem? Chris mentioned that we had production issues with her company, The Pinky Corporation Inc.," she laughed. "Sorry, I did not mean to be rude about her. I just thought it was funny."

"Forgiven, but for God's sake, don't ever call her that to her face or World War Three will break out. She is a powerful Party Member. You need to remember that if you want to be part of the team, do you?"

"Ah, not that again, Jack. I am studying for my Master's in History and Politics. For the last time, no, I do not want to be a team member. Is that clear enough for you?"

"Okay, I'll ask Chris, see what he has to say." He picked up his phone. "Don't you dare. I will never forgive you if you do."

"Calm down. I am calling Eric."

He did not get a chance to call. It was Eric calling him. 'Barry must have mentioned his call with me earlier.'

"Good morning, Eric. I won't beat about the bush my day-nurse Katie, is keeping an eye on me, making sure I am not overdoing things," Eric laughed.

"Fire away. I think I know what you want to talk about."

"The figures Barry has given me seem too good to be true and having spoken to him, he assures me they are in fact realistic, so what's your take on his projections?"

"Jack, I will give it to you straight, fanciful, no definitely not neither are they too optimistic. I have taken it on myself to ensure that the projections and costs will stand up in today's market place and I have held a morning briefing every day since your accident. You should know I am not into bullshit, self-praise or any other perceptions people may have. It's the figures at the end of the day that writes the story, my view probably the best set of figures we have ever produced prior to a new launch. So, there you have it, the figures stack up. I will make sure everyone understands what you are expecting."

"Well, put me in my place. Well done. I will look forward to breakfast on Friday."

"Ah, before you go, there is one thing bothering me and could cock up the whole launch and that is Yang Li. What have you done about her? I expect Chris has told you she refuses to take calls from anybody but yourself. We need to sort it, Jack, without deliveries our cash flow will dry up and you can kiss goodbye to a good launch for the Decadence Range, and after you have spoken to her, please let me know what you have agreed."

"Eric, thanks. I will call you within the hour." He hung up, glancing across at Katie. She smiled back.

He looked across at Katie again, her face tucked up inside a glossy magazine, House the country life and her fairy-tale notions. "Katie, can I tear you away from your daydreams for a few minutes? I have a job for you."

She pulled her head out of the magazine, staring back at him. "What have I just told you? No, for the very last time, no, I am not interested. Now go away and let me have my daydreams as you call them." She was angry.

"It's not that kind of job, Katie. I just need you to be my secretary for five minutes unless that is too much of a bother for you." He was equally annoyed with her.

"Sorry, I thought it was the other thing. What do you want me to do? Ring your wife and tell her you will be staying over tonight, and you will not be home, business pressure and all that crap." She laughed.

"You little sod. No, I'm deadly serious. I need you to call Yang Li and pretend you are my secretary and if she asks you why you have called her on this number, tell her that we have tried calling you without reply."

"Okay, give me your phone. I take it. Her number is in your log?"

"Yes, be polite please. It's very important."

The phone rings.

"Jack, how are you?"

"No, it's not Jack. It's me Katie, his secretary. He would like to talk to you. Can I hand him the phone?" she paused, surprised.

"Yes, please. We need to talk. Can you put him on?"

"Yang Li, good morning. How are you? Not happy I am being told. Why is that?"

"I am sure you know the answer to that question, Jack. Stop playing with me. You are better. That's good news. Now perhaps we can sort out our differences, can we?"

"Differences? I am not sure where they have come from. Tell me why you are unhappy and then we can perhaps resolve these differences we may have between us, if any that is."

"You are not being fair, Jack, and that will not help us to resolve our problems, will it? You know I am unhappy about losing the order for the Decadence Range you are not thinking properly, are you? You have made me very angry. Why?"

"Yang Li, I am running a successful business and buying from you at inflated prices will only bring disaster to both of our doors and that will not be good business for either of us. Is that what you want?"

"No, it is not, and my prices were competitive, and you cannot deny that, can you?"

"Yes. Competitive but not the cheapest. You seem to forget I am buying, not selling. There will be other contracts I want you to work on. In fact before my accident, I was putting together our Autumn Range and I was planning a visit to Shanghai to discuss my proposals with you. That deal is still on offer, so not everything is lost. You have to learn how to lose as well as win Yang Li."

"I do not want to lose, Jack. You seem to forget we have been supplying your company for many years now and your actions are like a slap on the face. Does loyalty not count for anything anymore? You should be ashamed of yourself."

"Now that kind of talk will not get us anywhere and you know that, Yang Li. So I ask you to accept that loss in good faith. You have been our best supplier and this is the very first time you have lost an order from us, so I think you are being a little unreasonable and you need to complete the outstanding orders you have for us. Refusing to deliver will not help you. In fact it will only work against you in the long run. I think it will be better for both of us if we end this call now and get back to each other later today. Please call me. I will be waiting." He waited for her reply, hoping he had not pushed her too far.

"Jack, let me think about it. I will call you back later. Please make sure you are around to take my call. Goodbye for now. I am glad you are on the mend. By the way that cheers me up and it has got nothing to do with our quarrel. We are good friends remember."

"Jack, what was all that about? Do you want to lose her? I did not think you were that silly."

"Well, for someone that only ten minutes ago told me that they did not want to become one of the team. I think you have got a cheek judging me like that. I know what I am doing, so I prefer it if you kept your uneducated views to yourself and stop interfering in things you know nothing about." He was angry, and she was upset, almost in tears.

"Come here. I'm sorry that was uncalled for. Do you forgive me?" He held his arms out, wanting to give her a hug and apologise for his outburst and his rude behaviour.

They hugged. Jack kissed her cheek.

"Don't treat me like that again, Jack, please. I was only expressing my point of view. I was not giving you instructions. You don't need my help there, but you should apologise to Yang Li for your bad manners and by that, I do not mean you should climb down and give in. All you need to do is be a little less aggressive, for my sake, Jack."

"You are a funny girl but I agree with you. Perhaps I was a little hard on her. I will apologise when she calls me back. I certainly do not want to lose her. She is far too valuable to us. She has been our number-one supplier since day-one and she deserves my loyalty. Perhaps I ought to take you with me on my next trip and then you can judge her for yourself. It will be good for you to see what kind of a person she really is in her own environment and then you would perhaps have a change of view."

"Let's go inside, Jack. It's getting chilly out here and I will make you a fresh coffee and a sandwich. We won't have time for much else and you definitely cannot miss her call." They held hands, walking back to the house.

*****

"Sometimes, Jack, you sound like a parrot. You won't change my mind. You are just wasting your time."

She put the coffee and sandwiches on the kitchen table and sat down beside him.

"Well, it was an open invitation, so let me know nearer the time. I can live in hope. Mum and Dad would have wanted it."

"That is not fair, Jack, playing that card and you know it." There was anger in her voice. She frowned as she looked across at him and picked up her magazine, burying her face behind its open pages.

"Mm… Beef, that's nice. You forgot the English mustard though."

"Well, you know where it is. Get up and get it yourself and stop being lazy. I can't remember the doctor saying no heavy lifting, can you?"

Jack got up from the table and walked over to the wall units behind where he had been sitting. He reached up, opening the cupboard door, his eyes searching for the mustard.

He fell to the floor, his right hand pulling the cupboard door from its hinges, crashing down to the floor on top of him, his limbs shaking. He had lost all control of his body, his feet kicking the legs of his chair. His eyes were closed, his face blue like a child's, holding its breath, his head rocking from side to side.

Katie threw her magazine to the floor, pushing her chair away, her hands reaching down to him, screaming. "Jack, Jack. Oh no, not again," she screamed, again kneeling beside him, taking his head in her hands, her mind telling him to answer her, fear gripping her body, almost fainting. She closed her eyes to keep control, shaking her head. She needed to stay alert.

As she opened her eyes, Jack's body had stopped shaking. He lay there like a small child sleeping, a smile on his face. The colour had returned to his cheeks. She placed her hand across his forehead, her ear listening to his breathing, her head lying across his chest.

A sigh of relief showed on her face as she listened to his heartbeat drumming away inside the walls of his chest, telling her he was still alive. He opened his eyes slowly as though he was just stirring from a heavy sleep. Katie looked at him, tears rolling down her cheeks, "Oh my God! Jack. It's happening all over again. I thought you had got over the worst of it." Her hands were gripping his arms, holding them tightly to the side of his body, taking control of him. "Get help, Jack. I'm so scared. I am going to lose you. Please, Jack, help me." She was sobbing, her words becoming garbled now. Jack was frightened for her.

"I'm okay. I just fainted. That's all. I just looked up and collapsed. I'm okay now. Believe me, I feel great."

She let go of his arms, pulling herself up, away from his body. "You have said that too many times now. This is the worst attack so far. You are not getting better. It's getting worse and you are just hiding the facts. You can't face the reality of your condition, can you?"

"That is unfair. This time, it just sounded worse. That's all. It was the cupboard door crashing down with me. Surely you can see that, can't you? I'm not hurt. I am okay, so it's just you panicking. That's all." He offered her his hand, asking her to help pull him up. That is when she noticed the stain on his trousers leg, blood seeping through the tear just above his knee.

"Jack, you're bleeding." Her heart leapt to her mouth, her stomach muscles tightened. Her fear returned to her eyes.

"It's nothing really. It's probably just a scratch. I can't feel any pain. It will be okay, so stop worrying yourself."

"Let me look. Take your trousers down. Let me see." Jack's face was blank, not quite believing what she was telling him. She reached over, pulling him towards her as she gripped his belt, undoing it and pulling the zip downwards, together with his trousers. "For God's sake, Jack, we are brother and sister, not some total strangers. Take them off and stop being so bloody stupid." Her face was flushed, and there was anger in her voice as she looked at the gash in his thigh just above the knee, the open wound frightening her. "Let me look." He kicked his shoes and trousers off. "Get me the first aid box please from the end cupboard and find the butterfly plasters. They will hold the skin together so that it can heal. It will just leave a small scar. That's all. It's nothing."

"This you mean, Jack?" She held them up for him to see.

"Yes, but I need something to wash the blood away first. There should be a bottle of TCP and cotton wool pads next to them in the same cupboard. Can you pass them to me please?"

"Let me do it for heaven's sake. Just look at the mess you have made."

"Me, cor, I can't seem to do anything right, can I? Ouch! Do you have to be so rough?"

"Stop being a big sissy and let me do it properly."

"Oh, you little sod, that stuff stings."

"Ha, ha! Baby," she grinned. "That will teach you to swing on cupboard doors, won't it, eh?"

"Now who's not taking things seriously?" She ignored the question, continuing to clean the open wound and apply the butterfly plasters.

"There. Now sit down there and relax. Do nothing whilst I make us both a nice cup of hot coffee. I think we could both do with one, then you can tell me all about it, can't you? And no lies please. I want the whole truth this time round. I know you have been keeping things from me, concealing the truth." Jack looked away, not saying a word.

All Jack was thinking about was exactly how much he should tell her, not because he did not want to frighten her but because he wasn't absolutely sure himself what was happening to him. All he was positive about was that he just knew everything would turn out alright in the end. He could not explain that to himself even so there would be little point in telling her about it, or even attempting to explain it to her. He would have to play it by ear judging her reactions but telling her as little as possible.

"Thanks," he smiled, waiting for the inevitable questions.

"Those sandwiches have had it by the look of them. I will cook some makeshift supper later. You must eat something."

"I will be okay," he took her hand, searching her eyes, still full of fear, not knowing how to ask him what had happened.

"Tell me, Jack. What happened, will you please?" she sighed.

"There is nothing to tell really as I have already said. There was more noise than accident. That is what frightened you, not me, fainting part of it just the crashing sound. I will have a bruised back and a small scar on my thigh at the very worse."

"You are doing it again. Stop bloody lying to me and tell me why you fainted. You're not helping me by lying to me, Jack. Now come on, tell me before I call Doctor Doogood." That alerted Jack. That was the last thing he wanted, her telling him all about it.

His face was flushed now and there was a hint of anger in his voice now. He took a deep breath, looking straight into her eyes.

"I saw a face inside the cupboard when I opened the door, a sad face gripped with fear, a ghostly white colour like a ghoul, a vampire perhaps, except that she was screaming. Her eyes were a fiery red. She was a young girl. Who it was, I have no idea. She just kept screaming and screaming and that is all I can remember like my other visions. Her face meant nothing to me, nor did her voice. I collapsed, and you know the rest." He gave her a blank stare, waiting for the next question from her.

"There must be some connection, a correlation between the events. Things like this just do not happen, Jack. You must know her, know them." She raised his voice.

"That is the whole point, Katie. I do not know. It scares me as much as it does you. I can tell you, I'm bloody scared."

"Can't you hear what she is saying? Surely even the odd word would give us some sort of clue."

"No, and that is the whole point. Nothing makes any sense, the visions, the voices, the places, where events have taken place, nothing adds up. I wished it did." He was lying again but she seemed to believe him this time and it was the truth, just not the whole truth. He had to spare her that.

"I'm going to call the doctor. I have had enough of this not knowing, the fear, the waiting for the next time it is going to happen, wondering if you are dead or alive. I can't handle it, Jack, anymore and you must help me, please."

She was distraught, sobbing. He took her in his arms, kissing the top of her head. "I love you," he whispered, leading her to the sofa. How long he held her in his arms, he had no idea.

*****

Jack's phone rang, the vibrations against his arm alerting him. He stirred, being careful not to wake Katie, thinking it would be better if she was asleep.

"Hi, Jack Cambridge. Jack, it's me, Yang Li. How are you?"

"I'm good. I have been waiting on your call. Thanks for calling back and before we talk about our differences, I would like to apologise for my rudeness earlier. I am truly sorry. I hope you can accept my apology."

"That is kind and manly of you, Jack. You have surprised me and yes, I accept your apology. That pleases me."

"So where do we go from here? I have checked my diary and I will be free after the first two weeks of May and I could visit any time after that, three weeks probably. I would want to bring finished samples back home with me so can you select a range of prints and fabrics for me to choose from? You should know what I like by now, not forgetting trends of course."

"You were serious. Then I thought that was just a softener for losing the Decadence Range, so tell me what you want. I am sure I can please you," Jack smiled to himself. Was there a metaphor in that statement somewhere?

"I do not give softeners. I stand on my reputation and I can tell you now that I owe a lot of my success to you and your workers, loyalty that is what I value and that is what you give me, so like you it should be quite easy for you to satisfy me."

"You please me, Jack, and surprise me and I too want to continue with our relationship. It is very good for both of our companies."

"If it is agreeable with yourself, I will send you the artwork and the Solid Works' videos of the complete ranges. There are five ranges. We want you to look at and sample, so there will be a lot of work for you which was another reason why you did not win the Decadence order. There would have been too much for you in the time frame available and I am sure you will be pleased when you view the files. You will need to complete the formalities, rights, copyrights and the usual contractual agreements including a new comprehensive Non-Disclosure Agreement. My guys have just Tweeted last year's copy. That's all, but the changes should not pose a problem, I am sure."

"Thanks, Jack. That sounds great. You will be sending schedules and running dates I hope, will you?"

"Yes of course, but I can tell you now the total spending will double your last year's turnover with us. Now, do you begin to see things in a better light?"

"I could kiss you JACK Cambridge. You lighten my heart with your words. When will you send the documents?"

"Later today, this evening probably. I will call the office after our call and have them sent on twenty-four-hour Express delivery. Nice weekend reading for you."

"Now tell me about my deliveries. Where are we with those? Are they ready to go?"

"Yes, and please accept my apologies for the delay. They are being shipped as we speak."

"The news you are waiting to hear. There will be a bank to bank transfer for £300,000 against site of shipping documents and bills of lading and a further payment of approximately £410, 000 within seven days from shipment date and then that should bring your account in line ninety days following delivery. I hope that will tidy everything up to date. I have told my people to waiver all late delivery penalties, so you don't have those to worry about and I think that's about all for now unless you have anything else you wish to ask me, is there?"

"I just need to say thank you, Jack, and make it two kisses. I owe you. I'm blushing now, but you are worth it. You have made a lot of people happy today and we will show you our appreciation when you visit. You are most welcome."

"I'm smiling. I can't admit to blushing. That would show a weakness. I will probably do that in my sleep. Who knows?"

"That just leaves me to say goodnight, Jack. Please call me next week. I will look forward to hearing from you."

"Goodnight, Yang Li. You too are most welcome."

*****

Jack tiptoed back to the sofa. Katie was still asleep. He checked the refrigerator for wine and started preparing the beef stroganoff for supper, perhaps something with ice cream for pudding.

He picked up his phone and dialled her number.

"Jack, what a surprise! You have rung to cancel everything?"

"Yes, how did you know that? Has someone from my office called you? Not a sound."

"Why have you done that?" Panic in her voice, he could see her face, smiling to himself.

"Yang Li, it's okay. I was just teasing you. I have called to give you some good news. I am not cancelling anything. Ha, ha, just the opposite. I have just put the phone down following a conversation with Eric. He will be sending you under separate cover this evening top up orders for the Poppy

Range which you are currently producing for us. These orders should keep you busy until the Autumn Ranges kick in. I should have mentioned it when we spoke earlier and accept my apologies for the joke. Remember you started that conversation, so you must share the blame."

"Jack, thank you. That's three kisses I owe you. You will wear me out."

"Then on that note, I will say goodnight young lady. Three kisses, is that all?"

The call ended.

Jack was busy with his cooking, busy pouring the cream over the strings of best Scottish beef and the Chanterelle mushrooms.

"I need a cuddle, Jack." He felt her arms around him, her head in the middle of his back, pulling herself close to him. He turned to face her, engaging her eyes, his arms around her, kissing her cheek. "Hungry?"

"Give me my cuddle first. I am frightened, Jack. What is going to happen to us? Tell me please."

"There is nothing going to happen. You must get that silly notion out of your head. I will be fine. I will be seeing the doctors on Monday and they will give me that all clear, probably keeping me on my present medication for a couple of weeks and that is at the very worst, so no more worrying and let me go before dinner is spoilt." He touched the end of her nose with a kiss on his finger.

"I just hope it will be that simple and I think I should still call him and tell him about today. You scare me, Jack. It shouldn't be like that, should it?" she said, sadness in her eyes.

"No, it should not be like that, but you and I can change all that by just thinking positively, so let's organise dinner and get an early night. You haven't forgotten we are off to Grassington on Thursday morning, have you?"

"You always manage to talk me out of everything, don't you?"

"Well, not everything unless of course you have changed your mind about joining me in the company." He kissed her lips.

"Off you go and set the table please. There's wine in the fridge. Do you fancy broccoli spears or asparagus with the kettle chips? I've made a lemon jus unless you prefer something completely different," she grinned.

"You are a wonder, Jack Cambridge. I can't lose you. Will you promise me that much?"

"Come here." He took her in his arms. "You must stop this worrying, okay? Let's just enjoy dinner and our day out in the Ridings. No more negative thinking, young lady. Now you promise me, will you?"

"You win and that is broccoli spears and no wine for you by the way. Shall I do you a lemonade?"

"Yes please."

There began shouting in his head. He turned, steadying himself, his hand gripping the edge of the cooker, his mind trying to block the screams ringing in his ears, her piercing eyes forcing him to look away, his mind searching for the answers. 'Was he getting better?' he asked himself as he stirred the stroganoff and Katie laid the table. He turned around, putting the frying pan on the marble slab ready for serving. He raised his head, his eyes looking up to the cupboard facing him. Her face was staring down at him, the screams piercing his ears.

He closed his eyes. She was gone. "Ready, Jack?"

*****

Chapter 25
A Lesson Learnt

The Clock Tower Skepton

"Can you hear that noise, John? It sounds like someone screaming but I can't see anyone, can you?"

"No, there's nobody around. I can hear shouting, though it's hard to tell sometimes. That noise could be coming from anywhere around the Square."

John and Thelma were standing under the Clock Tower in the town centre, waiting for their daughter, April, to arrive. They had arranged to meet her there for lunch.

Thelma was waving. She saw April on the other side of the Square. "There she is, John. She's coming over and just remember to be nice to her, please."

"I will. Stop worrying. Everything will be okay." He frowned, *nagging again.*

"Hi, you found a car parking space then." She kissed her cheek.

"Yes, I've parked behind the Argos Store. I'll pop in there later before I go home."

"Dad, hi, are you okay?"

"Yes, I'm fine. How are you?" he replied, smiling. "Yes, I'm okay, busy as always. I can't be late. I have an appointment later back at the office." She kissed his cheek, giving him a warm smile.

"There's that sound again, John. It is someone screaming. I'm sure it is."

"There's nobody here except the three of us. I thought I heard it earlier, but I couldn't see anyone," he replied. "April, can you hear that screaming sound? We heard it just before you arrived. Your dad says the sound could be coming from anywhere around the Square, but where?"

"It's coming from inside there, the Clock Tower. I can hear it quite clearly. That's strange. The doors closed behind those railings look. I'm certain it's coming from inside but the gates got a padlock on it. Perhaps someone has been trapped inside and is shouting to be let out." She pointed to the railings and the padlock.

"Can you hear it now, John? It's getting louder. There is definitely somebody locked in there. Listen, there it is again."

"Yes, I can hear it. We better get some help, Dad."

"Well, we need to find the person with the key to that padlock. There, look. Does it say anything on that sign on the railing just behind you, Thelma? Perhaps there's a phone number."

"Forget that. I'll call the police. Let them sort it out. It's pretty obvious. We can't sort it out ourselves." April was dialling the emergency number 999.

"I'll try this number here. There is one. It says: in emergency, dial." John dialled the number, listening for a reply.

April spoke to the Emergency Services, Police, giving them the details.

John held up his phone. "No reply. What do you expect from the Council? What did the Police say, April?"

"They're on their way. They want us to stay here. They will want to take statements from all of us, so there goes our lunch," she frowned, disappointment written all over her face.

"It can't be helped. You can't leave whoever it is trapped in there all alone. I would never live with myself if they died."

"I know, Mum. It's just that I have looked forward to it all weekend. That's all," she replied, touching her arm.

"Never mind. There will be other days."

"It's all gone quiet. The shouting has stopped. Listen, nothing."

"Oh my God! I hope that doesn't mean what I think it means. Does it, John?"

"I honestly don't know. The Police should be here anytime. They will be able to sort it out, so don't worry. It's not your fault." He put his arm around her, smiling, trying to tell her everything will turn out alright.

"Look after your mum, April. There's a good girl."

As he spoke, he could hear the Police siren. He looked towards the High Street. It wasn't a Police car but an ambulance. It pulled up onto the pavement. John signalled to the Paramedic as he got out of the vehicle.

You could see the relief on Thelma's face.

"The Police are not far behind us. Tell us what the problem is first. Then we can see what we can do to help."

"Well, what we can do is nothing until you can open that padlock there, locking the chain to the railings. She's inside."

"You've spoken to her, haven't you?"

"No, but I think it sounded like a young girl or woman but it's all gone suddenly quite. We haven't heard anything for the last five minutes or so."

He walked back to the ambulance and started talking to his co-worker when a police siren could be heard heading towards them.

"Here they are, Thelma. We will soon have the answer to what this is all about, a prank by students gone wrong I should think."

"I hope so. I still can't hear anything. She's probably collapsed or worse even. I don't know. Will they be able to open the gate?"

The police officer was stopped by the paramedic who explained the situation as he knew it.

The officers walked over towards John. "Sergeant Dilkes from Kempton Road Station. This is PC Watson. Are you the one who made the 999 calls earlier?"

"No, that was my daughter. We are all here together. We heard the girl screaming and not being able to access the door, we decided to call for help. That's the problem. That padlock on the railings holding that chain."

He pointed to the chain and padlock. "Well, that's not going to be easy, is it? Look at the size of that padlock, Pete.

We will never shift that. Did you call the council? They are the key holders."

"Yes, but unfortunately no one answered the phone. I did call it. Shall I try again now you are here?"

"Yes, do that please and I will phone the emergency number. Someone will answer that, and they should be able to give us the answers we need. When was the last time you heard her screaming?"

"It must have been at least fifteen minutes ago I think."

"Thelma."

"Yes, I keep listening, but I am not hearing anything. I hope she hasn't collapsed or something worse has happened to her."

Sergeant Dilkes was talking to someone on his mobile. He walked around the tower looking for alternative access.

He walked over to John, putting his phone back into his pocket. "They are on the way, twenty minutes they said."

"What about the keys? Did they say they had them?" asked the paramedic, obviously concerned about whoever was trapped inside the tower, hoping they were not too late.

"They have got the keys the Town Warden on his way with them. What about your side? Is everything ready just in case?"

"Yes, we will bring the stretcher, the necessary equipment nearer the doorway, so we will be prepared."

"Thanks," he replied, walking off towards PC Watson.

"Pete, as soon as we get access, your first job is to get some identification, wallet, handbag, whatever you can get your hands on. It's important that we contact the next of kin just in case, so until the Warden arrives, you can start taking statements from these witnesses. Do the mother first. She's the one you will get the most detail from. Find out what you can and give me a heads up on anything important. And keep an eye on the crowd. It's already building. I'll call in for another car to assist us, okay?"

"Yes, Sarge," he replied, notebook in hand, walking towards mother.

"No luck with that call to the council again. There still not answering the phone. How did you get on?"

"Good. The Town Warden's on his way here with the keys, so it shouldn't be too long now I hope, and then we will have the answers we are all waiting for," he replied.

"Right, Warden. You shift that padlock and open the door to the tower and then move out the way and let myself and the paramedics take over. We have been trained for these types of incidents. Then you will need to stay around until a forensic team arrives and only when they have finished with their examination of the crime scene will you be able to lock the tower back up again. I will have a constable stay with you until the incident is declared closed, so if you wish to call your wife and tell her you will be home late, I am sure you know how these things pan out, never as you expect."

"Thank you, Sergeant. I'll call her now. It's her Bingo night. She'll play bloody hell if she misses that, my life won't be worth living next week," he replied, laughing.

"Thanks, we will need a statement from you before you leave. PC Watson will be dealing with that," he smiled, pointing towards him. "That's him over there."

A second car had arrived and Sergeant Smythe was briefing them on the incident. The crowd was beginning to fill out. The Square was almost full, everybody waiting for whatever the police were waiting for. The gossip was growing by the minute.

"I need you pair to keep this lot under control until this whole thing is over. Hopefully things should begin to happen once the Warden has opened up the bloody tower. We think someone is trapped inside, pranksters from the university probably but who knows it may surprise us all, so keep the crowd under control and the traffic moving, okay? Off you go."

"Yes, Sarge," they both replied, grinning. They had been pulled off another job, hoping this was the better of the two.

Things were beginning to happen, the sound of the gate creaking as it was pulled open and the jangling of the chains told everyone that progress was being made.

The Warden unlocked the padlock, allowing the chain to fall away to the pavement and pulled the gate open. He paused as he searched for the key to the Tower door.

He unlocked the door, then stepped back whilst Sergeant Dilkes attempted to push the door open. It stopped, leaving him just enough room to put his head around the door whilst holding a flashlight in his hands. He stepped back. "It's a girl alright. She has collapsed. I will have to push her with the door until there is enough room to climb over the body."

It seemed ages for him to open the door wide enough allowing him to step over the body, pulling the door shut behind him.

Thelma already had tears in her eyes. "Oh, my God, April, what if that was you?" April pulled her close to her.

"Just be patient, Mum. We don't know anything now. She has probably fainted, dehydration I would think. She will be alright."

The door began to open, the flashlight throwing shadows around the room inside the Tower. The paramedic moved towards the door to assist Sergeant Dilkes as he appeared at the door with the girl in his arms. Her body and clothing were emaciated. There was blood on her fingernails and around the uppers of her trainers. It was difficult to see the girl's face that was hidden most of the time by a double helping of Shirley Temple curls bobbing up and down on her head as Sergeant Dilkes carried her to the ambulance.

"She will be okay I hope. She is still breathing. She did open her eyes but then relapsed. Let's get her inside the ambulance. Then you can take over." The paramedic followed behind him.

Sergeant Dilkes stepped down from the ambulance and walked over to the mother. "She's going to be alright. She is on a saline drip and they will take her off to the hospital as soon as they have stabilised her, so you are not to worry, and thank you by the way. That young girl owes you her life." Thelma burst out crying, allowing her emotion to take over.

PC Watson reported to Dilkes. "I have called the father, explaining the situation to him and told him to go straight to Skepton General and we can interview him there, Sarge."

"Good. Well, finish taking statements from the family and the Town Warden. He's not to leave until forensics have finished okay. And then when you have finished up here, meet me at the hospital. There's nothing more I can do here now. I need a black coffee. I'll get you one when we catch up later."

"Thanks, Sarge. I'll tidy up here and get a statement from the key-holder once forensics have finished and meet you there."

"You take the car. I'll go with the paramedics to the General. See you later. Oh, just keep your eye on Gabby Hurst from the Gazette. Don't let her earwig the witnesses, I want this case shut tight until we establish all of the facts. Don't let me down," he frowned.

As the sirens sounded and the ambulance drove away, the crowd began to disperse, going about their own business, leaving just the hard-core few to dawdle about the Square waiting just on the off chance something else would turn up. That did not happen. The family and the Town Warden left, and the Monday night carried on as normal. It was all over until it hit the news headlines and the local rag the following evening, The Skepton and Grassington Echo.

*****

Chapter 26
That's Ludicrous

Routine, that had always been the start of Belinda's day and today was no exception, coffee, shower, breakfast in that order, then back to the bathroom brushing her teeth and then the bit she enjoyed the most sitting in front of her dressing table mirror. You know the story from there on.

Mirror, Mirror on the wall, who is the fairest of them all, ME.

First the face plan, this side, that side, teeth, smile, dollop and circles with her forefinger, the cream spreading itself across her cheeks, chin and forehead, nothing to be missed.

Switch the TV on, catching the news and weather.

She checked the cream, then pencilled her eyebrows and fixed her lipstick, a tissue kiss and one last check. She allowed her dressing gown to fall off her shoulders and on to the floor.

She cupped her breasts, wishing they were twenty years younger, stroking her nipples as she stood up.

A frown, always a frown knowing there is nothing she can do that she wasn't already failing at. She patted her stomach and made a wish, a shake of the head before she headed to her knickers drawer, thong. Bra and a slip this morning, she wanted to avoid any hint of being tarty.

A two-piece suit, the smart businesswoman image, going places, she told herself feeling good, ready for the office crap that would be waiting for her, she began rehearsing her excuses. She already knew the questions, from how are, feeling better, how's your dad? Bill told us...

She did not want to believe it. What her thoughts were telling her, she realised she would have to try harder to close her mind of those emotions.

"Err... err... err..." The car would not start. She took the key out of the ignition and inspected it, turning it around in her fingers, wanting something to blame. *Fucking hell! What a start to the day before it's even begun.* Her face and neck coloured a bright pink before she decided to call Bill.

"Belinda, where are you? Is everything okay?" He was almost shouting, panicking. Then he remembered what he had told himself over and over during the last three days. *Whatever you do, stay calm, treat her properly, be nice to her.* He was already wanting to take his words back.

"Hi, Bill. Are you okay? Sorry, the car won't start. What shall I do?" she said, with tears in her voice. "What shall I do?" She began panicking, repeating herself.

"Where are you?" he replied, glad that she was not shouting back at him.

"I'm at home, Bill, outside on the drive. I put the key in the ignition and nothing, nothing at all."

"Stay where you are, put the kettle on and I will be over to sort you out. I'll just make my excuses, let Linda know what's happening and then I will be on my way, so don't worry. Everything will be fine."

"Thanks, Bill, biscuits with your coffee?"

"You know just what I want. Thanks. Chocolate Bourbon if you have any of course. I won't be long."

Choices. That's what was racing through her thoughts right now. *The biscuits can wait. Shall I fuck him before coffee and biscuits or after a grunt? Did it really matter? He would be hungry for anything he could get. He will be horny by the time he gets here. That's for sure.* She knew just exactly how his dirty mind worked.

She dashed upstairs to the bedroom, slipping out of her suit and kicking her shoes off before she even made the bedroom door, she threw her jacket and skirt on to the bed, then searched her wardrobe for an instant sex number. She held it up to her body looking in the cheval mirror, smiling.

Mm, that will do. She should be able to slip out of that without any difficulty. She pulled at the zip and then grabbed a new pair of shoes from the wardrobe. *Red.* She slipped them on as she made her way to the knickers drawer, changing her thong for a pair of red lace knickers, Bill's favourites.

She had another look in the mirror. *That should do it. His eyes will be popping out even before his dick was hard*, she told herself. There was more breast out than in, and this was a game she could not afford to lose.

She was excited by the thought of him slipping inside her. Why? She had no idea, lust I suppose. "Just close your eyes, dear," – that is what her mother would have told her. Now she had decided it was over between them. Her attitude had shifted significantly. Now he was paying for his lust. It did not seem so cheap and dirty. He wouldn't realise that of course. He was her victim.

The kettle was whistling. The Chocolate Bourbons were on the side plate waiting for afters that is. There was no chance of snogging him after a bourbon, chocolate tongues and all that mess. She shuddered at the thought.

She had just about got the plan set out in her head when the doorbell rang. Her face began to flush. She wanted him but, on her terms. *Remember that,* she reminded herself.

"Thank God, you're here. I was beginning to worry that you had changed your mind."

"No, everybody wanted me at every desk. I passed until I was pissed off with it and just ignored them all. We won't have time for coffee and biscuits I'm afraid. We need to get back to the office and that means you had better slip out of that dress. Head Office are on the way as we speak. I'll explain everything on the way back to the office."

Fuck, she panicked as she raced up the stairs, Bill's words spinning round in her head, beginning to wish she was still with Neville, the fear of her plans falling around her ears, her face flushed. She was fucked now and not in the away she wanted to be. Dick changed to horror. 'Oh my God, what am I going to do?'

Bill gave her the car keys back. "Better not lose them. Let's get going. We need to make it back to the office before they arrive or there will be bloody hell to pay."

"Your tanks on empty by the way. That is why your car wouldn't start. I checked it whilst you were slipping out of that sexy number you were wearing five minutes ago, a bit naughty. You obviously had plans," he grinned. She was lost for words, too many thoughts that were not making any sense spinning around in her head.

The car sped from the drive. Her mind was dancing faster than a quick step with all kinds of thoughts bouncing around in her head. She was almost in tears…

"You had better explain what's going on. Have you been sacked?"

"No, it's bad but not quite that bad. It's your leaving that is causing the alarm at Head Office and I am getting the blame for it all, so you can understand if I am a bit pissed off at the moment. We need to get our stories straight, fuck things up and we are both for the chop and make no mistake about it." There was fear in his voice and anger was in his eyes. She had to be very careful what she said.

"It's all my doing, Bill. Let me take all the blame. After all, it's not your fault. It's Neville's, so use that as your excuse. Just explain it away as a domestic. Tell them I will be available to offer my help with any outstanding contracts after I have left if you think that will help, will it?"

"Well, there hangs the problem. It's not so much your leaving but where you are going to that concerns Head Office, our main competitor surely. You can understand their concerns about that. It's not too late to change your mind you know. I will match the package they have offered you if you are prepared to listen." That did not fit in with her plans. Panic returned. She needed a solution but had no idea where that would come from. *For fuck's sake,* she couldn't think clearly. *This is turning out to be one almighty mess.*

She wanted to run away. She wanted Neville, her comfort zone.

"They won't buy the domestic bit or at least I can't see them showing any sympathy towards you or me. This is Corporate, pass the parcel and if we are not careful, we will be sitting in a sorting office in Timbuktu sorting mail before you can say Jack Robinson."

"As bad as that is it," she replied, a sadness in her voice. Then the idea came to her. She smiled at him. Yes, a plan was there but would he have the bollocks to go along with it. That was the only problem. Money on two fronts, those spinning reels already dancing before her very eyes.

"I'm afraid it is. Any ideas?"

"Well, at such short notice, I have a solution, but can we get away with it?"

"Well, start by telling me what you have in mind and remember, it must be good or we are fucked," he replied, irritated.

She paused. "Dare I?" she asked herself and then the words were out of her mouth. She had no time to think. "Tell them I am going there undercover to feed you their secrets. It's as simple as that, providing we can sound convincing, can we?"

"They are never going to buy that. A spy, never, forget it. It's a ridiculous suggestion."

"Well, you have got about twenty minutes to get your head around it and change your mind," she grinned. "Come on, Bill, we can make it work. It may even improve your prospects for promotion, a Directorship a seat on the board."

"Now you are stretching my imagination too far. It's ludicrous of us to think that we could get away with it."

He was panicking now, his neck and back drenched in sweat, his face a warm pink. Those sods would be thinking they had been shagging. That was also playing on his mind.

If we get away with it, surely, that would be a bonus for her. *Bill would think he has got me anchored in-between the two companies.* So, a loan would be easier for him to come to terms with. Her new plan was already taking shape.

"Well, what do you think? We haven't much time left. We are nearly there."

"I don't like it but I cannot see that we have much choice now. Who came up with the idea by the way they are bound to ask. Why, you of course, Bill. You don't think I was that clever surely. You take all the credit. Just make the incentive stick that should add some truth to the proposition."

"And what about the story of you and Neville splitting up? We can't have two stories floating around." He was panicking again.

"Of course, we can. One for Simpson & Smith and the staff here and the truth shared only with Head Office. Just use my break up as a scapegoat. That's all. We can't change that. Everybody here knows all about it. We can't change it. It would look too suspicious. We would be hanging ourselves."

"Okay, leave the talking to me. You just play the Chinese nodding cat bit, agreed?"

"Yes, agreed, fingers crossed then," she laughed.

"Here, you better take my car and keep your appointment at your bank. That will give me chance to break the news to the guys at Head Office. Clifton's coming. He will be the lead, so that's good news. Just make sure you get back here before lunch. I will arrange to take them to that Spanish tapas in the High Street. I'll handle the girls in the front office. Best of luck." He waved as she pulled out of the car park.

*****

She turned the words over in her mind. *I'm always in the shit. It is only the depth that varies,* she laughed. Her Dad's favourite saying but this time it just happens to be true. *Last week, I was married to Neville, reasonably happy and led a comfortable life-style in suburbia. Now I need a mortgage, a new husband and a crash course on how to become a spy. Bloody great! What else can go wrong?* she blushed. A slight shiver ran down her back, a Lesbian chasing her lust, wow. It just gets worst. Her face and neck were a bright pink, panic filling her thoughts.

She parked at the rear of the bank in the private car park. She was a little early. She phoned Bill. "Hi, is everything okay? Have they arrived yet?" She was panicking.

"No, not yet and I'm still inventing my storyline. Wish me luck. I better go. They will be here anytime now. Best of luck by the way."

"Thanks, see you later." He seemed quite pleased with himself which surprised her. Perhaps the challenge will do him good. He probably thinks there will be a good shag in it later when he drops me off at home. She smiled. She felt horny. Perhaps being a spy could be fun.

"Good morning, please take a seat, Mrs Scrudge," he pointed to the chair in front of his desk. She cringed at her name *Scrudge*. She hated it.

Early forties, well-dressed, good-looking, straight out of finishing school, Mr Fogerty, David Fogerty, the wooden plaque on his desk was telling her. She grinned, *Fuckable.*

"I have been reading your file. A mortgage, you hold the freehold on the property, is that correct?"

"Yes, we paid the mortgage off in 2003 I think."

"Yes, that's correct. How much are you trying to fund, Belinda? You don't mind if I call you by your first name, do you?"

"No, of course not," she lied. She smiled. *Anything for a mortgage and yes, including that if necessary.*

"Have you had the property valued recently?"

"Yes, last week. Penrose did it. They are keen to put it on the market."

"You're selling then. Have you another property in mind?"

"I better explain. I only told Pembroke I was selling to get a free valuation. I'm not selling. I am buying my husband's share of the property. He's moving to Milan with his job and his new life." Her voice sounded upset, showing her embarrassment regarding her request.

"Oh, sorry, I did not realise but there's no need for you to worry. The bank is always impartial in these situations. Equity, that is what the bank considers and that is supported by your earnings. I take it, nothing has changed and that you are still with the same employer?"

"Yes, I've been there ever since we last met which would be 2003. You are exactly as I remember you."

"Thank you. It's nice of you to say so. I don't think there will be a problem, but I need to take some details from you and then I should be able to give you a decision before you leave today. Things have changed a lot over the past two or three years. The decision can be made here by the bank without referral as long as you can tick all the boxes. It is just a formality."

"Thank you," she replied, not believing her luck. "You will need to pop into the bank and sign the necessary papers in the next couple weeks providing everything stacks up that is."

"Relax, Belinda. We are nearly done. Yes, the bank will offer you a mortgage. You should receive confirmation of acceptance through the post within five working days, from completion of all the necessary paperwork."

"Wonderful, you have been marvellous. Thank you."

"A coffee whilst we tie up the loose ends?"

"Yes please, that will be nice, Thank you." *You Bastard,* she lied, hating him and his fucking bank. "My pleasure and thank you for giving the bank the opportunity to be of service to you."

She laughed, almost in tears as she closed the car door. *Oh my God, the days going from bad to worse. I won't get it. They will pick up my BACS salary payment details and realise that I have lied about my employment. I'm just digging the hole deeper. Perhaps it's time to change my mind about leaving. I daren't tell Bill.*

*****

It had started to rain by the time she parked the car back at the office. *An omen for tears. I hope not,* she said to herself. The visit to the bank had broken her spirit and scattered her thoughts to such an extent she did not want to carry on, but she knew she had very little choice in the matter. Perhaps she could use the bank's deferment of her mortgage to her advantage, a carrot to dangle in front of Bill the next time he wanted a shag.

I had better call him before I enter the lion's den I suppose.

"Do I look like a spy? I'm not sure. What do spies look like?" she asked herself. Her mobile was calling him.

"Belinda, where are you?"

"I'm sitting in the car, just got back from the bank. Have they arrived yet?"

"Yes, just come into reception and then go straight to your own office and avoid talking to anybody. The gossiping has already started. I will find you when the time's right. Just act normal, okay?"

"Okay. I don't think I know how to do that anymore, so you will owe me one big fucking gin and tonic tonight and no excuses." There was intent in her voice. Bill hung up.

Belinda went through her mail, nothing exciting, one from Neville saying he would be away for a few days, hoping I was okay, Milan presumably wishing she was with him right now, all forgiven and forgotten. It couldn't be worse than the situation she finds herself in today.

Back to the reality of the day as her desk phone rings, an internal call, she hesitated. *Is this the summons to the boardroom?* She could feel her neck and cheeks colouring, a tightening of her stomach muscles, fear. Mmm, maybe she just wanted to get it over and done with.

"I need you in the boardroom. There are answers required and you are the only one who can give them, straight away please. We are all waiting." The phone goes dead. She puts it back down. A slight sweat began to creep down her back.

"Fuck it," she whispered to herself. "I hope he told a good story. There's no time for a rehearsal, just stand by your words I suppose."

She checked her makeup, a spread of lipstick, a click of her hand mirror closing, signalling time to move on. She grinned. She wanted Jasper and Neville fuck the corporate. She wanted to shout but the spinning dollar sign said to her,

'Compose yourself. Everything will turn out just fine. Play them at their own game. It's easy. Let the dollars come to you.' She smiled as she walked into the lift.

Level 10, Ping

"Belinda, come on in. How are you?" Clifton said, offering his hand. "It's been a long time. You're looking good," he smiled, a get-your-knickers-down scan of her body, a wanting in his eyes.

"Hi, Rupert. Good to see you, still carrying your good looks I see," she smiled. Bill frowned not too pleased to hear those words. The last thing he wanted right now was competition wherever it came from.

"I believe you've met Simmons."

"David, good to see you again. It's been a long time."

"And this is Roger Tate. He's the new guy on the board, poached from Winslet. You know them of course." They shook hands. Not her style. *Slimy she would say.*

"Sit down, coffee?"

"Yes please." She was a little nervous. She wanted time to assess the situation. She had no idea what Bill had told them except that she was going undercover. She shivered at the thought.

"Tell me, Belinda, why you want to leave us? You've been with us, what thirteen years, time to move on, is it?" He was trying to get to the truth. It was obvious from the question that something was not quite right.

"No, not at all. In fact completely the reverse. I am moving on, as you put it, at Bill's request really. As you know we have been working on the Schroder account together for a long time now and it seems it was beginning to slip away from us. Bill wasn't going to let that happen and asked me for my help. Where he got the notion or the inspiration from for me to go undercover, I am not quite sure but we spoke about it at length several times before I approached Simpson & Smith. Bill pointed me in the right direction. He knew Brendon Rudd from way back. The rest was straight forward puffed out with the usual corporate crap. They wanted to know what I knew about the Schroder account. It was quite easy really. In fact I enjoyed stitching them up and that's it in a nutshell, plus whatever Bill has told you of course. Oh, and before I forget, I will expect a good bonus; that goes without saying." She gave him a how-much frown. "You say."

"Well, some people say honesty pays, so tell me about your break up. I believe you and Neville are going your separate ways these days, just the basics will do." That completely threw her. She knew he was a crafty bastard. That's how he became top dog. She thought carefully before she replied.

"Honesty, Rupert, purely and simply we were both held together through convenience, going nowhere. We both did it without pain. He got what he wanted and I got what I wanted. He's moving to Milan to start a new life. There are no lovers involved on either side. It is just a journey that had come to an end. Yes, there was a little sadness but that is to be expected after twenty years of marriage." She frowned, looking down at the table, waiting for him to pull her to pieces. He would enjoy that, hoping that the word 'honesty' would confuse his thinking, a completely ambiguous statement that may just throw him off-track.

"Let's leave that there then. Now tell me, what experience have you got to becoming a spy Miss Moneypenny?" he grinned. They all laughed, making him feel good.

The coffee arrived. It could not have come at a better moment as far as Belinda was concerned, just the breathing space she needed.

"Milk and Sugar, Belinda?" enquired David, playing Mother. He smiled.

"Milk. No sugar please, David," she grinned, returning his smile.

The conversation over coffee was more personal than corporate. It was hard to say who fancied her the most. That is other than Bill of course. Rupert was not comfortable with the way the conversation was moving.

"Right, people. Let's get back to being corporate, no more passing the parcel."

"Belinda, why do you want to spy on our competitor?" There was a little menace in his voice, his eyes searching her body, hoping there was perhaps a little something in it for himself.

Belinda had used coffee time to her advantage. She could handle him now with her confidence restored, or was it purely shit or bust for her?

"I am not a spy. I do not want to wear that mantle either. I just want to help protect the company that has been a large part of my life all these years. I have made many friends here. I enjoy coming to work and I think I am good at my job and I am not the person that will let all our hard work slip away without a fight. I know what corner I am in, who I can trust and the people I am comfortable with, and that is what made my mind up really. I like my job. I want to keep my job. It's as simple as that, guys. Take me or leave me. The rest is up to you." She enjoyed the lies. It was like a game now. She stared at Rupert drawing his eyes to her breasts.

"David, what's your take on the situation? You have been noticeably quiet and that's not like you, is it?"

"I am quiet, Rupert, simply out of surprise. When we were driving up here, I thought it would be a simple matter of containment, protecting our interests, how wrong could I be now we want to control the market by deception not by our ability to achieve, so that just throws our strategy for success out of the window. I need more time to think and the three of us ought to consider the implications in a more private conversation."

"I'm surprised too, but today seems to be a day of surprises, doesn't it just?" He turned towards Roger.

"Roger, now you address your concerns. Let me hear your views or like David. Can't you make your mind up?" There was a great deal of sarcasm in his words. He frowned. David looked away, wanting to swear back at him but remembering whose company he was in. *Bite your tongue,* he said to himself.

"Thank you, Rupert. Let me begin by putting the emphasis on you, Belinda. I will come to the point. I don't believe in hiding my views. What is the situation with you and Bill? I would say you two are shagging now. Tell me the truth because that will have implications beyond our present discussion. The truth please. I have already had the gossip." He frowned.

You could feel the silence. It was that bad. Nobody expected that, not even Rupert. Bill's neck and face became a decidedly pink colour, his eyes searching the carpet. He had no idea that was coming. That's for sure. However, Belinda took confidence from that, knowing they had not discussed or even thought about that situation whilst travelling up here.

Belinda was determined to give him as good as she got. "You don't trust anybody, do you, Roger? Your eyes give you away, don't you think?" She put him down, now she had the upper hand.

Roger was furious. Anger flashed in his eyes. *You bastard! How dare you?*

"Well, guys, I feel that is the best word to describe you all. Let's get down to the nitty-gritty, shall we? Bill and I have been good friends. The office put us down to shagging many years ago. That's normal. It happens in all corporate companies of this size, so there was never any point in trying to deny it. They are entitled to their own views after all."

"Yes, we have shagged." And that comes straight from the horse's mouth, not office or corporate gossip, the truth as asked for.

"Now let me set the records straight. We are not having an affair, sharing beds, shagging or whatever label you want to tie around our working relationship. If it is an issue, I will leave today and let you all get on with it. Satisfied now, Roger, are you?" Her stare told them everything.

My God! That took all of them by complete surprise. It even had Bill sitting up admitting his part in it all. He was grinning now. *Good on you, Belinda.*

Rupert spoke first.

"Well, well, young lady, that told us I suppose, my verdict. That conversation is finished. Thank you, Belinda. Now I think we should have our private meeting and reach a decision.

No doubt we will have further questions for the two of you, so you go about your business and we will call for you when we are ready, okay?"

Roger stood up, determined to have his say. "Sit down, Roger. I'm not in the mood for any amateur dramatics. We will discuss your issues and then you can have your say. Now sit down." He sat down, put down corporate style. David grinned. He enjoyed that bit.

*****

They took the lift to Bill's office.

"Well done you, talk about a put down that was fantastic. I never realised you had it in you. Thanks," he smiled.

"I meant every word, Bill. I had nothing to lose, certainly not to that sanctimonious bastard, Roger Tate. Anyway we will see what they have to say later, shall we?" She frowned, her mind exhausted by it all for the moment. No doubting she would recover, ready for the next barrage.

Roger will be after my guts, but I will survive. I have nothing to lose.

"Come to my office. I will organise some coffee. I have told Linda no calls today, so we should not be disturbed."

"Sit down and relax. You are like a coiled spring. Are you okay?"

She laughed, "Fucking hell, Bill. I hope there is not more to come like that."

"There will be. Just do as you have been doing. I think you handled yourself admirably. I better watch my step. Otherwise, I will be sitting where you are right now. Rupert was very impressed I can assure you. He will be on your side. I don't mean that everything's okay, certainly not, so we need to stay alert. I think I will be the ball they all want to kick about in round two," he laughed. "Bugger them. We will come out the other side whatever they decide." That surprised her.

"Here, put that in your bag. I have had it here too long. It's the money I promised you for your dress." He removed a plain envelope from his inside jacket pocket. "And I thought you would forget. Thank you. I need it right now," she said, slipping the envelope into her handbag as she spoke.

She lied, looking away towards the door. Linda was on her way with the coffee, nosing no doubt.

"Hi, Belinda, good weekend?"

"Yes, fine. Thanks, Linda. I will catch up with you tomorrow when corporate have gone," she smiled. Linda put the coffee down, knowing there was no gossip to harvest. Bill thanked her, and she left the office, disappointed.

"I'll make it up to you one way or another," she smiled. He wasn't as bad as she painted him; sometimes he could be very kind.

Bill handed her a coffee. "Tell me what you are thinking right now. Don't pull any punches. Just give it to me straight." He frowned, not wanting to push her too far.

"I am not quite sure. Rupert, he will decide at the end of the day, and it is obvious that David has very little time for the newcomer, Tate, so I think our problems are likely to come from them rather than from Rupert himself. What do you think?"

"Well, we know what they are not going to ask about and that's our love life, so it can only be about your position and my thinking behind it. Tate won't be satisfied until he has got his own back. David, I am not quite sure about him. He is the dark horse, so be careful."

"I'm not worried. I just think we need to be very careful with our words and thoughts or we will be in Timbuktu," she laughed. "Bollocks, I am not going there, and neither are you. If all this falls through, we are off to the Bahamas, one suitcase each." It was his turn to laugh.

"Well, I don't suppose we will have the opportunity to share each other tonight, so keep your evening free tomorrow. We have a lot of catching up to do." She gave him a naughty smile. She enjoyed feeding his ego and that was all it was, a means to an end. He knew exactly what she had in mind. "I will. You can be assured of that but let's get today over with. After all, we may be packing for the Bahamas."

He finished his coffee. It was a good hour before his desk phone rang.

"Brevit."

"Come up, Bill. Leave Belinda there. We will deal with her later." Corporate had taken over again.

"Bill, sit down and let's make some progress." Rupert pointed to the chair at the opposite end of the table from where the three of them were seated.

Ganging up, aye, he whispered to himself. Bill took his seat. It was Rupert who spoke first.

"I don't want to draw this out, Bill. We have several questions that we need to put to you."

"What makes you so sure that we can get away with it?"

"This Industrial spying I'm talking about. It could become very messy if it ever got out of hand. Have you any thoughts on that?"

Bill took his time. He walked over to the booze cupboard and took a tumbler and a bottle of whiskey over to where he was sitting. He raised his glass, "You don't mind." He raised the glass and the bottle. "Anybody joining me?" It was silent, Bill's cue to answer the question.

"Gentlemen, we seem to be missing the point here, avoiding the issues that brought us here together today, so my view is this. Let's analyse our market position as of today. Right now, we sit comfortably in second place behind Simpson & Smith, agreed?" No comments, just stares.

"I do not need to tell you that we cannot survive much longer on the arse of those sods once the Schroder contract has been awarded. There will be no prize for the runners up. They will need to shut up shop. There will be only one winner out of all this and I intend to be on the winning side. That is where I will be and that is why I came up with my plan to get the information we need to win the day. I have spent weeks persuading Belinda to help me. Now we are ready to go and you lot want to be difficult," he scowled.

"It's not a matter of being difficult. There's a matter of ethics involved here. Doesn't that concern you?" asked David.

"Never mind about ethics. What about involvement, when the shit hits the fan? Are you going to pick up the pieces? Are you?" Roger was angry, wanting to get his own back.

Rupert was watching and listening like a hawk on his perch, waiting to pounce on his prey, which one?

"Ethics, yes, let's talk about ethics, David, shall we? It seems you have forgotten the Bowler Incident 2013." *Fuck them.* "Your words and we did not hear another word until today."

"Involvement, starts at the top trickles down to the likes of me, and believe me I built plenty of fucking jigsaws out of the bits and pieces you lot have left behind, so don't preach to me about ethics and involvement and listen to what I have said for a change. I am not seeking glory and I realise I cannot do it on my own without Rupert and your help, but I can stop you in your tracks if you continue along these lines, so make your mind up exactly where you want to be, in or out." They could all see the anger in his eyes and hear the determination in his words. Their minds were spinning, each one of them concerned by his words.

"Where did all that come from, Bill? Have you been taking lessons from Belinda? I haven't heard you talk like that ever."

"Well, there is always a first time I suppose." He snapped back at him.

Rupert walked over to the drinks cupboard, two glasses in his hands. He walked over to where Bill was sitting. "Whiskey David?" He said, offering a glass to David. Roger held out his hand, ready to take his glass.

"Not you, Roger. You will drive us to the hotel later." If looks could kill, he bit his lip. *Bastard,* he looked away towards the door, hiding his embarrassment, his face reddened by his anger, knowing there was nothing he could do except bide his time. There would be another day, his day.

Rupert took a swig from his glass. "I had forgotten how good this was, your favourite, Bill?"

"Yes, it is, and it has got me through a few bad days. I can tell you and this may be one of them." Rupert topped up his glass.

"I am serious, Bill. We need to understand this spying business a little better. We are not having a go at you, but I have shareholders to consider and they couldn't give a fuck who's shagging who. Dividends, that's all they understand, so I have to protect my own position and everybody else's."

"Roger has a question you need to answer. Can we deal with that and then we will ask Belinda to join us and thrash out a strategy we are all in agreement with. Are you comfortable with that?"

Bill walked towards the centre of the table and lifted the foil on the sandwich plate removing a beef sandwich. "Still fresh, I'm starving." He was playing for time getting his confidence up. Roger was not about to pull any punches.

"Bill, have you had any experience on the other side of the fence? I'm talking about prison because that is where you are leading us with this silly notion of yours, undercover, industrial espionage, spying on our competitors. You can call it what you like but it's not me and if I have my way, you will be finished, your employment with us in the morning holding Belinda's hand."

Rupert was furious. For a moment, he thought he was just about to throw his half full tumbler at Roger. You could see the rage in his eyes.

Bill spoke first. "Mr Tate, how on earth did we end up here together in this boardroom? I have no idea but before this is over and I put my wife's photograph in the cardboard box, please let me put a question to you if that is in order. Is it, Rupert?" he said, passing the parcel to him.

"Go ahead, Bill, whilst I calm down. I will have my say in a few minutes' time. The floor's all yours."

"You were with Kingfish, Detroit, spin doctor no less is that correct?" His face flushed, he wanted to shit his pants. "Where did that come from? Answer me, will you?"

He did not know where to start, floundering, struggling for the answers, his thinking ravelled up and in total confusion.

"Let me refresh your memory, Mr Tate. You were moved on for inappropriate behaviour. That was the official line of course but when you dig deeper, you were told to quit suspected of industrial espionage, reference page three of your personal records." Bill removed a folded A4 document from his inside jacket pocket, throwing it down on the table in front of Rupert.

"Page 3." He pointed with his finger, staring him in the eyes.

Bill left the room, taking the lift back to his office. He wanted to talk to Belinda before the shit finally hit the fan.

They sat for what seemed a lifetime over a cup of coffee.

He had explained what had taken place to her. "Were did you dig that dirt up from? Do you know somebody at Kingfish?"

"Yes, I met the Personnel Officer in New York a couple of years back at a conference. Tate just happened to come up in the conversation. It's a small world sometimes."

"I called her about three weeks ago and she offered to send me a copy of his file, pure luck you might say."

"Did she have a grudge against him or something?"

"Yes, she did. He came on to her and got angry when she told him where to go."

"Revenge then?"

"Yes, you could call it that," he sniggered. "Served the bastard right. He deserved it the way he ripped into you," he smiled. "It shouldn't take much longer now." He looked at his watch as the phone rang.

"Belinda."

She put the phone down. "Five minutes. They want us both this time," she laughed. "Shall we just go and pack our cases and leave them to it?"

"I must say I am tempted but that would not be the answer. Let's just play it out and see what they have to say for themselves, shall we?"

"Okay." She stroked his arm, surprised. She had seen a new side to him today, feelings that surprised her and made her feel good inside.

Level 10. Ping

"Come in, Bill. Belinda, take a seat."

Back where we started a couple of hours ago, Bill said to himself.

"Belinda, no doubt Bill has brought you up to date regarding the situation, we find ourselves in, so I won't go over all that again but I would like to thank you for your loyalty and dedication. All three of us are unanimous on that score. We also agree to go ahead with Bill's plan, so over the next couple of days we will thrash out the detail and I am prepared to stay here for as long as it takes, not too long I hope, so my first question to both of you. Are you with me or is it the end of the road for you two?"

Bill looked cross at Belinda and decided that it was his place to state their case, take control so to speak.

"Rupert, I can speak for the two of us and it is our wish to go ahead as planned but with some reservations, but you would expect that, wouldn't you?"

"Bill, let me make one thing crystal clear before this goes any further. I need you and Roger to shake hands and put your differences behind you or I will drive back to Head Office on my own and call it a day. You choose."

Roger held out his hand. "The best man won. My apologies." Bill reluctantly shook his hand, looking over to where Rupert was sitting, seeking his approval.

"Well, let's make for that Spanish Tapas you have been telling me about, Bill. We can book into the hotel and meet you two there, say eight thirty."

"That will be fine. I'll just check my desk in case there is anything I need to deal with and we will meet you there."

Bill and Belinda left the room.

"You are one lucky fucker, Roger. If Bill had turned you down, that would have been the end of us three, so thank your lucky stars. How he found out about you, well, there hangs a tale for both of you. He did his homework. You didn't perhaps. We ought to consider a position on the board for him as a thank you and a vote of confidence. Let's all think about that."

*****

Back in Bill's office, Belinda closed the door behind her and took the chair facing Bill already seated behind his desk, sorting his messages.

He looked up after sifting through his mail. "Crap mainly to add to all the other crap. We have both suffered today." There was disappointment in his eyes as he spoke to her.

"Before we chat just nip to your own office and check your mail whilst I organise some coffee for us, that should give us about an hour to chat before we take a taxi to the restaurant and meet up with them." He shook his head as she left the office. She was pissed off and she was not disguising her thoughts. He would just have to ignore it, giving her time to collect her thoughts. *She will be fine by the time we hit the restaurant. We will be a little late. Let them buggers get a couple of drinks in front of us. They are going to need it,* he told himself as he picked up the phone.

Belinda's messages were much the same as Bill's, a nice message and a picture of Neville sitting in the sunshine outside the Café Royale in Milano Square, HI. The message read. She smiled, missing him already.

"Shall I be mother then?" Belinda was pointing to the coffee tray sitting on the office sideboard. She gave him a smile.

Bill looked up from his paperwork. "Yes, please, Belinda. Sorry, I just need to send this urgent mail and then you will have my undivided attention for the rest of the evening, okay?" He smiled, his eyes searching her breasts, wanting her.

"Right, fire away. What do you make of it all?"

"That, Bill, is a question too far at this moment in time. I have not got a clue and I mean that. Have you any idea because I would love to hear it," she frowned, keeping her eyes focused on his face, searching for any tell-tale signs that he was not telling her the whole truth.

"You will come out of this and get a lot of credit. Me, my patch up with Roger is exactly that and I cannot see it lasting. He is a vindictive bastard and he hates suffering any type of defeat, a mardy arse, shall we say? He will come after you again, but Rupert won't let him hurt you. David on the other hand still has cards to play. He's a cunning sod and his knife is hiding in his pocket out of sight, but he will strike when he can be assured of victory and not before. Rupert, I have always liked him, although I would never admit it openly, respect, he knows what he wants and he will get what he wants and trample on anybody who gets in his way which makes him the easier one of the three of them to deal with. He is the open book. Roger is hiding somewhere in the book cover and you will find David hiding somewhere in the fine print." He grinned. "Let's just play it by ear, agree in principal between ourselves. We already have a suitcase plan, so let's enjoy ourselves."

She laughed, "You amaze me, Bill Brevit. You absolutely do. You have shown your true colours today and they will not go unrewarded I assure you. Shall we have a dirty date tomorrow evening, on the company that would be?" She pushed her breasts out, wanting him to look at her, wanting him inside her. *Perhaps,* her mind went blank there.

"Do you really want an answer?" He laughed aloud.

*****

Tapas for five. "Bill, Belinda, come and sit down. Let me get you a drink. It has been a long day." Rupert held out his hand, a smile that said it all.

"Table rules first, people. There will be no business talk this evening. This is an enjoy-time-only dinner. Do you get my point?" Silence fell, not a word, only a large grin from Belinda.

"Well, it seems that Belinda's with me you lot. Just do as you're told perhaps that is clear enough for you all."

"Your table is ready, Mr Clifton," he said, pointing towards the restaurant proper.

"Shall we?" Rupert led the way. "You sit this side with me. After all, we know we are on the same side. The boys can sit facing us," he grinned, enjoying himself.

The wine water was asking Rupert which wine he would like to start with. "Just give everyone the choice. Let them decide for themselves."

There were three choices a 2002 *French Chablis*, a 2008 *Chilean Merlot* and a 1999 *Italian Borolo*.

"Your health, Rupert, and thanks for the memory." Bill lifted his glass of Borollo. "Cheers, your good health."

"My pleasure, Bill," he smiled, pleased with himself. It did not go by unnoticed. David shot him sarcastic grin whilst Rupert looked on disapprovingly. Favouritism, sulking for attention that was not coming his way.

Rupert tapped the table with his fork. "Gentlemen, Belinda, I know I said there was to be no corporate chat this evening, but I have a few words to say to you, Bill. I have listed your name in this year's nominations for appointment as a Director of the Board. David and Roger have seconded my nomination. Congratulations." He stood, raising his glass. "Bill Brevit." Everyone stood and joined in with the congratulations. Belinda offered her hand. Bill squeezed it lovingly. "Thanks."

As Spanish Tapas goes, it wasn't bad although Roger would not agree but there was not a lot that he agreed with anyway. Rupert said his goodbyes until tomorrow.

Bill's taxi arrived, taking him and Belinda back to the office. They held hands, both wanting more but that would have to wait.

"I will collect my car and I have told the taxi driver to take you on home. I will pick you up in the morning at 7 pm, early I know but we need to be prepared for round two. I will send someone to collect your car, so let me have your keys please."

"Thanks, Bill," she leaned over, kissing his cheek.

Bill got out of the taxi and walked around to his window, handing the driver a ten-pound note. "Stay until she is inside, okay?"

"Yes, Sir. Thank you. I will," he replied, tucking the note into the top pocket of his jacket, smiling.

Bill waved goodbye, tired, ready for home and bed.

Belinda kicked her shoes off in the hall, threw her jacket on the chair and went straight to bed wondering what tomorrow would bring as she closed her eyes, thinking of Bill.

*****

Chapter 27
Grace Nightingale

St Clarence's Nursing Home:

Gerta drew the blinds in room 21. 'Mrs Grace Nightingale,' the door sign read.

"I will say goodnight then, Grace."

"Goodnight, Gerta. Thank you. See you in the morning." Gerta, the senior nurse on the night shift, left the room with the supper tray, ticked the medication record, slipping it back into her tunic pocket as she closed the door behind her.

Grace had been a resident at St Clarence's for three years now. She liked it there. She had made many friends and had several visitors throughout the month, always cheerful and caring for some of the less fortunate residents at the home. It was 8:30 pm, time for the home to take a rest and prepare for breakfast and the day that lay ahead. Gerta enjoyed the boredom of night duty.

"Anything nice for supper, Rosie?"

"The same old story, Gerta, whatever Gobby has left over from breakfast, lunch and supper, crap as usual. I shan't bother. I've brought a sandwich and a bag of crisps and if I am hungry at the end of my shift, I will see what's for breakfast before I sign off in the morning. You?"

"I can eat anything me. I'll have something later. You stick the kettle on and mash the tea. I just want to have a quick walk around. Percy's not been sleeping well and one or two of the others, so I will just make sure everything is okay. Five minutes." She left the room, leaving Rosie to put the kettle on, picking up the morning paper. "Five minutes," she said.

She put her head around the door of room 21 and crept over to the side of the bed, closing the door behind her. Grace was fast asleep; the sleeping pill she had slipped into her milk earlier that evening had taken effect as she knew it would.

She searched under the bed, knowing exactly were Grace kept her handbag. She grinned to herself as she walked across the room to the dressing table, placing the handbag near the table lamp and checking the curtains were closed properly, no chinks of light peeping through before switching on the lamp. She had tested it earlier that evening when she started her shift.

She had spent several weeks planning the theft, knowing which days Grace had visitors and the days she did not. She also knew which days Grace would not use her cards. She was after all a woman of habit.

She knew exactly where she kept her cards and cash. She even knew the card pin number, memorising it from the last time Grace received her new card the month earlier. She would put the card back in her purse tomorrow night, sticking to the same routine as this evening and nobody would be any wiser.

She carefully removed the purse from the bag, selecting the visa debit card inside the zip pocket. She would need it for two days at most. She added a twenty-pound note for good measure before stuffing them both into her tunic pocket.

She closed the handbag, turning out the table lamp and slipping the bag back underneath the bed where she had taken it from. She smiled, a smug grin as she left the room, heading back to the rest room for a cuppa with Rosie.

Gerta finished breakfast and her shift, checked her pockets tapping then, making sure she had not left her cell phones behind. She smiled and left for home.

Without her uniform, Gerta dressed quite plainly, a uniform so to speak more in keeping with a prison guard, the same colour without the shoulder flashes. It suited her figure, broad, overfed, overweight, five feet five tall with short blonde hair and piercing blue eyes. 'Ugly' best describes her, a vicious ugly thug disguised by her uniform during the night, a nightingale.

She was already on a spending spree, having spent most of her shift memorising the sixteen-digit number, expiry date and the card security code number on the reverse side of the card for Grace's debit card. She already had her credit card details filed away in her head somewhere from previous visits inside Grace's handbag.

Her first hit on the card was at the ATM in the High Street just around the corner from St Clarence's. She drew out the maximum allowed. She would hit the card again at another ATM on the way to the nursing home in the morning. Martin Street Co-op would do. She smiled. Greed rolled around in her eyes.

She parked her car in the road outside the block of flats where she lived with her cat, Jekyll, an evil-looking tiger cat, her best friend, her only friend.

Taking the stairs to LEVEL 7, the lift was out of order for the third week, running and at forty-four years old and two stone overweight, she hated every step.

Gerta threw her handbag and coat onto the sofa, then switched on her laptop, checking for flights from Manchester and cheap holidays in the Argentine, a daily visit to familiar airlines and travel agent's sites. Her excitement was growing. She looked at the half-filled suitcase sitting on the floor at the bottom of her bed. *Not long now, Rudolph*, she said to herself grinning. *Ready to go. Nearly there.*

She had not seen him for seven years. Today, she would have enough savings to buy a couple of new outfits and purchase a one-way ticket to visit her brother, Rudolph.

*****

Chapter 28
The Contract

Belinda finished her coffee. She had been awake since the early hours of the morning, pondering. At four o'clock, she wanted Neville and Jasper to come home. By four thirty, she wanted sex again with Julie, and for the last hour, she had thought of nothing but her and Bill and their long running relationship. Were they both ready for change?

The hurdles seemed to be getting higher. She had thought of inviting Bill over for breakfast. Well, a good shagging was preferred. She could grab a breakfast in the office canteen. Now she was just hanging about, waiting for him to pick her up. When she heard the car pull into the drive, her thoughts were far away. She had a cardboard box tucked up safely under her arm, going somewhere when Bill beeped his hooter, telling her he was waiting. *That's not like Bill. I thought he would be here, his hands all over me. I hope nothing's changed since last night.*

"Hi, Bill. Good morning. Thanks for coming," she smiled.

She leant over her seat, kissing him on the lips. Her eyes were telling him, *Later.*

"Hi, you look nice," he replied with a smile.

The car pulled out of the drive and Bill was in a hurry. "Is there anything wrong you seem agitated?"

"No, you know why," he paused, searching her eyes. "Surely, you don't need me to spell it out, do you?" he grinned. She grabbed his thigh, stroking him. "No, tonight we agreed you know what happened the last time we did this in the car?" It was her turn to laugh.

"We know the remedy for that, don't we, darling?" His grin was rude and big, lust floating in his eyes as he looked down her cleavage.

She wanted to change the subject. She was still feeling horny from her dirty thoughts about Julie having oral sex with her but that was at four thirty and now she was about to play a more serious game with her future at stake. She would need to concentrate on that. Sex would come later. She smiled at her thoughts.

"Do you want to drop in to McDonald's for a coffee and a breakfast bap? We have time?"

"No, do you mind if we get to your office and have breakfast there instead? I will feel more comfortable there." Her smile said 'please'.

"Okay, that's fine. We need to discuss tactics wherever we eat breakfast. It will be a big day for the both of us."

"Are you expecting problems then?"

"No, but there is a lot at stake for all of us and Rupert will not be giving anything away. You can rest, assured about that."

"Anyway, it's not him I am worried about. It's that slimy bastard. I hate Roger bloody Tate. He won't give in until he has got his own back, a bad loser. I knew it the first time I saw him."

"Well, you worry about him too much. The rat in the wood pile is not him or Rupert. It's... *I've been very quiet,* David. He is the one that worries me the most."

He parked the car. "I've got someone on the way over to your house to fix your car." He glanced at his watch. "So you will be back on the road by the time this is all over."

"Good. I'm lost without my car and it looks bad you keep coming to my house with Neville living nearby."

"Well, hopefully he will be off to Milan in the next couple of weeks and then it won't be an issue, will it?" She did not reply.

"Close the door please and let's talk about terms. I think that will be the first issue they will want to put to bed. All that bit last night about me becoming a board member may have just been a bluff to take us off guard. That's just the kind of tactic David would have suggested, so think hard and talk hard and if you are not sure, go for a pee or something, okay?"

"Easier said than done, Bill. We will see. I need a coffee."

"Your friend is on her way." He pointed to Linda and her tray of coffee. She was almost at the door as he spoke.

"Good morning, Belinda. Bill, your breakfast is on its way. Is there anything I can do?"

"Not yet, Linda, but there will be before the day's over no doubt. Oh, can you just make sure the Boardroom is tidy and everything has been put away and I will catch you later, okay?"

"Thanks." She left the office none the wiser. She wanted gossip. It was written all over her face.

"It is going to be a long day. Is there anything you need to ask? We best sort out our differences now. We will want to be showing a united front. Those buggers will be looking very hard for any divisions between us. Remember what Rupert said? Bottom line, that will be his bone, David. He's the oddball, so beware of him and Roger. I think will be kept in check by Rupert. He won't want him falling over again, another day perhaps."

What could David's angle be? Where will it come from? That's the million-dollar question for today. Perhaps it won't happen, and we are being too pessimistic.

He sniggered, "No, Belinda, Rupert and Roger would have piled everything up on David's back. That poor sod will carry the can, should things go decidedly wrong. Today, tomorrow or in the future, it will be two against one as far as David is concerned. He is trapped, I'm afraid, between Rupert's ego and Roger's vanity with not a lot of wiggle room in between them."

"Well, you seemed to have worked that out well. Is there something I'm missing or is there something you aren't telling me. Which is it?" she asked with a slight hint of sarcasm in her voice.

"I have told you everything. There is nothing I have missed out or overlooked. I have done my homework and you should have done yours." He frowned, pouring himself another coffee.

"Yes, please, Bill." She offered him her cup. "Ah, here's breakfast, muesli and yoghurt for you and sausage, egg and tomatoes for me. Good."

Breakfast did not take long.

"Do you seriously think that the balance of power rests with David, Why?"

"Believe it or not, Belinda, it is not a well-known fact. Certainly never spoken of except behind closed doors but David is one of the founder members and the largest single shareholder of CERAMIC 5. Now do you begin to understand? You are not to repeat any of this. Is that quite clear?"

"My God, yes, well, that's a shock I can tell you. So why does he let Rupert and Roger get away with so much? Well, Rupert. That's easy. He has turned in good yearly profits since he took over as CEO. He can't do a thing wrong as far as the shareholders are concerned. The balance sheet never lies, and the dividends have paid out handsomely for the past six years. Now Roger, he sits at the other end of the seesaw and holds the balance between the three of them and even I must admit he is bloody good at his job, pinching clients to you and me headhunting on the balance sheet. He has a very large budget. Japan and China don't come cheap. He has the knack of finding people's faults and uses them without mercy against them. He is what you said about him, a slimy bastard, but that is the name of the game I'm afraid. Accept it or move on. Even the weak have choices."

"My God, I am learning fast and I never believed Corporate was ever this bad," she grinned.

"Fucking hell, I want out."

Bill almost choked on his coffee. "No, I was only joking, Bill. I love it. It's going to be a good day. I just know it is." She wanted to kiss him. I mean, have sex with him here over the desk. Her face flushed as she looked into his eyes. "Who's being a naughty girl then?" He grinned. Erection was not very far away…

*****

"Let's get back to being serious. We still have a lot to do. Let's start with your demands on my budget. Can we say £2000 per month?" He frowned, hoping she was going to agree this time round. He had posed the questions several times without receiving a reply.

"That is cash of course. I don't want it showing up anywhere. You do understand my concerns I hope?" He held out his hand. "Agreed, and the payment will begin after your first month's engagement at Simpson & Smith."

"Thanks, Bill. You won't regret it. I promise you."

"Right. Let's balance it out then. Your position, benefits to yourself, working relationship to be agreed. Anything I have missed?"

"I don't think so. Me, I'm the easy bit. It's the others that concern me."

Bill turned her words over in his mind. *I'm the easy bit.* He did not like those words one little bit. Jealousy was written all over his face and it did not go a miss on Belinda. She reached over, touching his arm. "There's no need to look like that. I am yours. Just remember that when they are kicking us around the boardroom floor. I'm yours." He looked away, hurt, but he would handle it.

"Well, then we will play it this way." The desk phone rang. He picked up the phone thinking it was Rupert. "It's your wife, Mr Brevit," the girl on the switchboard said.

"Jill, I can't talk. I told you I will see you when I return home. I don't know when that will be, so why are you calling me?"

"Don't be like that, Bill, please. I'm just calling to say mother has rung and would like us both to visit this weekend. Shall I tell her I will go on my own? I could be there this afternoon. What shall I tell her?"

"I'm sorry, Jill. It's probably the biggest crisis in my working life and I cannot be with you, so call me later. I shall probably be tied up to the early hours. You know what Rupert's like, the night owl. On second thoughts, it's best I call you. Take care. Give your mother my love." He hung up. "A good day you said. Well, that's tonight's freedom sorted," he grinned. She replied, smiling. They were both having dirty thoughts.

"This Corporate feeling good. I've been feeling horny since yesterday and it's getting worse, so you had better behave." Mischief was in her eyes.

"Well, don't let's celebrate just yet. We still have to work out David's take on all of this. Rupert and Roger, I will look after that pair. We both need to concentrate our thoughts and at least come up with our own plan. Any ideas, naughty girl?"

"We can start by not mixing naughty with Corporate. They don't fit together until after the event, over a night cap, pillow talk that kind of girly thing."

"Yes, you're right of course. I will behave."

"I don't mind you being naughty, Bill, but not here. Put the phone down right now." She smiled. She wanted him inside her.

"I don't bloody know what David's game is. I wished I did. So what are your thoughts? You handled yourself very well yesterday. Surely you have given it some thought?"

"Yes and no is the answer to your question. Yes, I have given it some thought and no, I haven't a bloody clue as to what to do about it. I was hoping you would be able to tell me. Will that fuck everything up? Do you think?" She looked concerned now, almost afraid.

"It's laughable. We may have just overplayed our thinking. It may just come to nothing but I have a nagging thought in the back of my mind. He's a cunning little fucker, clever and my view is for what it is worth is that he will just want to show the other two how powerful he really is and if that is the case, we could both become the victims in all this power play because that is what all this is about. They have agreed to back my scheme and offered their commitment and support, so there is not much else to consider is there. Do you think that is a rational assessment of the situation?"

"Bill, I can't honestly answer that, except that I agree that David is the problem. In fact there actually is one and it is not just the two of us feeling insecure about our own personal situations. I hope so but like you have said we will cope with whatever they chuck at us. Suitcases?" She grinned.

He laughed, "Suitcases." He laughed as the desk phone rang. It was the switchboard. "Mr Clifton would like you and Belinda to join them in the boardroom, sir."

"Thank you, Melanie." He put the phone down, smiling at her. "Ready?" he laughed, taking her hand and gently squeezing it. "Come on, let's get it over with."

Level 10. Ping

*****

"Good morning, help yourself to coffee and then we will get started." Rupert walked over to them and kissed Belinda. "You are looking well" he smiled… "How are you feeling this morning?"

Bill looked away, annoyed. Belinda's cheeks blushed.

"How are you feeling this morning, you." *What's his fucking game?* he wondered.

Bill helped himself to coffee. "Good morning, David, Roger. Sleep well you two?"

"It was heavy last night."

"I'm fine, thanks," David replied. "Nearly there, Bill, better after my coffee," he smiled.

"Good, all we need now is some sensible thinking and then we can all go home happy." He grinned.

"Have you and Bill agreed upon everything or is there something you would prefer the two of us had a more private conversation?"

She smiled back at him. "Thank you, Rupert. That was a kind thought but I think we should be okay and speak as one, so I hope we can get this over with quickly and then perhaps the two of us could take lunch together. I am sure you could fix that, couldn't you?" Her eyes left him little choice.

He grinned, "Let me ponder. Is that the correct word?" He laughed.

"Not for too long I hope?" she replied, looking across at Bill and the other two already seated around the table, waiting for them to join them.

Rupert and Belinda sat down facing each other. "Who's holding the whistle then, Roger?"

"Hmm, well, let me start by saying that I agreed to put everything behind me any bad feeling or grievances I had with, Bill and Belinda I am talking about. It was my misconception of Bill and Belinda's involvement that muddied the waters for me but listening to their side of the story, I am afraid to admit it but I got it all wrong and for that, I wish to apologise for my misgivings and I sincerely hope we can all move on from there." He offered his hand to Bill. Then Belinda kissing her cheeks, Rupert looked on, 'surprise' written all over his face. David looked down at the carpet, thinking. About what? His secret, and he certainly wasn't ready to share it just yet, but it would happen. Rupert was sure of that.

"Roger, did you have humble pie for breakfast or did you have a wet dream? Which was it? It's definitely not like you to apologise. What's your angle?" He looked him straight in the eyes. They were all watching, waiting for his reply and without hesitation, he replied.

"I don't. No, I never eat humble pie, Rupert. I am genuinely apologetic about the comments I made to Bill and Belinda yesterday and that should be an end to it." He looked towards Bill and Belinda, a warm smile on his face.

"Enough said. Let's move on. David you have the floor."

David got up from his seat and walked over to the window, pulling the blinds apart with his free hand. Silence, not a murmur from anyone; you could hear a pin drop. David looked out across the skyline. The blinds fell back into line as David removed his hand and turned to face them all.

He walked back towards the table and picked up the desk phone from its cradle. "Melanie, have someone bring the files I left with you earlier and bring them straight to the boardroom." He put the phone down and sat down waiting for one of them to ask a question. Complete silence, everyone in the room watched each other, waiting as someone knocked the door, pushing it open. All eyes watched the door as Melanie came in with the files he had asked her to bring to him.

"One to each person present in the room please, Melanie." She placed the blue folder in front of everybody and left the room. "Thanks, Melanie," David said as she closed the door behind her.

David started to talk. He stood up taking centre stage. He was enjoying himself, in control, not a situation he could enjoy very often, and he had every intention of enjoying himself this morning.

"In front of each of you is your contractual agreements covering our discussions here yesterday and today. I worked late having prepared the draft several days ago, finalising it after our Tapas evening last night. I finalised what I think is a contractual agreement to be agreed and signed by all of us. I had a courier deliver them this morning ready for this meeting. My people worked the twilight shift. That's how important this document is. The signed documents will be kept safe and secret by myself. These are the terms and conditions you all need to agree to without further debate. You have no options. The document is non-negotiable, so I will give you two hours to read and discuss it amongst yourselves as you wish and we will re-convene this board meeting at 1 pm. No signatures, no agreement to move forward."

There was complete silence. Even Rupert was momentarily lost for words. "Fuck me, David. You do not often bang your drum but where did this come from? A little fucking sly, wouldn't you say?" Rupert was very angry but not at all surprised. This was quite the norm for David. However, it has never been as bad as this, demanding, no fucking options. He wanted to shout but bit his lip.

"Let the others have their say first," he told himself.

"Yes, it fucking well is. Why, David, why?" he was shouting his anger. Bill and Belinda looked on.

Roger was standing now, waving the file about as though he was lecturing atomic physics at Harvard as the professor. Rupert smiled at his antics.

"Shouting, Roger, will get you nowhere. Sign or fuck off and that is my last word on the subject." He walked to the door. "1 pm gentlemen and don't be late," he said, slamming the door shut behind him as he left the room.

Everybody wanted to talk all at once. "Wo, wo, everybody, let's discuss it properly. Otherwise, we will get nowhere. Let's have a coffee and agree a way forward. Belinda, would you?" His eyes pointed to the desk phone.

Bill laughed, "I for one am not at all surprised and I think you were also expecting something along these lines Rupert, so what's your view?" Rupert sat quietly in his chair, thinking before replying.

"My suggestion for you, Bill, is to take Belinda to your office and come to your own conclusions and I will sit here with Roger and do the same. Meeting back here at 12:30 would that be agreeable to you both?"

Belinda spoke first, smiling. "I knew Corporate was over talked about, but this bombshell has me wondering where I really want to be, so yes, I agree that is the sensible approach now. I just hope you can keep your hand on the situation, Rupert, for all our sakes."

"Come on, Belinda. Let's get out of here and consider our options in private. See the two of you at 12:30 then." Bill guided her to the door. "Gentlemen, 12:30."

Rupert and Roger started their own debate.

*****

"Well, what did you make of that then?" he grinned. "The crafty bastard, I knew he was planning something. I just knew it."

Belinda grinned, "Do you know I thought you were exaggerating a bit when you told me David was the one for us to keep an eye on. So, I apologise. You certainly have done your homework."

"Do you know you have only become Corporate for two days now and you are already thinking like one of us. Where you get your confidence from, I am not quite sure." His eyes wanted her.

"It's not so much confidence, Bill. I assure you it's more like going with the tide but I will get used to it, then it will be time for you to start worrying about it. Until then, let me just enjoy myself." She gave him a sexy smile. This Corporate definitely did wonders for her sex drive. She was already wet and it wasn't ten o'clock yet. *Perhaps I'm turning into a morning girl*, she said to herself.

The coffee arrived. Bill threw his copy of the contract on to his desk. "I suggest we read and talk our way through this bloody lot. Let's have a look," he said, opening the file.

Belinda copied him, taking her seat on the other side of his desk.

They remained silent for some time before Bill spoke.

"I will say this about the wily sod. It's good, chapter and verse. It's good there isn't much the crafty bugger has left out. How are you doing?"

"About the same conclusion as you, Bill. Good," she sighed, sitting back in her chair, stretching both arms above her head. "Have you a pen?" she sniggered, awaiting his reply.

"You agree then?"

"No, Bill, but we have very little choice. Well, we haven't got a choice and he knows it, the smug little fucker. He's got all of us by the balls unless of course there is something I've missed."

"No, there is nothing you've missed. You realise this is a contract lasting for perpetuity, don't you? There will be no walking away after you have signed on the dotted lines, so be sure it is what you want to do first. There is still time for you to reconsider your position." He frowned, ogling her breasts to take his mind off the seriousness of the situation facing him.

Before he allowed her to say anything, he dropped the question to her. "What's with this lunch business between you and Rupert?" His eyes were telling her to be careful. How she replied, he was in no mood for any competition from the likes of Rupert.

"Bill, I know you have only just pointed out my shortcomings of joining the corporate culture but I am a quick learner and if I am going to survive, then playing up to him is just part of the game. There will be no sex involved. I can assure you of that. It was just a ploy to keep him off our backs. It's you I want, and don't you forget it," she smiled, reassuring him of her desires, her lust.

"Tonight, remember?" he grinned.

"Yes, I do remember."

"I just wished we were here all alone. I would have your knickers down and be on you in a flash, you naughty girl."

She laughed. "I shall just have to stay wet a little longer. I am afraid, Bill, you will have to be patient. After lunch with Rupert, sorry, there's not a lot I can do about that apart from making it up to you later," she grinned.

"So, we are signing, are we?"

"Yes, unless you don't want to of course. Do we really have a choice?"

"No." He threw her his ballpoint.

Level 10. Ping

"Well, Roger, that came as a bit of a shock. I know he can be very assertive when he wants to be. This is not about cloak and dagger, espionage and all that crap. This is David's way of keeping the two of us in check. If we sign this, we have got him for life and the cunning little bastard knows it, so what are your thoughts?"

Roger walked over to the drinks cupboard and took out the bottle of Courvoisier brandy and two glasses. "Join me, it's early I know but I need one right now."

"God, he's got where he wants us in his hand. We are like a pair of humans gripped in the hands of the giant in Gulliver's travels, helpless, completely fucking helpless."

"Cheers!" Rupert lifted his glass.

"Cheers to you, Rupert," he replied. There was anger in his voice. Concern showed in his eyes.

"What option have we? Sorry, let's put it another way. Are you going to sign?" He turned the pages of the contract on the table. "Here on page 5. Terms and conditions. There is nothing else to consider. This page is what we are signing up to. All the rest of the crap is just padding out copied from a HMS stationery document available on line. Just carefully read the wording. He must have spent the remainder of last night and the early hours of this morning just altering page 5. The crafty old bastard is concentrating on this page alone knowing that we cannot do a thing about it. Cleverer than you thought, does that sum it up?"

"Too bloody true. It does so. I suggest we sign up or walk away. We don't have any other choice so far as I can see and that is my advice to you. Put up or shut up." He laughed at the calamity of it all the last two days that is.

He gulped his drink, emptying the glass. He took his pen out of his inside jacket pocket and signed on the dotted line, then threw the file down in David's chair seat. "And you, Roger," he said, offering him his pen. Roger signed and placed the file on top of Rupert's. Before walking to the drinks cupboard, he returned with the bottle offering him a top up.

"We need this, don't we? They had given in to the power of the pen."

"We had six good years now. Let's play to his tune for a while. He won't use that document to take control of our lifestyles. He will let us carry on as before the only difference now is he is wagging the dog's tail and not us." Fucked explain their expressions as they finished their brandy.

*****

Early on parade that was Bill and Belinda.

"Signed copies on David's chair, unsigned copies in the bin over there next to the door. You can make your own way down to the car park." Sarcasm just a little. They both put their copy on David's chair. They all burst into fits of laughter.

"Open another bottle, Roger. Let's get pissed," he paused, staring at Belinda. "On second thoughts, I have a lunch date. Leave me out of it. You three can celebrate before David turns up 1 pm sharp. He said, didn't he?" she said, looking at his watch. "Twenty minutes…"

"Shall I book a table for the two of us, Rupert, or do you want to forget all about it?"

"Please, Belinda. Go ahead. I will be hungry by the time this is all over. We missed breakfast of course. Oh, here is David. He's early." He had heard the footsteps in the corridor. He knew straight away by the sound of the footsteps.

"David, you are early. Any reason for that?" asked Roger.

"I couldn't keep away, Roger," he replied with a smirk on his face. He knew he had won. All he wanted to hear now was the bullshit and he could make his way back to London.

Everybody was watching everybody else, wondering who would be first to have his pennyworth. Belinda stood up and walked over to David, her thoughts telling her to get it over with. It would not get any easier and she was right. David offered his hand. "Belinda, thank you, Miss Money Penny," he laughed. She laughed and then there was silence. Who would be next? It most definitely won't be Rupert. He wanted to be Play God by rights.

Roger looked towards Rupert before shifting his eyes towards Bill. He wanted to be next to demonstrate that he was the right guy in the right position to help in moving the company forward and grabbing the Schroder account from under the noses of Simpson & Smith. He wanted to be the one who plunged the knife. There was more than his own vanity at stake here now. He needed to survive by putting time between his mistakes and final victory.

Bill followed. Roger at least he had the common sense to realise that it was David who had rearranged the landscape as well as who sits where on the fence. He was just glad he could see himself up there with Belinda and the others. Yes, there would be room for Belinda. David would make sure of that. Rupert had no choice and no say in the matter anymore.

Finally, Rupert took centre stage, watched by the others. Has the bullshit begun to flow? It was that thick, you could see the embarrassment on everyone's faces, their eyes drifting to the floor, waiting for it to end.

David grinned, a sweet victory. He accepted Rupert's hand, his final gesture having accepted defeat at the hands of the better man. After all, David was a manipulator. It had taken him six years, so this victory was especially sweet.

David left the boardroom with the signed contracts safely in his hand. Roger drove him to the train station for the two o'clock train to London and home.

Rupert took Belinda as winner of the consolation prize to the Italian restaurant and Bill returned to his own office, a phone call to Jill and catch up with his desk and his work.

*****

Chapter 29
Reunion

Skepton General Hospital:

Ward 21, Room 3 Intensive Care Beryl was connected by an IV line to a saline drip. Only her arm and the tubing were visible, not a pretty sight as the monitor blipped away, signalling that life still had a presence here.

Her father and mother were talking to Dr James, the duty doctor in a consulting room further down the corridor.

"There is not much more I can tell you at this stage. Time, I'm afraid, is in charge for the time being anyway. The effects of dehydration are our main concern right now. Unfortunately everything has been hindered by the drugs your daughter took during her period of captivity. Three days the Coroner's report says. She is very lucky girl to have survived and we still have no idea how she came to be inside the Tower. That is still unexplained, even the coroner and police are baffled by it and I don't suppose either of you have any inkling why she should have been there?"

"Sorry, doctor. We unfortunately have the same information as yourself. We have no idea either," he said, repeating the Doctor's words. The police sergeant did hint that it could well have been a stunt by university students but there is no proof to substantiate that claim now, although over the last couple of years, there have been several similar incidents involving a hard core of students running under the banner: ***"Fuck you, Jack. We're in charge."***

"They are still treating it as attempted murder but they did mention a case for kidnapping but they would not elaborate on that, and that's really all I can tell you, doctor," replied William, Beryl's father. He squeezed his wife's hand as he spoke. Jain was taking it very badly, her constant tears making it difficult for him to cope with the situation himself at times.

"You can see her now but I advise you to think in terms of the worst happening. It is very much touch-and-go at the present time but she is in good hands here at the general, so please don't give up yet. Things could turn for the better. She is young and relatively fit, so that's a big plus on our side. Let me take you to her." Doctor James led the way down the corridor to ROOM 3.

"Any change, sister?" They chatted privately before sister allowed them into the room.

"I suggest you have five minutes and then perhaps we can have a chat. Can I get you a cuppa, coffee, tea?"

"No, thank you, sister. We will be fine," he replied. Jain just cried on his shoulder, wanting some comfort from him.

William and Jain sat waiting for Sister Smart back in Consulting Room 3.

"Hello, sorry I am late. I have just checked your daughter. Everything is fine at the moment, although there is no change just yet. However the signs are encouraging. I expect to see a big improvement within the next four hours or so. Her medication should have worn off by then so. I suggest you nip to the restaurant and have something to eat and drink. It will be a long night. I will keep you both informed of her progress and you know where we are. Just report to the duty nurse when you return to the ward." She gave them both a warm smile.

"Thank you, sister. We will take your advice," he replied, smiling, encouraged by her words.

"Come along, Jain. You need a cup of tea." They both left sister to her notes and followed the directions, taking them to the restaurant one floor up.

*****

William was finishing a chicken korma and a glass of cold milk. Jain was still crying over a cup of cold tea, but progress was being made there as she was now blaming herself for Beryl's wayward lifestyle.

"We could have done a lot more for her. We did not try hard enough, Dad, and when we did, it was all too late. She won't die, will she, William?" Tears flooded down her cheeks. He took her hand.

"No, my dear. She won't die, and we will take her home with us and do whatever it takes to give her a happy life again." He fought back his own tears, gently squeezing her hand.

"Mr Heatherley?" the voice said. William turned around, facing him. "Sergeant Dilkes, Kempton Road Police Station. May I have a word?" He offered his hand.

"Yes, certainly. This is my wife, Jain." He turned to face her.

"Hello." She looked away, embarrassed. She did not want to involve other people. She wanted him to go away.

"Sister told me you would be here. I won't keep you long, just trying to piece together the events that have brought you both here." As he spoke, Constable Watson joined them at the table with a tray of tea cups for himself and Sergeant Dilkes. "This is PC Watson. He attended the crime scene when we found your daughter."

"Hello," William replied.

"I know it will be difficult for you both but nevertheless I have to pursue the lines of enquiry. I am sure you understand that. All I want to do at this stage is establish the known facts until such times that we will be able to talk to your daughter in person."

He frowned, hoping they could contribute some information, however small, to help them with their enquiries.

"Some background information would help. How did she become involved with drugs? Can you tell us that much?" enquired PC Watson.

"There's not much we can tell you about that I'm afraid. I know it sounds a little odd, but she ran away from home, from school and her family. I tried several times to get her to return home, but it just seemed to drive her further away. We could never understand why," William replied, confused, wishing all this was not happening.

"Talk to her grandma. She was close to her. She will know something. I know she will. Please help us, will you?" Jain spoke quietly, hiding her face in her hands.

"Do you have an address? That could be a good lead. I need to check it out." He took his notebook from his pocket, waiting for her to give him the address, pencil ready in his hand.

"Three, Walnut Close, at the back of the Wallis supermarket somewhere," replied William.

"Yes, I know it. Thank you." He wrote the details down in his notebook.

"You had better call it through Pete and tell them to get straight back to us, so we can follow that up after we finish here."

"Yes, sergeant." He walked away to make the call.

"Thank you for that. It should help us we have very little else to go on. You are sure there is nothing more you can tell me? Anything, however small it may seem?"

"No, I am sorry, sergeant. I can't think of anything that could help," replied William.

"Try the school she used to go around with a boy called Jed. He went to her school. Kingstone High School. He's the one that got her on drugs in the first place, a bad person he was," replied Jain. She did not move her head, finding comfort in her own thoughts.

"Good. That's very good. That should help. I don't suppose you have an address for this Jed, do you?"

"It's somewhere on the Rushey Mead Estate. I remember dropping her off there once they were going to a local disco. Brent Road. Sorry I cannot remember the number, but you should be able to find him there or, at the very least, his parents would still be living there. Perhaps they may have an address for him. I don't know," Jain replied, again desperately wanting to help her mind, confused by everything happening around her.

PC Watson finished his call and re-joined them at the table.

"They are sending a car around there now, Sarge."

"Thanks, Pete. Sort this out. It's the drug dealers last known address. See what you can dig up. Then we will finish off here and make our way to Walnut Close."

He finished his tea. "Thank you, William. Jain, you have been very helpful. You will be staying here at the hospital tonight, won't you?" he asked.

"Yes of course, sergeant," William replied. "I will call in later then and let you know what progress we have made. What ward will you be on?"

"Twenty-one."

"Thanks. Everything will turn out okay. I am sure of that." He smiled and left with PC Watson, heading for Walnut Close.

*****

Number 3, the corner house of a row of terraced housing was a reminder of past years still awaiting the demolition man. It had started to rain.

Sergeant Dilkes spoke to the officer in the patrol sent to the scene from Martin Street Station. "Nothing's happened, sergeant. Nobody in or out since we arrived."

"Okay, you call in and get back to the station. We will take it from here, Goodnight."

Dolly Parker answered the door, pulling against the safety chain. "Hello, who are you? What do you want?"

"Mrs Dolly Parker, Police, Sergeant Dilkes, Kempton Road Station." He showed her his ID card. "I need to talk to you about your granddaughter, Beryl. She is in Skepton General. Her parents are with her. Can we come in and talk to you?" She pulled the safety chain clear and opened the door, still holding on to it, taking a good look at the officers before opening the door and letting them inside.

"Come through to the parlour. I'll put the kettle on. I suppose you will want a cup of tea, won't you, sergeant?" she enquired with a friendly smile. "She is alright? Beryl I mean. I haven't seen her for a few days. When she left here, she was going to university, a very clever girl, my Beryl. She should qualify this year as a solicitor. Has she had an accident or something?" She put the kettle on the gas ring as she spoke.

"I am afraid she is very poorly now, but she is in good hands. I spoke to the ward sister about an hour ago. She's on the mend I'm told. We would like you to help us if that's at all possible. Do you think you could help?"

"I don't know. What is it that you want?" There was concern on her face. She looked frightened by the news.

A Persian grey cat jumped up on PC Watson knee. "Oh, don't mind, Percy. He just wants a bit of fuss. That's all. He likes visitors," she grinned as she started to lay out the cups and saucers. PC Watson stroked the cat's back.

"Meow." The cat raised his tail, wanting more attention.

"No mugs here, sergeant. I do not agree with them, too modern for me. My mother would never have approved. You don't mind a cup and saucer, do you? I'm far too old to change my ways."

"That will be fine I ought to bring my missus around to see you. She will never believe me, cups and saucers," he laughed. "You should bring her then for a cuppa. I wouldn't mind. I would enjoy the company."

"Do you know your daughter's boyfriend, Jed?" PC Watson asked.

"He's not her boyfriend. She is far too sensible for that kind of thing. Her studies are far too important to her. No, she just buys drugs from him now and again, not very often. She says it helps her concentrate on her university work. No, he's not her boyfriend," she spoke with confidence. It was obvious Beryl was her ray of sunshine and she would not betray her in any way and she was making that abundantly clear.

Dilkes grinned at PC Watson.

She poured the tea. "Help yourself please, to sugar and milk. I'll just get the biscuit tin. You can't have tea at this time of night without a digestive or a malted cream." She put a selection on a side plate and sat down at the table with them, stirring her tea.

"What can you tell us about this Jed lad? When was the last time she saw him?"

"That morning I should think. There was twenty pounds missing from my purse. That's how I know. She is not a bad girl. She just needs a little help now and again. That's all."

"What day was it then, Dolly?" asked Sergeant Dilkes.

"Thursday, about ten o'clock. I think, yes, it was. It definitely was. She had a lecture at eleven o'clock that morning. I remember her telling me now." Sergeant Dilkes looked across at PC Watson. "Thursday Pete almost four days. Call the hospital and let Sister Smart know. It may be helpful. I'm not sure but best be on the safe side. Ah, do it now." There was a certain panic in his voice.

PC Watson walked through to the hall to make his call to the hospital.

"Thank you for the tea and biscuits, Dolly, and thank you very much for helping us with our enquiries. You have been most helpful. I will say goodbye for now. We need to return to the station and see what else has happened, see if there is any more good news," he exaggerated, a white lie, knowing it would not do any harm, help cheer her up. "I will let your family know what is going on."

"Please tell William to come and see me. I want to go and visit her. She will like that. Take her some flowers, shall I?"

"Yes, that would be very nice," he replied, holding her hand in his, comforting her.

She walked to the door behind them, closing it shut and securing the safety chain before returning to the parlour, picking up Percy. She sat down in the chair with him on her lap before bursting into tears, weeping at the bad news the sergeant had brought her.

*****

Jed Wallace sat in the interview room, playing with a plastic tea cup, fear in his eyes. 'Attempted murder they said.' He turned the words over in his mind. Beads of sweat began to form on his upper lip, his neck and face beginning to colour.

This is big shit, he told himself. *Not the drugs they found on him, but the murder wrap.* Those thoughts hurt and he didn't like that. He would squeal if it came to it. 'I am not going down for murder. That's for fucking sure,' he said to himself.

The door swung open. "Wallace, is that you?"

"Yes," he replied, staring at the cup in his hand, not wanting eye contact. 'Let him read the riot act first.' The usual crap, he had heard it too many times before to let it worry him. He was just waiting for the heavy stuff to start.

"I am Inspector Crisp, the Lead Officer in this case." He threw a file down on to the desk. "Not your first visit here, is it, Wallace? I lost count after page one. You'll get two years on the drug wrap, so we can leave that there. I'm only interested right now in the more serious charge of attempted murder against you." He sat down facing him.

PC Watson read him his rights

"You do not have to say anything. But it may harm your defence if you do not mention when questioned something which you later rely on in court. Anything you do say may be given in evidence."

"You are facing very serious charges, so my advice to you is to cooperate fully with this enquiry or take the consequences. We are looking at adding the kidnapping of a person to the charge sheet. That means you could be facing life. Is that what you really want or would you prefer to remain a fringe criminal, either way you will do time. For how long is really your choice." He pushed the telephone towards him. "You had better make your call." He picked up the case file and left the room with PC Watson.

Wallace stared at the phone. He stood up and walked around the table considering his options. *What fucking options! I haven't got any and that bastard knows it. I'll just tell him what he wants to hear and do twelve months with good behaviour. They can't pin the murder wrap on me. Kidnapping, where the fuck did that come from? Bullshit! He's just trying to scare me, slimy bastard. I was not there, and I am sure he knows that as well. Let's get it over with*, he told himself

He sat waiting for them to return. It seemed like forever. They were not in a hurry. *The solicitor can fuck off. I will do a deal on my own.*

*****

It was Friday. Beryl was on the mend, sitting up in bed. The nurses had changed her bedding, showered her and got her looking as best as they could. They had re-bandaged her hands and feet. They would take some time to heal, especially her fingers, where she had been scratching on the door. She lost five of her nails completely. Her feet suffered much the same as her hands but being very badly bruised hindered the treatment. Two weeks and she should well on the way to a complete recovery but would require psychological therapy to mend her internal wounds. The consultant said she could leave hospital on Saturday, but he would make a final decision during his morning rounds tomorrow.

Beryl's parents had gone for a cup of tea in the cafeteria. "About an hour whilst we get her ready," the nurse had said.

"Can we go yet, Dad? Surely it's been an hour since the nurse asked us to leave, is it?"

William looked at his watch. "Not yet, dear. We've only been gone twenty-five minutes, half way," he smiled. "It won't be long and then we can see her and then I must go and fetch her Gran. That will be the first thing she asks us."

"The doctor said she could come home on Saturday. She can come, Dad, can't she? You do want her to, don't you?" She looked scared, waiting for him to reply. It showed in her face. The tears in her eyes was begging him to say 'yes'.

"Sometimes, you do not understand me at all, do you? A silly question asking me if she can come home. You already know the answer. I want her home just as much as you do but I warn you now. There are no guarantees she will want to stay, so just treat her like a normal child. Let her be in charge. She will make the right decision for herself in the long term. Let's go. We can stop at the WVS shop and buy a morning paper that will waste some time." He held out his hand. She smiled for the first time in days as they left the cafeteria on the way to the lifts.

William peeped through the window into Beryl's room. She was sitting up in bed, her bandaged hands outside the bed covers. She looked good.

"You go first, love. It's you she will want to fuss over," he laughed. "That's better. Let her see we are happy to see her." She pushed the door open, letting go of his hand.

Beryl looked up her, smile struggling to fit her face. She was happy to see them and held out her hands.

"Mum," she burst into tears. 'Dad' holding out her hands, she threw them around her mum, sobbing, "I'm sorry, Mum. Please forgive me." She struggled slightly to say the words. "Dad, hold me. Don't leave me again." She was confused, hurt, her mind full of horrors.

A few tissues later, everyone cried, just the relief of it all for Dad, Mum just carried on where she left off this morning, and Beryl, well, she wanted to go home, for good this time she said.

"When is Gran coming, Mum?"

"Dad is going now. I had better call her and let her know she will be excited you know what she is like. It won't be long. You can tell me all about it whilst he is gone. We haven't a clue what has happened." Dad leaned over and kissed her cheek. He smiled as she spoke.

"I'm coming home this time, Dad, for good if you will have me." She began to cry again.

"You are a silly girl. Your room's all ready for you. We will invite Gran to come and stay for a few days and Mum will bake a cake. We will have a party. You just wait and see." He kissed her on the lips. "My silly girl." He wiped his tears, "I best get off and fetch Gran." He left the room, waving through the window before he finally left.

The file read 'PENDING' further enquiries. Wallace got sentenced to two years. Beryl was back at university, much to the pleasure of her Gran. Dad and Mum were just pleased to have her back at home.

Chapter 30
The Ridings

Katie was preparing breakfast. You could hear the sausages sizzling in the frying pan, a plate of freshly cut bread on the table next to the teapot, almost done. 'I had better go and see what Jack's up to, see if he is still asleep,' she said to herself.

"Who's a busy girl then? How long have you been up? I could hear those sausages sizzling in the pan as I came down the stairs."

"I didn't want to wake you and I couldn't sleep thinking about our chat last night and whether I should call Dr Doogood or not."

"No, you shouldn't. Just forget all about what happened the other day and let's start the day on a positive note and enjoy ourselves, shall we? What's for breakfast? Apart from the sausages that is. I'm starving."

"Tell me when you are not. Just sit down and do something useful for a change and pour the tea. There's a good boy."

"It looks like it will be fine today. It won't be long before those clouds have drifted away, and the sun comes out."

"Oh, good. I will feel better when we are on are way. You did tell Chris, no calls today?"

"Not exactly. The last person I spoke to was Eric and I told him, so we should be able to enjoy a quiet day together to make up for the time we didn't spend at Brancaster." She plated breakfast and joined him at the table.

"Sugar?"

"No, Jack. You know I don't take sugar. A little milk though please."

Jack took his second slice of bread. He smiled at her.
"Enjoying that, Jack?"

"But of course, why wouldn't I? Breakfast is the best meal of the day, didn't you know?"

"I will remind you of that when you are eating your sandwiches for lunch later," she grinned.

"Sandwiches, we haven't got sandwiches surely, and here was me thinking I would buy you a nice lunch as a thank you. Never mind, eh."

"A Nice lunch, in your walking boots. Is that it, Jack? A nice restaurant, Jack, McDonalds perhaps or Burger King." Her grin turned to laughter.

A McDonald's or a Burger King out there in the Dales. Is she real or has she planned something different for today? He frowned as he took his cup of tea to his mouth and there was her face, an evil face framed in the rim of the cup. He turned cold, his thoughts fighting her, attempting to hide his emotions that would only bring an end to the day before it started. He closed his eyes and she was gone. Her face meant nothing to him like all the other faces and voices. They never told their story.

"Well, you could have a burger with a large portion of chips and a serving of sticky toffee pudding with ice cream for afters. How does that sound?"

"That may be okay for you, Jack. I will be going for a nice pub lunch on my own. I can drop you off at McDonald's on the way and pick you up later."

"You would, wouldn't you? Okay, I'll buy you lunch as long as you forget the sandwiches, okay?"

"Okay, Jack."

"Well, I feel a lot better now. Shall we leave the pots and do them when we get back?"

"Typical, Jack. You can put everything in the dishwasher whilst I go and brush my teeth and get ready, five minutes. You should be all done by the time I come down and ready to go, so as Dad would have said, jump to it." She ran upstairs, not giving him a chance to argue with her.

*****

The doorbell rang:

"That will be the taxi, Jack. Grab your coat, and we will be off."

"A taxi, what happened to the car?"

"It's staying here, Jack. The taxi will take us to the station and we will take the bus to Grassington and then we can choose where we want to go when we get there. I thought you would enjoy that. Mum and Dad used to take us on the bus, remember? Don't pull faces. We haven't got time for all that. Start the day in a positive mood. Isn't that what you were telling me earlier, remember?"

Katie picked out a couple of tourists guides from the display in the entrance of the bus station. "We can read these on the way there. Your face," she laughed.

"I'm fine. My mind is everywhere. I am sorry. I will push my problems and my work to the back of my mind." He held out his hand. "Come on. Let's make this a special day." She took his hand and they both joined the queue for the Grassington bus, boarding.

"It's just like old times. I wish Mum and Dad were with us. I need to make this journey, Jack. They would have wanted us to." She handed him one of the brochures. "You see, if you can find anything in that one you would like to do, and I'll do the same in this one." She waved the brochure in her hand. "Excited, Jack?"

"In a funny way, yes. Strange as that may seem and you are you?"

"Just being with you for the day is enough reward for me and hopefully it will do you some good and take the pressure off you. Then I will be happy. Ask me this evening in the pub," she grinned. "Half of bitter for you."

It was market day, so they spent the morning walking around popping in to every shop possible. Katie was enjoying herself. "In here, Jack." She pulled him inside another trinket shop. "I want to look at that cat they have got in the window. I thought it would make a nice present for Aunt Kathryn. It's her birthday in a couple of weeks' time. She'll like that. I am sure she will."

"Shopping trip now, is it? By the time we have had lunch, we will both be worn out; so I can't see us getting much walking done, can you?"

"Spoil me, Jack. Does it really matter shopping or walking as long as we are enjoying ourselves?"

"Yes, mother."

She grinned. "There's no need for that, Dad."

"I just thought I would join in with the fun. It's nice to see you happy. It's your day after all. How much is it?" She showed him the price ticket £49.00. "For a pot cat?"

"It is a collectible," replied the lady assistant. He returned her smile. "I wasn't being rude, just teasing my sister. I like it. It's very nice."

"Do you mean that scrooge or are you just saying it to please me?"

"I will pay for it. Does that say it all?" She took his arm, giving him a big smile. "Thank you, Jack. I will tell Aunt Kathryn it is from both of us."

"I will take it. Thank you, Jack. Your card please."

"Right. Lunch, all this walking around has tired me out."

"Seriously?"

"No, I just wanted an excuse. That's all, and a pint of beer."

"Half, Jack. We agreed."

*****

Lunch was a bowl of hot wild mushroom soup served with crusty bread and a shared bowl of crispy whitebait to follow, half a glass of bitter for Jack and a glass of white wine for her.

Katie finished her wine. "Watch this please, Jack. I need to go for a pee." She put her handbag and the paper bag, holding the porcelain cat for Aunt Kathryn on the table in front of him.

Curiosity got the better of him. He took the paper bag in his hand, holding it in front of him and looking down at it. He opened it and removed the tissue paper parcel from inside it.

His eyes dimmed as he peered inside the empty bag. She was there inside it, staring at him, the old lady from the hospital trolley, tears in her eyes, her face still disfigured and bruised from her fall, a sadness that disturbed him. What did she want from him? He had no idea, and then she was gone and a younger violent face took her place, evil etched into her face, fierce dark eyes staring back at him and gone in a flash like the first face. All he could see now was what looked like a black polka dot dress. He clapped his hands together, collapsing the bag just before Katie returned to the table.

"Nosey, couldn't keep out, could you?"

"Just looking. It's nice," he lied to her. The cat was still wrapped in the tissue paper. He put it back inside the bag and gave it back to her. "Ready?"

"Ready. Where are we off to now?" he replied.

"Back to the market if you don't mind. I want to look at the dress material."

Jack laughed, taking her hand. "Let's go."

"I may as well give you this back. I don't think we will be needing it today, do you? It will be dark out there in the Ridings by the time the markets finished." He handed her back the brochure she had given to him on the bus that morning.

"Great Escapes in the East Ridings," he grinned, gently squeezing her arm.

She looked up to him, her eyes full of apologies. "Sorry, Jack. Am I spoiling it for you? You did say it was my day, didn't you?"

"I'm okay but whilst you're looking at dress materials, I will…"

She grabbed his arm in both hands. "You will stay with me and help me choose the fabric for my dress, won't you, Jack? You are not wandering off. Stay here beside me, alright?"

He never had a choice really. He smiled. "You are right. Of course yes. It is your day, so stop worrying about me. I'm fine."

He stared at the figure at the other end of the stall. She was staring at him, her eyes full of evil, wanting revenge. You could see the anger etched in her face, the face that had no meaning for him. Was she trying to tell him something? And almost in an instant she had gone. Was she just another image conjured up by his imagination? He had no idea and that concerned him. *It appears all these events, voices, faces are linked together somehow.* It was more than just coincidence. That much he did believe.

"Jack, are you with me or have you lost interest already?" She waved a fabric in front of him.

"Sorry, I thought I saw somebody I knew, but they had gone before I had chance to say hello," another white lie.

"Who do you know here in Grassington, a secret girlfriend perhaps." She gave him a mischievous grin.

"No, and yes." He looked away from her, his eyes searching the other end of the stall again, seeing if she was still there. *No, I must have imagined it*, he said to himself, disappointed.

"What, Jack?"

"No, I am sorry. There is no mystery girlfriend and, yes, I like the fabric very much."

"Stay with me, Jack." She held up a sample of navy blue fabric to show him. "I thought this would go with it. What do you think?"

"A good contrast a strong colour to balance the patterned fabric. That one there." He pointed to the fabric she had laid out on the stall.

"Are you sure, Jack? You are not just saying that to please me, are you?"

"No, and just so that you know I am telling the truth, I will pay for it. How's that?" He grinned. His apology was lost in his words. She held his arm, looking into his eyes. She smiled, pleased with him. He did care and that meant more than anything to her right now.

"Thanks." She turned to the stallholder. "I will take both of those and the dress pattern. Thank you and these two please.

How much?" She handed him a zip and a button strip to go with the navy-blue fabric and the dress pattern.

Jack paid the stallholder and then she dragged him away two stalls down. Jack was wishing they were out in the open countryside getting some fresh air and exercise. They had both been in short supply since his accident.

"Cotton reels and needles." She handed them to the lady to wrap. "Why didn't you buy those at that last stall? He had the same thing, didn't he?"

"Not quite, Jack. He never had the right price. That was his problem. He's better with fabric. The other girl, she is cheaper on the accessories, so I buy from both. That is what shopping is all about, Jack. I thought you would at least had learnt that much in the last six years." She grinned. "Come on. It's time for a cuppa. Let's pop in the plough. They serve tea in there on market day and most of the people will have left by now, so it will be nice and cosy in there. Dad always took me in there whilst you were off with your head in the bookshops with mother. Remember?"

"Shopping, is it? You could have done all that down at our warehouse and it would have saved us both money. That's thinking before you shop, Katie."

"Stealing, you mean, from the taxman," she frowned.

"Yes, you can look at it like that. I know what you say is true. I just do not want it that way. My clothes are mine and I only want to share them when I am wearing them, not whilst I'm stealing the materials to make them."

"I'm not going there. That is your choice."

"Good. That is the end of that then."

"Well, that's your excuse. I will have a pint of beer and no arguments please, before you dare say another word and that's that. You've had your fun. Now let me have mine for a change," he grinned back.

She squeezed his hand. "I love you, Jack Cambridge."

"You too, mother."

"Well, have you enjoyed your day? Got everything you need?"

"A woman never gets everything she needs. There is always something she can't afford, wants but cannot make her mind up, or forgets entirely but I am happy it has been a nice day together, just the two of us. That is the most important thing. Sorry, I have dragged you all around today. Ah, here's your pint of beer."

"Table 6, one pot of tea with an almond slice and one pint of Stringers Bitter for you, sir," she said in a cheerful manner.

"Will there be anything else, sir?"

"No, that will be all. Thank you very much," Jack replied with a smile.

"Thank you," she replied, returning his smile. "You've still got an eye for the ladies, I see. Your accident hasn't stopped that, not that you were the chasing kind, too busy making a success for yourself. Dad would have been so proud of you, you know."

"Oh, I don't know that to be true. You were always his favourite. And now I have you looking after me, will I be your favourite?"

"There is no 'will be' at all. You are my favourite. You are all I have got. That's how much you mean to me." She touched his arm. "I know, and I love you too," she smiled.

"Would you like to stop in town tonight and have a meal? I thought perhaps we could go to The Owl and Coot. They do a very nice American noodle dish that you enjoyed the last time we ate there. Put your beer down and give me an answer please."

"I will let you know after we get back to Skepton. Depends whether I fall asleep on the bus on the way back or not."

He grinned.

The bus left on time.

Jack took a window seat half way down the bus, Katie taking the seat beside him. "You can catch fifty winks if you want. I will be boring and put my head in this dress pattern. I don't suppose that will interest you. It's a girly thing."

Jack turned in his seat, facing the window. He closed his eyes trying to relax but the voices and faces invaded his mind, blocking out all his other thoughts. He opened his eyes and there in the dim evening light were the faces dancing about in the bus window, the voices shouting and screaming at him, making no sense. His body froze and for the first time he was frightened. The garbled messages and the images somehow were threatening him. He closed his eyes. He opened his eyes but the noises in his head just got louder and that is all he could remember. He closed his eyes as the invaders had taken control of his body and his mind.

Katie was too busy with her dress pattern to have noticed anything. That is until she saw his clenched fists, their knuckles white, caused by the pressure of his grip. It scared her then. She told herself that he was asleep, perhaps having a bad dream and there was nothing for her to be frightened about. She returned to the dress pattern, keeping an eye on him in case he had another turn.

Jack lifted his head, a thumping headache and stiff neck. His whole body bathed in sweat, his thighs hurting from the cramp, rubbing them to ease the pain, his mind trying to keep up with his body. His thoughts were all over the place. He could not concentrate, and it showed in his face.

"Are you okay, Jack? You look in pain. What's the matter? Tell me?"

"Katie, it's nothing just a touch of cramp. That is all. I should have sat upright instead of sitting with my body all twisted towards the window. It's my own fault and there is nothing for you to worry yourself about. I'll be fine as soon as the cramp eases. Did you make your dress?" He lied to her. He was in severe pain and his head was throbbing. He just needed to keep his calm and hope it passes before the bus arrives at the station.

"Jack, it's only a dress pattern. I won't be wearing it tonight, so don't worry. Do you still fancy the Owl & Coot for supper?"

"Okay, if that is what you would like. It's a date then."

*****

The taxi dropped them at the bottom of the drive, Jack laden with the day's shopping and a pocket full of receipts. 'Not bad for a day out walking,' he said to himself as Katie opened the door.

"Don't stand on that, Jack. Mind your step. Someone has slipped a letter under the door. I wonder who that's from. It must be urgent," she said, bending down to pick it up.

"Just drop those things over there, Jack, by the door. I will look at them later." She was too busy ripping open the envelope someone had left. "Jack, that's all it said." She didn't even look at who it was addressed to. She just wanted to find out what they wanted whoever they were.

"What does it say?" Jack now got interested in the contents of the envelope. "Who is it from, Katie?"

"The envelope is addressed to me." He took the torn envelope from her hand. She was still busy reading the letter.

*****

Chapter 31
Digital Decadence

HIDE AND SEEK HOLLOW:

It was five o'clock. Jack was laying the breakfast table, two orange juices, two yoghurts and toast with Strawberry jam. No, it's real life. Proper breakfast would be served at six thirty in the offices of JACKatie Enterprises Limited, a working breakfast discussing the launch of the Decadence Range to be followed by the filming of the floor show and the showing the first draft of the Decadence website.

Jack had stayed up late preparing himself for the meeting. Katie had fallen asleep watching a Rom Com. They said their goodnight at eleven o'clock.

"Set your alarm, Katie, for five o'clock sharp," he shouted to her as he passed the bathroom door before hitting the pillow himself. It had been a long day.

"Goodnight" came the reply just as he was opening his bedroom door. His mind went blank as he held the door knob. He felt dizzy but managed to force himself inside the room, pulling the door shut behind him before throwing himself on to his bed, his head full of flashing lights and voices screaming at him.

He held his breath hoping the voices would go away but that only made things worse. He blacked out, his mind a total blank. He would remember nothing of the incident in the morning.

"Hi, coffee?"

"Oh, yes please. I can't even remember going to bed last night. It was that silly film I was watching, complete rubbish," Katie replied.

"Well, you were well away; did you sleep okay?"

"Like a log. I must have needed it. Looking after you seems to be a full-time job these days," she laughed, giving him a warm smile.

"Well, not for much longer now. You will be able to get back to your routine at university before you realise it. I'm feeling confident that I will get the okay to return back to work next week or the week after," he replied, returning her smile as he finished a slice of toast spread thick with strawberry jam. He drank the last of his coffee as he got up from the table.

"Five minutes, Katie. That's all the time you have left, so hurry up. I will see you in the car and don't forget to lock up and set the alarm. We have got a busy day ahead of us," he shouted as the front door shut behind him.

Katie got in the car fixing her seat belt. "I hope you are ready for a long day, are you?" he smiled.

"Yes, I'm fine. Thank you, Jack. You just worry about yourself. After all, you are the invalid, not me." She grinned, seeing the funny side of the situation. She was excited, a first for her this film shoot and he will be there. Her heartbeat began to race away with her thoughts, her face showing her feelings which did not go unnoticed by Jack.

"I hope you are not thinking of flirting with one of my staff, are you?"

She blushed. "You are just wanting to get your own back, aren't you? Because of your boyish outburst with Pinky yesterday." She was annoyed.

"Don't do that, Katie. This is the second time I have had to mention this. Stop being disrespectful to her and let this be the last time I have to tell you off about it. Just behave, can you?" He raised his voice.

"Don't let start the day like this. I have been looking forward to it all week, so can we put all this behind us and be friends again?" He stared at her, wanting a reply.

"I'm so sorry, Jack. That was silly of me. You know I always let it annoy me when you talk about him like that. There is nothing between us I promise."

Jack was not convinced, and her blushes agreed with him. "I will be watching you but don't worry. I am not against your flirting. I will just see how things go between the two of you before I make my final judgement. After all, I am responsible for you and I love you and I will look out for you and you need to know I am always there for you, do you understand?"

She took his hand. "I love you too, Jack. Thank you. I know how much you care and it makes me feel secure. I'm just a silly girl sometimes. Forgive me please." Her eyes made her apology.

"I do." He gently squeezed her hand.

"Let's make this a special day. I'm a partner, now aren't I?" she replied, giving him a big smile.

"Is that official then? You really mean it, do you?"

"Yes, of course I do," she grinned, happy with him, happy with herself.

"Good morning, Jack. Katie on time, I see." Chris had been waiting for them.

"Am I ever late, Chris?"

"No," he laughed, smiling at Katie, a flirty smile.

Jack walked closer to his side. "This is a working day, Christopher. Okay?"

"Yes, I do understand, Jack. Don't worry. I will give you my all as usual." He frowned, having his arse kicked never pleased him but he understood. Jack was work, work and pleasure would only find a place after that.

Katie looked the other way, avoiding them. She knew exactly what Jack was telling him. She frowned, a little disappointed, a little embarrassed, a slight blushing of her cheeks giving her away, revealing her true feelings.

The team was waiting, five minutes early; that pleased Jack, a dedicated team. It made him feel good.

Eric took the chair. "Before we start breakfast, can I just have your attention please everybody?" he turned, facing Jack. "Welcome back, Jack. Welcome home." They all clapped. Katie blushed, proud of her brother. Her eyes did not forget Chris.

The doors opened, and breakfast was declared ready.

"Please help yourself to the buffet breakfast. Coffee will be served at the table." Chris was ready for the day ahead.

*****

Jack waited for everyone to be seated before he spoke.

"I am glad to be back, unofficially that is today, but it is definitely good for me to see you all here this morning, so let me begin. Firstly, can we discuss a couple of issues that have cropped up in the last few of days?"

"Eric, I was talking last night with Yang Li about the new Autumn Ranges we want her to produce later in the year and she mentioned she had asked for clarification on a couple of issues, so can we start there please?"

"It is nothing serious, Jack. She wanted clarification on range sizes. She pointed out something we have discussed amongst ourselves here many times and it concerns the size range, mainly the larger sizes we have asked for this year and I have yet to get back to her. I wanted us all to discuss it this morning. I considered that our best option. The other issue was cash flow projections for next year. She is concerned about our growth rate I think, and again that is something we can discuss here this morning and then I can put our explanations together over the weekend for your approval, Jack."

"Thanks, Eric," he paused, deciding who to engage with first. "Barry, talk to us about sizes. What is the final decision there?"

"Thanks, Jack. Glad you are back by the way. Let me just point out the obvious first. As you all know over the last five years, we have often been caught out with under sizing particular ranges. This happened again with the poppy range earlier this year. There are two influences, one, people are growing bigger, two, some students are taking advantage of our pricing structures and purchasing for the family and extended family and friends on far too many occasions for it to be anything other than deliberate purchasing. It most certainly is not incidental, good for business but we discussed the downside to increase in sales, our image, what importance do we have to attach to that. Let's talk about that please." He opened his folder ready for questions.

"Thank you, Barry. Let me deal with growth first. As you are all aware I have not been too idle during my convalescence, Katie has minimised my work time. That is something I cannot hide. It has been in my own best interests I might add but I did find time to discuss the issues with Eric and Barry and between us. We have come up with a strategy that will satisfy Yang Li and at the same time support our growth. Eric has done a brilliant job and takes this year's juggling honours. Don't worry, Eric. I will make sure you do not get another bouquet like the one you won last year for progressive management." Jack grinned. Everyone laughed. The comedy had begun.

"Barry and his team. Well, what can we say? Two thirds of our forecasted sales have already been taken up and that is before the first yard of fabric has been produced and cut. That is a fantastic achievement. Now it is down to all of you to make sure we deliver on costs, quality and on time."

"Can we do it? Of course we can. That is what we are good at. Who wants the floor next?" Jack sat down.

Chris took up the challenge as expected, and a half hour later had the answers to Yang Li's questions. He would finalise the rest of the report over the weekend and report back to Jack.

"Eric, call me on Sunday evening, early if possible. Then you and I can agree on everything. Then I would like you to take over and speak with Yang Li. I will be at the hospital on Monday, but we cannot delay in sending her the information, so we need to talk to each other."

"I will talk to Yang Li on Sunday evening, Eric, anyway. And tell her to expect your call, just CC me your report. I will find time to read it whilst I am waiting for my appointment at the hospital. I am sure you are all familiar with those kinds of situations."

"Will do, Jack. I hate mowing the lawns." He grinned. Everyone was amused. The comments kept coming.

"It's time to move on to the main event, the reason why we have all been summoned here today, the filming of the floor show. So, Chris, now is your big moment. Off you go. Tell us all about it please." His eyes were watching Katie. He smiled. He was having mixed thoughts.

Chris took the floor. His eyes immediately looking across at her and then back to Jack.

"The filming will take place in the staging room and you will all be given a copy of the working brief which outlines the parameters and guidelines for this eight-minute extravaganza. During discussions and briefings held with the film makers small improvements have been introduced, allowing for a more flexible approach to be made. I am sure I will have your approval, but let's wait and see, shall we? You are the audience and the verdict will be yours. So if you would all like to follow me to the staging room, everything should be ready. Enjoy. You will definitely be surprised. I can assure you."

Everyone was given a copy of the working brief as they entered the room. The film crew and the company workforce were seated along with guests and representatives of the press and television channels, awaiting their arrival. Barry had done his homework, lots of familiar faces, smiles and waves. 'That's a good sign,' Jack said to himself.

"Wow, you've got my attention already, Chris. Well done."

Everyone took their seats as the music began, a rhapsody sung by Manhattan Transfer, "A little street in Singapore." Jack smiled a very happy smile. They had paid a great deal of attention to the brief.

The eight minutes were over a breath-taking experience in Jack's words. The champagne corks popped. Everyone had been excited by the floor show. Its content and execution was brilliant, breath-taking, a joy to watch.

The first thing Jack did was to ask Chris to introduce him to the Film Director Felicity Sorrel and her team. "Brilliant felicity. My thanks. I am sure this won't be the last floor show you will do for us. Please call me next week. I would like to talk to you about our next project, just between the two of us that is. I am sure you understand."

Jack and Katie spent the next couple of hours meeting the Press and TV and his guests from the London crowd, Barry was flying. The whole thing had been a personal success for him and his team. He was up there, somewhere on cloud number?

Finally, the show was over. Jack and Katie said goodbye to their guest and broke up for a sandwich lunch.

"What did you think, Jack? Were they impressed? Do you think?"

"Yes, they were and just as importantly, our own people were knocked over by it and that is a good feeling. Is everything ready for the debriefing?"

"Of course, as soon as this lot is cleared away, I will get underway. Is that okay with you?"

"It's all yours, Barry. You take over from Chris and the floor is all yours. I just want to see the website please, after I have made my comments about the floor show that is."

*****

Lunch came to an end and the chaos and conversations subsided. Jack took the floor.

The meeting was restricted to the key players. Everybody else had taken the gossip back to their own departments and low-key discussions had begun, business as usual. The switchboard was already humming, and it wouldn't be long before stories hit the evening papers, a job well done.

"Well, what can I say to that? I would not know where to start, so I will make one small criticism. Can you believe that, a criticism? It could only come from me."

"The floor, Chris. No, I don't want it." The room fell silent, everybody looking at each other. 'Who will get the blame?' was written into their faces.

"I want a plain floor. Perhaps the words Decadence and Extravaganza could be evident in small doses across the floor, as it exists. It does nothing except distract your attention from the show itself. Its apparel, shoes and accessories, we are selling not MFI tiles, so get rid and come up with something for the final take. It's going nowhere until that is done is that clear?" Jack looked across to Barry and Chris. Floor was too busy.

"Let's leave that there and show me this website please."

"Is everything alright, Jack?" Katie whispered. She was concerned. Something had upset him.

"No, Katie. I know exactly what I want and how to get it. You will learn that over the next couple of years. I learnt the hard way, by my mistakes. Hopefully you will not have to go through that. It hurts, hurts a lot." He smiled, "I'm okay."

The website presentation took exactly seven minutes and that was the only part that was correct. Jack was bloody fuming, angry as they were all about to find out.

Jack stood up and it was obvious he was not happy, everyone could see his anger in his face.

"Great, seven minutes. That's the only fucking thing I can be pleased with. What happened to the brief? Nobody has listened to a word I said. You would wonder what the fuck we were doing, and I am one very unhappy man and I will try and explain my feelings, make sure you all listen very carefully because you have six days to get it right. I just can't allow this crap to go live. It's a bloody disgrace."

"Let me steer you in the right direction because at the end of the day, you will do as I ask. We, JACKatie Enterprises, sell apparel, footwear and accessories but so do another top ten fashion houses, not including competition from China, Bangladesh India and another twenty or so countries dotted around the globe. I could name each one of them after our business and what do we dish up? The same fucking crap we get from our competitors."

"I have spent several weeks going website after website until I have got Google eyes, boring yes but necessary. This is what you get, a moveable copy of a Mail Order Catalogue and that is not what I want and it is not what I am going to have. What you have to do to make it work is to listen to what I am looking for because it is obvious from this crap version nobody understood or listened to my brief, so I will start again and you better all pay attention."

"Think about USPs. Start there then. Open your minds. It's all their waiting for you to put it all together for God's sake."

"The theme is Decadence hence the name; Art Nouveau is the background the music is melody, my favourites, Manhattan transfer and TUXEDO JUNCTION even The Drifters. You can't really expand on that in the time frame, so put me something together that has a flow about it. You have all been looking from a white background, this colour, these size charts and God knows what. Play all that down, put it in the right place and when you have done all that, then you can begin to sell the Decadence Range."

"Let's begin, a dress a pair of shoes a belt, handbag underwear, bras, pants, get excited, upsell. Tell them what we have got that is what they want to see, add the music and graphics and you will have something that will captivate your target audiences, make things more appealing. Don't just sell them a dress. Sell them everything, get them interested and buying from us, then they will all be talking about us.
Seven days, ladies and gentlemen. Do not disappoint me."

Jack and Katie left the room. The team was picking themselves up off the floor, as 'Bollockings' go, that was big and he meant every word. Let's grab some coffee and talk about it. He's right. I have to admit that when it's spelt out like that it is obvious and I take the blame and I don't like that, so I know we can do better.' Chris led them out of the room. Nobody was very happy but that is how days go sometimes.

*****

Chapter 32
Life Begins Again

It seemed like a lifetime. Bill struggled to pull his thoughts together. He looked at his watch, almost six o'clock.

He's had her knickers down. That was his game from the very beginning. He's always fancied her. In fact this lunch could have been catch-up for all he knew.

Linda came in with a tray of coffee, wanting to harvest the latest gossip. What happened up there these last two days, she wanted to know. She put the tray down on his desk.

"I have put you a couple of biscuits on the tray. I thought you might be feeling a little peckish. Will she be back today? She was fishing, throwing her line in at the deep end," she smiled.

"Who knows, Linda? She could be anywhere. I'm not sure. She didn't say."

"Shall I?" She pointed to the spare cup.

He frowned. "Help yourself. You are working late this evening. Any special reason?" He knew the answer to his question of course. She blushed then. The lies began.

"I am just playing catch-up. That's all. Wondering if my new appointment has been agreed. Belinda did say she will let me know today but it looks like she has been delayed, kept busy. I saw her leaving with Mr Clifton just after lunch." She was shit stirring now, rubbing it in and enjoying every minute of it but his turn would come sooner than she realised.

"Linda, I have approved your new position but please let me remind you. Corporate is exactly that and it does well to keep your personal views close to your chest if you get my meaning. Close the door on the way out. I still have a lot of work to finish, catch up, isn't it?" He was angry, pissed off and she left the office with her tray, without saying another word.

His cell phone rang. "Belinda," he paused. "I am in the car park, Bill, two minutes." The phone went dead. He was confused. He shuffled the papers on his desk for the umpteenth time this afternoon, thinking of what to say to her. He told himself to let her do the talking, always safer that way he had learnt to regret many feet first conversations with her over the years. Today, he would keep his gob shut, wondering if she had been opening her legs to the dirty fucker she had lunch with, or did they have lunch? 'Did they have time to eat?' he asked himself.

The door swung open. Belinda waltzed in almost out of breath. "Hi, Bill. Sorry I'm late. Can I have a drink please? I feel exhausted. I hope that is not for the same reason I have been thinking of all afternoon. Whiskey?" He handed her the glass.

She frowned. "Not joining me?"

"Should I?"

"Don't fight me, Bill. If only you knew what kind of an afternoon I have had, you would not be questioning me like that."

"I'm not questioning you. It's that guy you have been with. I knew exactly what his intentions were. Did he get his own way?"

"That's fucking low, Bill, and you know it is." She was angry she wanted to hit him.

Bill looked away, reminding himself what he should have said. *Nothing,* exactly that but jealousy spoke for him now. It was time for regret.

"Fuck me, Belinda. You have been gone for hours. What do you expect me to think?"

"Not the fucking same as everybody else is thinking. For God's sake, nothing happened. To begin with, we were gate crashed by Roger. He was determined to spoil everything for Rupert. He had dropped David at the station and came to the restaurant to settle things with him. I was just the silly girl in the middle of it all. The meal was crap. The company was horrible. You had to be there to witness the bitterness of it all and I just gave up saying my farewells and grabbing a taxi and heading for home. I was even too shook up to call you. I just wanted you to cuddle me and here I am hating you right now. You are as bad those two. Is that what I can expect being Corporate? Because if it is, I'm out." She broke down in tears.

"God! Why do I always do it? Come here."

"No, Bill. I am going back home. I've had enough for one day. I even went home to change for dinner with you this evening. Now look at me." Bill couldn't find the words. *Shut up. Keep quiet. Let her go and calm down. Then pop around to hers later,* he told himself as the door slammed shut behind her.

*****

It was dark by the time he got there, a call to Jill keeping his card clean he hoped. He too had a crap day well sort of, most of it of his own making. Now he was hoping she would answer the door.

Belinda opened the door. She had been expecting him. She had dressed for sex, a silk dressing gown that hid nothing except her sexy underwear already wet from her expectations she had been playing with herself, desperate to feel him inside her. Her nipples gave her away. She didn't care. She just wanted dirty sex and a good hard fucking. She could already taste him.

"Hi, I knew you would come." She kissed him, inviting him in, taking the bottle of Chablis from him and closing the door behind him. She turned the key. He was hers, at least for tonight that is. She smiled to herself.

"She didn't give him time to speak. That would come later. You made me very angry, Bill, and now I am very horny. Fuck me. That's what I need. We can talk about our future afterwards but right now, I want you inside me," she pulled her dressing gown open, teasing him, showing him her pussy, purring, wanting inside her thong.

He pulled her to him. "Feel me," he said, excitedly taking her hand, wanting her to feel his hardness.

"Oh my God! Bill, look how big you are. That's what I want," she gasped, struggling with his belt, her greedy eyes wanting his big prick. As she began pulling his trousers down, he was kicking off his shoes.

God, I have never been this hard before, he said to himself, holding his prick in his hand ready to guide it between her legs. It would find its own way inside her. She would be very wet. She always was.

"God! Bill, just fuck me. Fuck me hard. We can play with each other afterwards. I just need you inside me." She took his prick in her hand, guiding him inside her. "Hard, Bill. Fuck me hard." Bill was inside her now like a rampant Bull, pounding her groin, satisfying her screams of lust as he slurped away inside her. "Ah, ah, you fucker. I'm coming. Harder, Bill, harder." She pushed herself on to his shaft like a desperate whore. He orgasmed as he forced himself deep inside her. "Oh God! Bill, that's good," she screamed as she felt the warmth of his orgasm inside her. They kissed, pulling himself away from her. She fell to her knees, taking him inside her mouth just catching the dribbles of his orgasm. She sucked him hard, greedily as he tried to pull away from her. He couldn't bear the tingling sensation. He pulled down harder, forcing her to let go. He gasped with excitement.

"That tasted nice. I want it fully load next time. A dribble is not enough. That's how much I like it, you naughty boy, big boy. Look at you, your massive prick. I hope you intend to fuck me all night." He was lost for words. Never had he experienced anything like it, a new woman. He wanted more of the same. *This was bullshit of course, fifty thousand pounds worth.*

"It's your turn now. Lick me clean." She sat on the stool with her legs spread apart, waiting for his mouth to taste her juices. He had to hurry to catch her fluids dribbling from her. He slurped hard first time, and then began licking her.

"Fucking hell! That's good. Keep going. I'm ready to come," she shouted, arching her back as she moaned, "Ah, ah, ah, you bastard. Get inside me. I need to feel you." Bill just did as he was told, like a sex slave. He had never had a helping this big before and he was enjoying every minute of it.

Belinda took the opened bottle of Chiraz from the fridge, pouring two glasses. They needed them. They were both bathed in sweat, blushed skin and panting like naughty puppies, shagged you could say.

"That was good, fucking good. Show me. Let me look at you." She spread her legs apart, her lips glistened with his come still dripping from her. She ran her fingers inside before taking them to her mouth, sucking hard, dirty sex. She gave Bill his share. He bit her fingers. She stirred her wine with her sticky fingers, then started sucking them like a baby's dummy stirring his dirty mind. Bill wanted her again. She wanted him. Where would the night take them?

*****

"I suppose we better eat. I'm starving. How about you?" She gave him a dirty smile.

"Later. You can play with me whilst I cook us something and if you are a really naughty boy, you can play with pussy whilst we eat."

Bill's eyes gave him away, although she found it very difficult to concentrate her thoughts properly. She was too busy looking at his prick dangling down between his big balls. She wanted more of that starting with her mouth. She was beginning to get wet again. She couldn't help herself. Then Julie's naked body flashed in front of her eyes. She went down on her knees, taking him inside her mouth, a generous sucking followed by a chorus of dirty words as she stood facing him.

"That's what days of waiting and wanting does for you, Bill. It's never been this good and I doubt it ever will be again, so let's make the most of it, shall we? Omelette, that's about all we will have time for, isn't it?" She gave him a begging smile.

He smiled, horny and fucked. He was still trying to get his mind working at the same pace as his sex drive.

"I don't know if that is the answer but give me as much as you've got. I like it when you are being this dirty. Come here. Let me feel you." She turned, facing the grill as he slipped his hand between her legs, feeling her swollen lips drenched in her come. He stroked her clitoris as she pushed her bottom against his groin, striking a rhythm, ready to orgasm. She swore like a whore, screaming as her orgasm gripped her body. She pulled herself downwards, forcing his hand away. "You fucker. It's never ever been this fucking good." Lust rolled around in her eyes. She was exhausted. It was the omelette that was fucked next.

They sat around the table laughing, gulping each other's wine, talking dirty, whispering until the bottle was empty. Bill opened the Chablis and the orgy started all over again.

It was four o'clock. The cockerel could be heard. Another day had begun.

Bill left the house to go home, shower and change, an early start. Belinda would be late and that is about all he could remember before they dragged themselves upstairs to bed. Sometime unknown, it had been a dirty day all round. He smiled.

*****

Chapter 33
Yang Li

HIDE AND SEEK HOLLOW:
Jack's mobile rang. He had been enjoying the sunshine in the garden, relaxing, reading the Sunday morning tabloids, a glass of shandy, his sister, her head buried in a woman's magazine, the odd giggle, the occasional stop for another round of sunblock oil.

Jack sprang to his feet, watching Katie as she put down her magazine, her eyes wanting to know who was calling him. He turned away from her.

"Hi, you are through to Jack. How can I help you?" He knew who it was. He just wanted to annoy Katie, nosey Katie. Mother. He grinned, enjoying every minute of it.

"Hi Yang Li. Sorry, I was just teasing my sister, Katie. How are you, good I hope?"

"Hi, Jack. Good morning. Yes, I am very well. Thank you. I just thought I would call you about the New Autumn Ranges you asked Eric have send us. We need to chat. Is now a good time, you say?"

"You say that beautifully, Yang Li. Don't you? Of course we can talk. You know I am always available for you, day or night, should you wish to call me. What is it that you want?"

"Jack, you are so kind to me. I just wanted to chat about the New Ranges and the new batch of orders for the Poppy Range that Eric has mailed me."

"I love you Jack Martin."

"Me too."

"You do realise the volumes and costs. We are still pulling everything together and trying to come up with a workable forecast, so I cannot promise you will have our final costs and delivery schedules until the end of this week. We still have a lot of work to do and we have raised a couple of important issues with Eric's team. Will that be happy for you?"

"Yang Li, that's fine. I will talk with Eric so there will be no kisses this time around. You still owe me three, remember?"

"How do you say that English word, stingy is that a correct word, Jack?"

"Let's say something like but that is as far as I am prepared to go," he laughed.

"Jack, you tease me. I am serious, kiss or no kiss, this is a business call. If you want to chat up, you should call me on my private number. Have you got it? No, because I have not given to you." She laughed. "You make me funny, Jack. Would you like it?"

"Don't you think that is something we should talk about on your private number?" he replied.

"Let me think about it. I am a woman, so you will wait." She was blushing now. *Have I gone too far?* she asked herself.

"The figures will do fine as long as I have them on Friday. I need to work on them and present my findings at a Board meeting scheduled for Monday and I will probably have several questions to ask you. Will you be available at the weekend I presume?"

"Thank you, Jack. Yes, of course. I will be here or you can get me on my private number (138766887619), although I am sure you will like my proposals and costings. Then I will demand another kiss. See, you cannot get away that easy."

"Perhaps I do not want to get away. Have you considered that?" He wanted her for the very first time. His heartbeat told him how much he wanted her.

Katie looked shocked.

"Until the next time, Jack. I have sent you a kiss on the wind, my regards best. Goodnight."

Jack put his phone down and took a sip of shandy, knowing Katie would now have a lot to say to him. He felt embarrassed, so he jumped in the deep end first.

"Before you tell me off, I apologise. Perhaps I went too far. I am sorry." He looked down at the grass, a little ashamed of himself.

"Jack, my brother, you flirt. You should have listened to yourself if you do not fancy her. I am a Dutch man, you flirt," she repeated herself. "Look at me, Jack. Stop being silly. You have nothing to be ashamed of. I am just surprised I never knew you had it in you."

"Was it that bad, that obvious?"

"That is for you to decide. All I know is she fancies you like mad and you just, well, I can't think of the words to describe your feelings. Wow! Am glad I am your sister."

"Jack Cambridge, I love you."

"Me too."

"That's too far now. You can do supper."

"Okay, I have embarrassed you and myself, so I won't make the same mistake again and I am truly sorry. You did not deserve that, entirely my fault."

"Jack, thanks. It's not all doom and gloom. Half of that conversation was her way of giving you her private number. For heaven's sake, she knew I would be listening. You told her yourself, so you have only yourself to blame, you silly boy. She was coming on to you big time." Jack put his hands up in the air, his cheeks a bright pink colour. His eyes sparkled in the sunshine.

"What's for tea?" Katie threw her magazine at him. He ducked out of the way, bursting with laughter. She joined in. "You sod," she continued, laughing, chasing him around the lawn…

*****

Chapter 34
Landlord

Jack and Katie held hands from the minute they left the consulting rooms of Professor Martin until she put the key in the car door. They didn't even want to look back. Jack held his sick certificate tightly in his free hand. They could not hide their happiness almost running away with joy and excitement down the long unending corridors of the Skepton General Hospital.

Jack had been given a clean bill of health following his second MRI scan and was told he was fit enough to return to work. His only conditions were to complete his course of subscribed medications and return for a reassessment in three months' time.

They both sat in their seats, laughing. "Give me a big hug, Jack Cambridge and tell me you love me." He kissed her cheek, smiling, happy.

"I love you, Katie Cambridge." She sighed with relief.

"Thank goodness that it's all over. I can't quite believe it yet, can you?"

"Yes, I can. I told you everything would turn out okay, didn't I?"

"Yes, you did. Now can we go somewhere for lunch and celebrate please, Jack?" she replied, squeezing his hand.

"Can I just say a big thank you because without you, I would not be here. You know that and as a thank-you present, I have decided to give you HIDE AND SEEK HOLLOW as a gift and before you say anything, I have made my mind up but you will have to put up with me as a lodger until I find a place of my own, would you mind?"

Tears flooded down her cheeks, "You can't do that, Jack. I won't let you. There is no need. You will regret it one day and I will never forgive myself for accepting your gift."

"Well, that won't wash. I know you have always set your heart on it belonging to you one day ever since we came to look at it with mum and dad. It's yours and I am not taking no for an answer." He gave her a generous smile.

"It's far too big for me anyway. It is a family house, you and two kids, a dog and a cat and him of course when you find him that is."

She laughed. "When you approve of him you mean," she frowned. "Mum and Dad would have been so happy for us both. Thank you, Jack. Let's go, otherwise I will sit here crying all afternoon."

They celebrated at the Goose and Feathers, a simple pub lunch of mushroom soup with whitebait to follow and a glass of champagne each.

Jack spent most of his time smiling, happy to be here with her, his landlady. He burst out laughing. "I want a rent book you know. Everything needs to be done properly."

She punched his ribs. "You'll be lucky, Jack, the lodger."

*****

Jack and Katie could not wait to share their good news.

"Chris, good morning. How are things back there?"

"Hi Jack, never mind us. How did you get on that's far more important don't you think?" he replied.

"A clean bill of health, Chris. I am pleased to say I am okay to return to work next week, so you still have the helm until then. Tell me how the rework of the Decadence website is going. Is it going?" There was a pause.

"Exactly, Jack. We have decided to start from scratch. The team has been working on it since your bollockings. It hurt them Jack and me, everybody. Actually if I am honest, I won't say it was not justified but it hurt nevertheless and we have put it behind us now. It's forgotten. I will make sure you are pleased with the new version; will you be free on Friday for a preview I hope?"

"I would not miss it for the world. We will be there. I will bring Katie along with me. She needs to be involved in these decisions. Now she is a director of the company."

"Good. We definitely can't let you down then, eh?"

"That's the spirit, Chris. Please ask Eric and Barry to call me," he replied.

"Thank you, Jack. I will. See you and Katie on Friday then." He sounded excited at just the mention of her name. Jack smiled to himself.

No, she is not ready yet.

*****

CERAMIC 5 Offices Skepton:

"Good morning, Belinda, and how are you?"

"Bill, you are late, any particular reason?" she replied.

"It's not you. That's all you are very rarely late, so what happened? Those two I suppose," she frowned.

"You got it in one, breakfast with Rupert and Roger, two mardy arses. I can tell you it was not easy listening to them calling David. It was bad. In fact the pair of them are just bad losers and they will never accept it but I suppose I have no doubt things will be back to normal by the end of the week. I have already heard from David. He has approved my seat on the Board, a formality he called it and sends you his regards. You have good allies there I can tell you. I have ordered coffee for the two of us. We could play catch up before this evening," he grinned.

She wasn't sure whether it was him talking or his dick. No doubt she will find out sooner or later.

"Congratulations, I shall expect champagne of course," she laughed, offering him her hand. He warmly accepted it, squeezing her hand, his eyes telling her his thoughts.

"So, what's next for us two, any ideas?" he paused, wanting time to think.

"Let's have coffee. Then we can talk. I need to make a couple of quick calls, five minutes. Keep the coffee hot." He turned and left the office.

Keep things at arms-length for the time being. See how things work out before you make any promises, he told himself as he walked back to his office. That wasn't what his dick was telling him. By the time he sat in his chair, he was almost erect, his dirty mind working overtime.

Belinda sat in her chair deep in thought when the coffee arrived followed by Bill. "That was quick?"

"David. That's all, and Jill asking if I am okay. She says she will be back Sunday night." He grinned.

"Of course, my dear. I will be fine."

"I know what you are thinking. It's written all over your face, playtime. That's what has got your attention now they have all gone back to head office but believe me it's not. We need to talk about other things first before we start playing." She finished her coffee. Bill was confused as always. *Since becoming Corporate, she has had a change of heart. It's all about 'how much' now.*

"I don't get it. What's wrong now?" He looked angry.

"Think about it, Bill, not with your dick. I am serious. We need to talk about you and me. Neville's gone. So you have got me all to yourself but only if you play your cards right, I will not be a pushover. I start my new job, so things are going to change. That is what we need to talk about, Bill. Shagging will come later. Close the door. We will do it now." Her stare told him he had very little say in the matter.

"I suppose you better start by telling me what you really want. Can we sort things out? Do you think?" He frowned. The anger had gone from his eyes.

"How serious are you about me, Bill? Will you leave Jill?" *She was lying. Fifty grand is what she had in mind and then he could fuck off. That was her immediate plan, laying on her back getting fucked was the easy bit. After all, she had her needs and masturbating was not the answer. Julie perhaps. No, my new lover. That's what I want.*

"Yes, I will but only when the time is right. You need to understand that. It is not in either of our interest to jump in with both feet. We need to think the whole thing through properly. Don't you think?" She was surprised. *He's lying. He just wants me for sex. That's his game.*

"Are you lying to me, Bill?" Her look told him how surprised she was.

"I expected you to say that. I just knew you would say something like that, but yes, I am serious. In fact, I have been thinking about it for some time, even before you split up with Neville. Jill and I just amble along. We put up with each other's faults. That's the best way of putting it whereas with you, I feel good when I am around you. Don't you feel the same?"

The dollar wheels were spinning. *The lies will be coming thick and fast. Now I can't turn back. I have come too far already.*

"Yes, I do but I have problems now which need sorting before I do anything. You have got to understand that, Bill. Neville leaving as quickly as he did put me in the shit really. I don't suppose you realised that, didn't you?" He was confused now, his brain doing overtime.

"Tell me. I'm all mixed up. What do you mean?" He was hooked. She looked all sad for greater effect.

"I did not get my mortgage. The bank refused my application in a round-about way. I need to wait six months. It's my new job that has messed things up. I need fifty thousand to pay Neville his share of the house and I have not got enough in my savings. I only have the equity in the house but without the bank giving me a mortgage, there is not much I can do about it." Her face had flushed. She told lies easily. She was used to it. There was no guilt on her part.

"Can't Neville wait? Have you talked to him about it?" The anger had returned. This is not how he wanted it to be.

"It's not Neville, Bill. It's me. I want things over and done with. Then I can concentrate on you and me. Otherwise, I won't have my heart in it and that would just be a recipe for disaster before we begin our new relationship. There is no alternative. I have thought of nothing else over the past few weeks. There is no other way, Bill. I am sorry. Perhaps we should call it a day." His face was on the floor. He was speechless. He stormed out of the office.

Well, that's fucked everything unless he just needs time to think. His dick will be telling him what to do. After all, I just need to keep him stiff until he hands over the cash. She grinned, 'Him and dick will be back.' She poured herself another coffee, smiling to herself.

*****

HIDE AND SEEK HOLLOW:

Jack took the call on his cell phone. "Hi Barry. Good morning. How are you?"

"I'm good, Jack. Glad to hear your good news. Chris tells me you're due back in the office next Monday. That is the good news we have all been waiting for. I have spoken to Yang Li and she is fine and has promised to have her report by the weekend. Do you want me to set up a board meeting for Monday or would you prefer a working breakfast?"

"Breakfast sounds more relaxing, so yes. Set it up and let's get back to normal. I shall be in the office on Friday for the re-run of the floor show and Decadence website review. Let's hope you have it looking good because time is catching up with us. I promised to send Yang Li a copy at the weekend. Is Eric about?"

"Yes, he is sitting opposite me. We have been playing catch up. The website, nobody wants another bollocking. I can assure you. I'll put him on."

"Good news, Jack. Thank God! Glad you are back with us. What can I do for you?"

"It's nothing serious but could you look at the costs involved in the floor show, just for reference I suppose. You have already discussed between yourselves that we will be doing a similar exercise for the Autumn Ranges with Yang Li. She needs to contribute, so it would be helpful if I can sit down with the two of you before the film show on Friday. Can you arrange that please?" he paused.

"Yes, that should be okay, Jack."

"Good. I will see you then." He put the phone down, a pleased grin on his face.

"Who was that, Jack? Chris?"

"No, pretty girl. It wasn't." She looked at the floor, a disappointed look on her face. Jack smiled. "It's hard being a Landlady, isn't it?" he laughed. She threw her magazine down on the floor and went to the kitchen, moody.

"I will be glad when I get back to university and get you out of my hair for a while."

Jack had his hands on her shoulders. He kissed the back of her head. "You do not really mean that, do you?"

She turned, facing him, leaning over, kissing his lips. "No, of course not, you silly boy. Coffee?"

"Yes, please. That will be nice and whilst I have got you, can we talk about you moving in here? We could start with you choosing your bedroom first I suppose and get that decorated and furnished. I'll take care of the costs, so you don't have that worry on your hands and if you want to drag me around the shops. Then this is the week to do it. Off you go and get your head in your magazines, okay?"

"Why do you spoil me so?"

"Because I am your big brother. What other reason could there be, landlady?"

They burst out laughing, happy together.

*****

Jack and Katie decided to grab some leisure time and after a light lunch of Brussels Pate and toast with fresh fruit to follow from the basket, they took a taxi into town, window-shopping. Katie said,

"What shall I do with my flat? Should I sell it?"

Jack laughed. "You have only been a Landlady for five minutes and already you're selling your assets. 'No' is the simple answer to that. You will let it out through an estate agent like I do with my other properties. That way, you are not involved with any of the hassle. Let them do it all for you and you pay their fees and they send you the rental income, all nice and simple. I will have a word with the guy that handles my properties and we can arrange to meet him at yours, say Wednesday. Will that be okay?"

"Are you sure, Jack? Is that the right way to go?"

"Yes, it is. You are a landlady now, so behave like one okay?"

"Like you, you mean. Do you?"

"Touché. I'll call him later when we get back home, alright?"

"Now, Jack, please. We can pop in here and grab a coffee. You can call him from here, please."

They sat at a table near the window in the Jack and the Bean Coffee Shop and Jack made the call.

"All done 3 pm, your place, Wednesday."

"Thanks, Jack," she smiled.

"That's what big brothers are for," he replied, laughing.

"Whilst I am here, I will call Yang Li and then I can spend a couple of days with you unless you have some lectures, have you?"

"No, I'm okay until a week tomorrow. Then I must hand in a dissertation. Can you believe it?"

"It's about time you did something." Jack dialled her number.

"Jack, good to hear your voice. How did it go? Good I am hoping?"

"Yes, I'm fine, fit and well and back at work from next Monday onwards. You will be pleased to know, I hope. How are you?"

"I am good, Jack. Still working on the samples and costings for the Autumn Ranges and I have spoken with Barry and Eric, so everything good. Oh, and thanks for your payment. No, I am not going to say it, you say?"

"No, I can't keep kissing you. I am here having coffee with Katie. She sends her regards. She is looking forward to meeting you very soon I hope. I will be sending you a copy of the Decadence Floor Show and website just so you have an idea how I want things to be with your floor show and website. You will have to let me share your thoughts and then we can meet up at your place with the film directors, Eric and Barry, if that is okay with you?"

"Wow! That sounds fantastic. Yes, I will call you over the weekend, unless of course you would like to call me on my private number, would you?"

"Wait and see. Goodbye for now." Katie grinned. "You chat up, merchant. I'm in love. I'm in love."

Jack blushed. "Ah, well."

*****

Chapter 35
Level 17

Brompton House was one of a number of Low Rise Tower Blocks that could be found in towns all over the north of England, built to a singular footprint in the seventies as part of the government's regeneration scheme. They were usually situated on the edge of industrial developments or next to a motorway or sometimes even crammed into an open space next to an over-crowded school, the block of flats now standing on what was once the school playing fields, nothing exciting, no green open spaces or kids play area, just the Tower. No, a breeding ground for disgruntled dropouts and immigrants, Gerta hated it and she was looking forward to her new life in Argentina.

Gerta was busy filling the rubbish bag whilst she waited for the House Clearer's van. She had not told them she was on LEVEL 7, or they would have probably not turned up but she would work that out with the guy when he arrived. Everything was going, not a stick to be left and whatever was not wanted would be taken by the night pickers. There would be nothing left before the night was out. She was satisfied by that thought.

She had purposefully not informed the Housing Department, her landlord, that she was leaving. In fact, the first indication that her neighbours would have was when the furniture was making its way to the removal van waiting downstairs.

The new tenants would move themselves in before breakfast time tomorrow and wait until the end of the week before the council caught up with the gossip. By then, it would be too late. The council would have new tenants.

The guy in charge was a surly bastard and was wanting to leave Gerta and her furniture and her possessions exactly where they were on LEVEL 7 after all Brompton House did not excite many people but after some very careful negotiating on Greta's part we did have the furniture finding its way downstairs, cash had changed hands and she was now £435 better off, folding stuff in her pocket. She smiled as she watched the procession of removal men racing up and down the stairs kept company by the nosey neighbours, taking note of everything that passed by their doors on the way down to the awaiting removal van.

The whole process took over three hours. Greta had a headache before it was all over. The flat looked twice the size now. It was empty. The dust and cobwebs would be left. She had already thrown the cleaning stuff into a plastic bucket which was now no doubt on the van downstairs. She never had any intention of leaving the place all spick and span.

Not much to show for her seven years as a tenant here, two suitcases a bunch of keys and a rent book, there was no sadness. It was always intended to happen this way. Even St Clarence's had no idea what was happening. The taxi driver taking her to Manchester Airport had a better idea. He was due in about half an hour's time. She checked her watch. It was a night flight to Buenos Aires, so she would have plenty of time to relax during the flight over.

She checked her tickets, her passport and wallet zipping her handbag, the first step in her journey to a new life in the Argentine.

She left the door wide open, placing the rubbish bag behind the door, no longer her property. She grinned, loving every minute of it. *Not long now, Rudolf,* she smiled.

The two suitcases were very heavy, her worldly possessions. She had already checked in online, paying the excess baggage charges. Everything had been planned down to the smallest detail and contingencies had been written into the overall planning. Her former life as an officer in the East

German Military had taught her that, the last time she had seen her brother.

She struggled down to LEVEL 5, hating every step. She dropped the flat keys and her rent book in the waste skip at LEVEL 6 on the way downstairs, stopping for a breather, her body weight punishing her now. Sweat rolled down her cheeks, her whole face a bright red. Her whole body bathed in sweat as she stood preparing herself to make for LEVEL 4.

She stood at the edge of the quarter landing apron attached to the flight of stairs taking her downwards, a suitcase straddled either side of her legs. She gripped the handles, her knuckles white waiting for the grab when it happened.

The flight of stairs lurched forward, breaking away from the landing she was standing on, twisting the hand railing, pulling it away from the connecting span and hitting her, causing her and the suitcases to plunge into the void left by the stairs. She fell backwards, the hand railing pushing her against the wall and trapping her left leg between the wall and railing, her body hanging down by her foot trapped by her boot, helpless, screaming as the stairs wrenched themselves free of the apron, crushing her body underneath them as it fell down on the lower stairs, killing her instantly. Her suitcases could be heard bouncing their way downwards, smashing to pieces on the lower landing. The pickers would be along before the dust had settled. She was lost in the cloud of dust and debris that followed the crash, covering the stairwell, forcing the nosey neighbours to shut their doors.

This story ends here. Flight BA 456 seat 41a to Buenos Aires would be empty on the evening flight.

Jekyll was rat-catching in an empty warehouse somewhere North of Skepton where Gerta had dumped him, his collar with name tag safely tucked inside a pocket in her suitcase.

*****

Chapter 36
Revelations

Jack looked over the Elspeth canal bridge, stopping on his way into town, preparing his mind and body for his return to work next week. He had done far too much relaxing and thinking under Katie's thumb these past few weeks and he felt it was time to shake the complacency away and get back into his stride. That's where his enjoyment lay in his work. It had taught him to be a hard taskmaster fair but firm. It would be his turn to look after her again.

The canal meandered its way through the centre of the town. It was early morning and a whitish mist hovered above the water. The toe-path was empty. The walkers and joggers were still in their beds.

He amused his thoughts with visions of Victorian workers walking the toe-path on their way to the cotton mills, dyeing and finishing houses and weaving sheds. That straddled both sides of the water their chimneys, belching their black smoke into the sky above, announcing the beginning of another day at work. The sound of machines the clatter of shuttles the hum from the belts that drove them created a magical symphony all of their own. It was given the name Industrial Revolution. Jack smiled, wanting to take part.

The perfect silence was broken by a man and his dog as they appeared from beneath the bridge. He saw the dog first followed by his master a non-descript dog walker of average build wearing trainers and a dark track suit, suburban a snob brand to make you feel good. Jack smiled.

Suddenly and without warning, the white polka dot cloth flashed by his eyes, wafting in the cold breeze, blowing up from the surface of the water and then it was gone. The dog, a Dalmatian, stopped and crouched momentarily on the edge of the toe-path, walking away having left a heap of dog shit, the steam curling its way upwards, joining the mist of the water.

Jack cringed. The pile was enormous and there was no way it would ever find its way inside a black plastic poo bag. It sat there like a pile of thick skinless sausages. The dog was almost in the standing position before the last sausage broke away. He was right. The walker looked around making sure he was alone and then satisfied, he pushed the crap pile into the canal with his instep, a slight splashing sound breaking the silence again. He took another look around before carrying on with his walk, wiping his shoe on the grass verge, the dog wagging his tail, panting, his eyes waiting for a pat on his head.

"Good boy, Jasper" was heard. Jack was angry.

Jack crossed the road at the traffic lights leading to the entrance of Caulder's Park once the home of Lord Springthorpe, mill owner and benefactor of the town.

A heavy dew carpeted the sweeping lawns. The tree branches drooping heavily from the weight of the dew. Closed daffodils waiting for the sun danced in the morning breeze when he saw the owl sweep down, taking a mouse caught in the open between to clumps of bushes. It reminded him of the girl at the Tower with her owl eyes and bouncing curls. His mind went blank then. The oak door behind the padlocked railings stood in front of him. He put both hands to his ears, wanting the screaming to stop.

The sound of a car horn snapped him out of it. The door and the owl had disappeared, leaving him watching the daffodils swinging in the breeze.

He made it to the other end of the park, crossing the road without incident, his mind back to work, Yang Li, Eric and Barry, Christopher and Katie occupying his thoughts, the tall Victorian College buildings reminding him of his school days. Then he met her.

It was her uniform that captured his thoughts, the Berlin wall, desperate people wanting to escape to re-join their families, lovers, or just to get away from the tyranny of the regime behind it. She was part of it, unrepentant, cold and heartless, the senior night nurse at St Clarence's nursing home. She passed by showing no emotion. Grace would still be asleep.

Jack made his way to the gardens facing the Town Hall, taking a bench facing the clock. He looked up and there she was, dangling from the minute hand, screaming, "Help me, help me." No one was listening. Her screams went unheard and as the minute hand reached twenty-five minutes past the hour, Gerta fell to her death as Jack turned his attention to the pigeons dancing on the cobblestones, flirting, mating, "Coo-coo-coo."

'Three miles,' Jack estimated, or forty-five minutes if you were a Yank. He felt good, itching to get back to work. Katie was away for the day shopping with an old school friend, so he was in no hurry to get back home. He would take the longer route, stopping at a news kiosk for a Mars bar and a bottle of water. 'Breakfast,' he told himself.

The way back home would take him through the Sefton Road Estate, a mixture of Victorian and post war properties grouped around industrial sites, old mills, railway sidings and a mixture of derelict buildings, then back across the river to home.

He reached Smitten Mill. He knew it by name only, painted in large black lettering on the side of the building when he saw her, three brick built shit houses and the thug. A cold chill passed over his body. The old lady, Daisie, was her name. The picture in his mind of her bruised face and the saline drip brought everything back to him. He felt physically sick. He was there standing next to her, wanting to hold her hand.

He closed his eyes, ashamed. Doreen, Vera, her mum and her dad danced inside his head. He wanted to scream at them. Then he saw her smashing into the wall. The vision had gone, and justice had been done.

Jack read the note she had left him on the Island Unit in the kitchen.

"Love you, Jack. Present in the fridge. Dinner at seven? Kisses, Katie."

*****

Chapter 37
Las Vegas

The taxi dropped them in the High Street. Katie could not be bothered driving around the town centre car parks searching for an empty space this morning. It was market day, a busy day and they had more than enough to do before lunchtime. Everything stopped after lunch, all except the pubs, restaurants, cafes and tea shops of course. They would all be full catering for farmers, visitors and the locals including mothers with their children straight from school. Market day was, after all, the day people met with their friends to catch up with the local gossip, swap stories, meet their lovers and other things better left untold.

You will find the **Las Vegas Café** on the High Street in Skepton town centre, a drab and dirty building wearing a well-worn white stucco overcoat hiding the pebble dash beneath it which comes complete with a large two-colour flashing neon sign, Las Vegas cafe in dazzling pink and green neon lettering taking you back to the swinging sixties. You could be forgiven for thinking it was a night club or dance hall.

It was on the first floor of the building, sitting above a Newsagents and a Cycle shop. It looked better at night time after a few beers in the Spread-Eagle Pub, a few doors down the street or any of the other pubs near the town centre.

You approached the Café up a flight of stairs with its Art Deco chrome-plated hand rails leading to a magnificent pair of swing doors complete with port hole glass windows and embellished with chrome fittings leading to a truly magnificent entrance hall complete with a 1940s Wurlitzer

Juke Box and an accompaniment of high back chrome stools and glitzy chandeliers.

Through the doors and facing you were more chrome handrails leading you down a short flight of stairs to the café proper with its breath-taking chrome chandeliers, hanging from the ceiling, illuminating the red Formica-topped tables with their chrome legs and matching chairs continuing the Art Nouveau theme of the café. Well-worn oak parquet strip flooring laid in a diagonal pattern completed its once extravagant interior.

A Little Richard song *Good Golly Miss Molly* blasting out from a digital juke box somewhere in the building created an atmosphere that would challenge any downtown New York café bar or night club. *Yea, yea. Electrifying.*

The tables complete with complimentary HP and tomato ketchup sauce bottles, salt and pepper cruets and a menu and napkin holder reminiscent of Woolworth cafeterias no longer with us that told you it was a cafe and not a night club.

Stretching along the whole of the back wall was the food counter, complete with chrome and stainless-steel herd rails, guiding the customers to the till at the other end of the line, another chrome wonder from Detroit 'The National' cash register company.

The whole effect was 1940s decadence, a time capsule taking you backwards in time, only the hustle and bustle of modern living spoilt the atmosphere.

"Two teas Table 4," a voice shouted. The clatter of pots and pans could be heard from the kitchen shouting out from behind the food counter gave the whole place a new meaning all its own.

It was busy 11 am on market day, the usual pensioner intake finishing a late breakfast or a pot of tea with a friend. Farmers and morning shoppers took the remaining tables. People were fidgeting and gossiping in the waiting area, queuing behind the 'wait here' sign.

A paraplegic in a wheel chair with his carer were at the head of the queue, several pensioners with shopping bags dropping in for a coffee before catching the bus home for lunch, and behind them were a trio of mouthy truant delinquents looking to make mischief.

Jack and Katie passed them as they left for the market. It was Jacks last convalescence day. He was due back at work on Monday and hopefully their lives would get back to normal. They were both looking forward to their Shanghai trip, a new experience for Katie, old friends and acquaintances for Jack, a working holiday.

*****

"I just need to get some tape for my dress, Jack. This way," she took his hand. "You haven't forgotten my sofa, have you? You promised, remember?" There was frustration in his voice.

"No, I have not. The market's on the way. Evington Gallery is on the far side of the Square. I know what I'm doing. Trust me. I'm your sister," she laughed. She was happy that Jack was on the mend. Dr Doogood had signed him off the sick, fit for work. The certificate said so. "Sorry, I should have known better but hurry up. There's a good girl. I want my sofa before the pubs are all full and then it will be no lunch for us, which means you will have to cook when we get back home later."

"Wrong again, Jack. I have already booked us a table for lunch at the Goose and Feathers for 1 pm sharp. Satisfied now?"

He grinned, "Okay. I will let you choose my sofa. How's that?"

"Now you're being silly. I will choose that one and you will want that one and on and on. It will go until you have your own way as usual. I am only coming to hold your hand. That is all." He did not reply. He stood behind her as she paid the stallholder for her tape, stuffing it in her handbag before offering him her hand, "Come along then, sofa boy." She giggled, her eyes sparkling, happy with herself, happy for Jack.

Jack's mind was full of images of the truants at the Las Vegas Café. *I will keep an eye on them. They are bad news waiting to be written, so I may have to write it for them if there is any wrongdoing,* he told himself.

"Where to now?" he replied, grinning. "Follow me. Just have some patience, will you?" she replied.

Evington Gallery was expecting them. Katie had told them that they would be dropping in just before lunch. They were met by Mr Jessop Senior, the proprietor and owner of the business. *A sofa, she said, better handle this myself.*

"Good morning, Miss Cambridge."

"Good morning, Mr Jessop. This is my brother, Jack, your customer now. I have just got him here," she smiled, Jack offering his hand.

"This way please. We have a very good selection of sofas and three-piece suites through here." He led the way. "I generally find it best if I leave my customers to browse the various ranges and then when they are ready, ask them to let me know when they have chosen what they want or require advice about the options available and I can fill in all of the details for them. We do not believe in pressing customers to buy only to choose. I like our customers to return over the coming years. That has always been our policy here at the Evington Gallery."

"Thanks, we will call you when we have some idea what we want. I can already see something I like," replied Jack.

They browsed. "Do you like this one? What about that one?"

"No, that's not the right colour. That's too small and no, that's too old-fashioned-looking."

Jack finally made his choice. "It has to be that one, Katie. I think the colours are right for the kitchen and I like the pattern effect that's embossed in the fabric. What do you think, good or bad?"

"I like the styling and the colour but do you think it is too clean a colour for the kitchen? Perhaps a darker colour would be better wearing. Don't you think?"

"Better wearing doesn't come in to it. The colour is right. I like the off-white colour and that is what I am having. I like the fabric and with a selection of coloured cushions, I think we could get there. We'll take it," he smiled, a happy look on his face.

"Before we tell Jessop, are you sure it is the right size? Perhaps the two-seater would look better." Jack cut her off short.

"No, don't be silly. It will look lost against that stretch of wall and I don't want it on that side either. It needs to be under the window, so you can look out over the lawns." He pointed to the two-seater.

"Okay, then both. Have both, one on each wall. That would look even better I think but it's your choice, not mine," she frowned.

"Brilliant! That's settled then, the two-seater, bright yellow and that one, in cherry red. Shall we fetch Jessop now?"

"Not yet. You will need a magazine rack or table for the corner, something that will draw them both together. A table won't do. You will have to keep walking around it, and you won't put up with that, will you? Knowing you, I saw a nice one in the other room whilst you were choosing your sofa. It's of American Shaker design in cherry wood. It will look great in the corner and keep everything tidy. You have a look at it whilst I fetch Jessop. Then we can tell him what we want and then you can take me for a well-earned lunch hard work shopping with you," she grinned.

"Okay, sounds good to me." He sat down on the two-seater, his hands one either side on the cushions. He closed his eyes. There was trouble a foot at the Café Las Vegas.

He could see the whole thing unfolding. Bert Stum, a tall overweight bully of scruffy appearance, was in charge. He was orchestrating abuse at the paraplegic boy, Johnnie, and his carer, Sarah Moffatt, from the moment he first set eyes on them. In his warped mind, they would be easy prey, ready for goading and torment. He would have to stay aware of the situation in case things got out of hand. It could only ever be a one-sided affair.

He needed time to adjust his thinking now having realised what powers he had. It still frightened him, the responsibility that is. His secret and all that came with it over shadowed his thoughts and that troubled him a great deal.

"We have decided on these two. Jack's just going through to the other room to look at the American Shaker magazine table, aren't you, Jack?" Jack seemed distant from the conversation. "Jack!"

"Sorry, don't forget the cushions and I will look at the table now."

"You want both the three-seater and the two-seater, don't you? That is what we agreed, wasn't it?"

"Yes, they are for the kitchen. We still have plenty of rooms to furnish yet, so expect us to be back."

"I don't want to appear disapprovingly, but wouldn't a darker colour be more wearable, suitable perhaps for a kitchen?"

"No, Jack doesn't think along those lines. I'm afraid when it's dirty, he will have it cleaned or throw it away but that would never happen. He's far too house proud for that kind of thing."

"No, the colour's fine."

"Your brother was saying you needed cushions. We have a huge selection through here." He pointed to the room where Jack had disappeared to.

Jack was sitting in an arm chair, his eyes closed. "Jack, have you decided?" she tapped his foot with her toe.

"Sorry, miles away." No, his thoughts were on the other side of the Square at the Las Vegas café. He lied. Of course it would not do to confuse her mind with his newly gained powers. That would have to remain his secrets and he still had to come to terms with it himself.

"Yes, I will have that as well and that light, I think, would go well with the table. What do you think, Katie? Do you like it?" She looked at the art deco lamp on the magazine table. She hadn't paid attention to it before.

"Yes, splendid. So I will begin choosing cushions and you pair can sort out the costs and delivery."

She left them to it, busying herself with the dozens of cushions with the girl assistant Jessop had sent to assist her.

Lots of cushions later and lots pictures on her iPhone, they left the store with a promise that delivery would be made this coming Saturday. After Jack had insisted the delivery was the make or break of the sale, Jessop took the debit card payment from Jack's card and after a couple of phone calls to Jessop's suppliers, the sofa company and the cushion makers were made at Jack's insistence. Jack had agreed to pay a small overnight delivery charge from the cushion manufacturer, and delivery was confirmed for this coming Saturday, much to Jack and Katie's delight and a very pleased Mr Jessop senior.

With smiles all round, Jack and Katie made their way to the Goose and Feathers Pub for lunch. They were a little early, taking a drink at the bar until they were called.

"Did you decide by the way what to do with the sofa already in the kitchen? It's almost brand new as though it has never been used, seems a shame. Can't you put it in the sitting room?"

"I have been waiting for you to ask that question. I have already decided. I called Chris at the office and it is being picked up first thing in the morning. It will be delivered to Lucy's house, a girl from his office. She works in research, Lucy Bent."

"Well, you haven't wasted any time. It is a bit of a big freebie; do you like her?"

"Well. Well. Well, I do believe you're jealous because your silly notion tells you I fancy some girl at the office, silly girl. I just mentioned to Chris that if he knew of anybody that wanted it, they could have it. He asked around and Lucy said 'yes' and before you say another word, she has just got married and they are moving in to their first home together. I said fine. I am glad. It has found a good home."

"You're mad sometimes, a two-grand settee just like that given away."

"No, not just given away at all. They will be charged for delivery and they will donate £100 to a charity of my choice, The Heart Foundation. You said it was too big for your flat, remember?"

"I suppose you're right. Ignore me. I am silly sometimes," she grinned. "But I am not jealous as you put it. I know who you fancy, don't I?"

"I am definitely not going there," he replied with a cheeky grin.

The waitress came and took their order, chicken curry with boiled rice and vegetables for Jack and a mushroom omelette for Katie with fresh baked bread and butter and a garlic dip, a white wine for her and a pint of bitter for him. Jack left the table, telling Katie he was off to the gents for a wee.

He closed his eyes, putting an end to the torment being handed out to Johnnie, the paraplegic, and Sarah, his carer.

It started from the moment the truants arrived at the table opposite them, the only free table available. Their choice was made purely by random activity.

Sarah put the menu in the holder on Johnnie's wheelchair, asking him to select his drink and burger meal. They always had the same meal every market day. It was more of a ritual now. They had done it so many times before. She would have what she always had, a chicken and bacon salad burger with garlic mayonnaise and a strawberry milkshake.

Johnnie, as expected, chose the cheese burger and the lemon milkshake. He smiled, excited. He was always excited. He loved going out and meeting people and the Las Vegas Cafe was always his favourite place to be. He felt comfortable here, excited by the people around him, the staff and the young girl waitresses always made him most welcome. He enjoyed the bright lights and the loud music, and it showed in his face, a happy face. He did not understand conflict or discontent. His biggest challenge in life was building his Lego castles.

Johnnie was tall, although his body form laying in his wheelchair disfigured from birth disguised the fact, dark brown hair with deep blue eyes with a rosy complexion and infectious smile at twenty-eight years of age. He had learnt to accept his misfortune being determined to get the most from life as he could. He enjoyed himself. He loved being alive, going places and meeting people. That is what gave him his resolve to survive in a sometimes-hostile world.

The trio led by bully boy, Bert Strum, were busy pouring salt and pepper into the brown sauce bottle and generally making a mess of everything else. Nobody took the slightest bit of notice, fear turning their eyes away. *Not our problem. Mind your own business. Get involved and invite trouble to your table.* That was not a choice most people wanted to make. Dennis Smart was an equally scruffy lout. He was lanky, being very tall for his age, although skinny with it. His eyes told you he was a nasty piece of work, his greasy brown hair completing his profile, a villain.

On the other hand, we had Vivian Pugh and as his name suggests, he was well out of his depth hanging around with that pair of thugs, expensive clothes indicating that he came from a good home. A short back and sides told you there was hope but time was running out. His bright blue eyes and angelic face also told you he was trapped in their world and could not find a way out. It kicked off with Bert Strum, goading Dennis Smart, nudging his elbow. It always started this way, a well-rehearsed routine. Vivian Pugh was waiting for his cue, nervous, his eyes giving him away.

"What are you staring at, bitch?"

"Don't you mean fucking ugly bitch, Den?" They all laughed, sneering at them, frightening Sarah. Johnnie swung his arm in a protest knowing he could do nothing about it. Sarah, a girl in her early twenties, devoted to Johnnie, she had been one of his carers for the past three years. It was a challenge she enjoyed. She loved him in her own way. You could see it in her eyes. She was tall, blonde and very pretty with bright blue eyes and an infectious smile, attractive, smart and tidy in her appearance and not a bit flirty but easily frightened. She ignored them, turning away from them to protect Johnnie, her body gripped with fear, wondering what she should do.

"Shall we go, Johnnie? We can go to the Cat & Mouse Café in King Street. Would you like that?"

"No, staying here, make them go away. They are frightening you. Bullies, that is what they are. I don't like them. Ask them to leave us alone." Johnnie did not understand fear. He wanted to stay. He had looked forward to it all week. "I am staying here. We are not leaving, Sarah."

"I've got just the thing for you, here." Den stroked himself, enjoying every bit of it, scaring her out of her wits when suddenly everything went quiet. You could almost hear a pin drop as the music stopped and silence took the stage.

Den's upper lip became twisted and, in an instant, he was the proud owner of a hair lip, unable to utter another word, his fingers stroking his lips. "Fucking hell, what have you done?" shouted Bert Strum, his eyes almost popping out of their sockets.

Vivian Pugh rose up from his chair, gripping his stomach with both hands, fear and pain showing in his face. Then he farted before slumping back down on the chair. A squelching sound could be heard as his bottom touched the chair seat. He immediately stood back up, frozen where he stood as his diarrhoea trickled down his legs, over the top of his socks and into his shoes before forming puddles on the parquet floor. He forced himself back down on to the chair seat, both hands cupping his face in shame. He rolled over on to the floor, receiving a kick to the side of his head from Den venting his anger and disbelief of what was happening.

The waitress arrived with a tray, holding three bowls of tomato soup and a stack of bread on a side plate.

"Table 47, three tomato soups," she ignored Vivian laying on the floor in the puddles of shit as she put the contents of the tray on the table next to each spoon, too frightened to dare to say a word. She hurried back to the kitchen out of harm's way.

Bert Strum held the spoon full of soup at shoulder height, ready to launch his attack on Sarah and Johnnie when suddenly and without warning, his hand and a portion of his forearm just above the wrist fell away from his upper arm, crashing down into the bowl of soup, the spoon and the soup splashing everything and everyone around the table.

Screams could be heard.
The Police arrived.

*****

The End